Gaia's Web

Steve Proskauer

This is a work of fiction. All of the characters, names, incidents, organizations, and dialogue in this novel are either the products of the author's imagination or are used fictitiously.

No part of this book may be reproduced, stored in a retrieval system, or transmitted by any means without the written permission of the author.

Because of the dynamic nature of the Internet, any web addresses or links contained in this book may have changed since publication and may no longer be valid. The views expressed in this work are solely those of the author.

Published by Gaia Press
December, 2012
923 Lake Street - Salt Lake City - Utah 84105 - USA

ISBN: 978-0-9860340-0-8 (sc)
ISBN: 978-0-9860340-1-5 (e)

Dedicated to

My late father, Richard Proskauer

A brilliant visionary

To my sons Dan and Tim

To my grandchildren Max, Francisco, Alejandro,

Lydia, Jose Ricardo, Daisy and Nicolás

And to all my descendants.

May they live auspicious lives in Gaia's Web

Contents

PART ONE
CONCEPTION

Our trouble is not the over-all absence of smartness but the intractable power of pure stupidity, and no machine, or mind, seems extended enough to cure that.

Adam Gopnik, "The Information: How the Internet Got Inside Us." The New Yorker, 2/14-21/2011

Chaos exhibits order yet is infinite possibility: it is contained and yet is unlimited. (p. 36) ...the chaos of the world can be seen as a pattern of endless possibilities in harmony somehow with the soul of the universe... (p. 19)

Rhea Y. Miller (1996). Cloudhand, Clenched Fist: Chaos, Crisis and the Emergence of Community. SanDiego: LuraMedia.

The STAIR Project

Daryl McIntyre paced back and forth in a small anteroom on the top floor of the Turing Building waiting to propose the most important project of his distinguished career. At any moment he would be summoned before the Challenge Committee to defend his theory. Daryl believed that simulating human creativity and consciousness had to be the next step in strong artificial intelligence, but not everyone thought such an ambitious goal was attainable – or even desirable. The power of computers had increased so rapidly by 2018 that even the experts were starting to fear them. If the growing dread of machines conquering mankind won out, Daryl knew the Earth was doomed.

The door in the far wall swung open and Dr. Gardner Reynolds stepped into the room, impeccably dressed in a dark double-breasted suit and maroon tie, every strand of his distinguished grey hair in place. By contrast, Daryl wore a sporty green shirt open at the neck with casual tan pants. Light brown tufts of his tousled mop stuck out over his ears. The two men differed just as much in body type, the stocky Reynolds a head shorter than lanky Daryl. Their faces reflected a mutual respect that overshadowed appearances.

"Welcome, Dr. McIntyre. After following your work for years, I'm delighted to make your acquaintance in person. The Committee is ready to see you now. Come this way."

"Thank you, Dr. Reynolds, it's a pleasure to meet you at last. Your recent work on eleventh generation data transmission is brilliant. Virtually unlimited signal density -- amazing!"

"That means a lot to me coming from one of our foremost visionaries," Reynolds replied with a gracious nod as he motioned Daryl into the large semicircular meeting room. Set into the curved outer wall was an enormous plate glass window affording a panoramic view of San Francisco and across the bay to Oakland on the east, Tiburon and Sausalito on the north, with the graceful arch of the Golden Gate Bridge to the west rising out of the morning fog. No problem keeping the big picture in mind from up here, thought Daryl as he followed Reynolds through the door.

The Turing Challenge Committee assembled once a year in San Francisco to fund advanced research projects too daring for academia and too abstract for product-oriented corporate labs. Eight Committee members, representing the largest computer firms in the world, sat four on each side around an immense oval table. Dr. Reynolds gestured for Daryl to take the chair at the foot of the table as he walked around to the head. Reynolds, his strongest ally on the Committee, felt uncomfortably far away, the full length of the twenty-foot shiny marble slab.

Glancing around the table, Daryl was relieved to see neutral and curious looks directed his way, except for a skeptical scowl on Isaac Nicholson's face. What's that old relic doing on the Committee? Daryl wondered. Maybe his lab enjoys getting rid of him for a few days.

"Dr. McIntyre," Reynolds began, "would you be good enough to summarize your proposal?"

4

"Yes, of course. I plan to create a strong artificial intelligence program capable of simulating human creativity and even consciousness itself," Daryl declared. "I want to realize Alan Turing's dream of a computer whose responses would be indistinguishable from those of a brilliant and creative human mind."

"Wait a minute!" interrupted Arnold Van Vector, the pioneering IBM software engineer, "You aren't claiming a computer can simulate creative imagination, are you? Even the powerful chess program Deep Blue played without any flair and triumphed over Gary Kasparov only by calculating every possible position many moves ahead. Those games bored me to tears. No pizazz at all. Machines have no soul. They can't bring any true originality to their output. Just workhorses, that's all they'll ever be."

"How do we know that, Arnold?" Daryl shot back. "Deep Blue is ancient history. Computers have only recently approached the capacity of the human brain. What if. . ."

Dr. Nicholson interrupted with a dismissive gesture. "Yes, yes – no doubt we have greater computation power than ever before, but even if we built a computer ten times as powerful as the human brain, how would we know how to program it for creativity and consciousness? No one understands these mysterious qualities of mind. We can't teach a machine to do a task we can't define, so why should we fund you to fumble around in the dark trying to do the impossible?"

"But suppose we could define the indefinable, Isaac? What then?" Daryl parried, "Consider, what is the essential process that distinguishes abstract thinking and creativity from blind

5

calculation? What's the critical difference between the chess master and Deep Blue?" Daryl looked around the table. Silence.

"The crucial advantage of man over machine," Daryl continued, "has been the ability to recognize and synthesize complex patterns from data and to discover the hidden designs in groups of patterns. This function allows human beings to make intuitive leaps beyond the reach of number crunching alone. My mathematical models use iterative equations to discover patterns within data, then take the patterns themselves as the data and find patterns within those patterns. The program repeats the same process over and over to discover higher order patterns embedded in the original data. This, I believe, constitutes the essence of original thinking and creativity. My theory defines consciousness as self-aware recognition and creation of higher order patterns. The conscious computer would see itself as a pattern seeker and pattern weaver."

Nicholson waved Daryl's idea aside like a pesky fly. "No equation, iterative or not, could come anywhere close to modeling creativity, let alone consciousness. There are too many variables and random elements even to begin designing a mathematical simulation. You're too talented to be wasting your time on a pie in the sky project. Pick a more approachable problem and come back next year with something at least plausible."

"Haven't you read my theory, Isaac? I use complex equations based on chaos theory, not some simple random number generator! Chaotic behavior may bear a superficial resemblance to randomness but there's a crucial difference. When chaotic equations are plotted, the points aren't just scattered around aimlessly – they fall into complex orbits, like the paths of satellites around planets – or the patterns of creative thinking."

The chastened Dr. Nicholson sat glowering silently while others raised legitimate questions about lack of experimental data to support this new model. Daryl sensed that the majority were impressed by his approach but hesitant to bet big bucks on an untested theory. This was the moment to bring up the most urgent application of his theory.

"Gentlemen, we could quibble endlessly about details of my proposal while life on Earth goes down the drain! The STAIR Project holds the promise of reversing the catastrophic decay of the biosphere. Think about it for a moment. A computer capable of creative problem solving in highly complex situations involving thousands of variables would be just what we need to resolve the rapidly worsening environmental crisis. Mankind has amply demonstrated its inability to cope with the many issues involved. Strong artificial intelligence may be our last hope."

To emphasize his point, Daryl presented ominous data showing that time had run out on a number of fronts – air and water pollution, global warming, extremes of drought and flooding, and species extinctions. He projected photographs of the disappearing glaciers and the ugly wounds left by strip mining. "Look at what our civilization has done -- whole mountains cut away, leaving shapeless piles of grey rock and sand – barren manmade slag heaps cluttering the horizon of sacred Navajo lands. The same savaging of the Earth occurs on every continent now.

"In the next photo you can see huge islands of floating trash choking the ocean as it meets the atmosphere, the interface where so many species come to breathe, feed and breed. These piles of debris occur all over the world now and have increased alarmingly in size. The largest is twice the size of Alaska. They are surrounded by dead zones of sterile seawater devoid of life

7

extending ten or fifteen miles in all directions. One of these poisonous floating junkyards has started to obstruct the Atlantic sea lanes. Nearby fish populations have been wiped out everywhere and many varieties of food fish have disappeared in the last five years. All of us are responsible for creating new continents of toxic waste that have disrupted the delicate balance of ocean life.

"Now look at this video I took from the window of my plane on a trip to the Amazon. You are seeing mile after mile of clear cut rainforest. Where the densest and most diverse biosphere on Earth used to thrive – the major producer of oxygen on Earth and the home of countless species, many still undiscovered – nothing but naked pastureland now remains to feed herds of cattle for fast food burgers. A priceless treasure lost forever. Half of the rainforest on our planet has disappeared now and the oxygen content of the atmosphere has fallen from 20% to 18% in a single decade!" Daryl noticed the Committee members turning pale and looking increasingly alarmed as they viewed this relentless parade of desecration.

"But at the rate we are going," Daryl went on, "most of the world's population will run out of drinking water long before they run out of oxygen. Private companies have taken over 85% of the aquifers and are quietly selling water to the highest bidder. The poorest countries will be the first to die of thirst, but many more will surely follow. Private corporations out for a quick profit have no interest in conserving clean water sources."

"For the STAIR Project to have a chance of preventing imminent environmental collapse, we must act at once. Should you dismiss or delay my proposal, you will not only be holding back research in artificial intelligence, you will be imperiling all life on Earth."

Daryl rose from his chair and leaned across the table, looking each man in the eye, skewering them with his words. "I propose to create a superhuman problem-solver that could help us right these terrible wrongs. Make no mistake, failure to correct our blunders and misplaced priorities within the next decade will lead to the extinction of the human race!"

Daryl sat down and continued to gaze into the eyes of the grim faces around the table. After a long silence, Dr. Reynolds cleared his throat and asked Daryl to wait outside. Ten minutes later, he ushered him back to hear their verdict. "Speaking for the Committee, I wish to thank you for bringing your bold proposal to us. We agree on the vital importance of acting quickly. The Committee has decided to approve the STAIR Project and to fund it in excess of what you have requested so that you can extend your research protocol and proceed to test its ecological applications immediately."

Daryl thanked the Committee and Dr. Reynolds escorted him out. At the door he shook Daryl's hand warmly. "Good luck, Dr. McIntyre. We're counting on you."

Early that evening Daryl stood on the deck of the Whidbey Island ferry from Seattle, gazing across the wooded length of shoreline ahead. He savored the salt breeze wafting over the bow, his pulse leaping in anticipation of his reunion with Samantha. As the ferry thrummed closer to the island, Daryl thought he could just make out her shapely figure at the end of the dock, red hair streaming in the wind.

Samantha spotted him as the ferry drew closer to the pier. She jumped up and down waiving excitedly, impatient to hear the news about the meeting. Samantha ran up to her husband at the bottom of the ramp and grabbed him by the shoulders, fixing him with her flashing green eyes. "Quick, tell me what happened!"

"We got the grant!"

"Already? What a coups, Daryl!" Samantha threw her arms around him and gave him a long hug.

"I still can't believe it!" Daryl exclaimed as Samantha dropped her arms. "They're giving us thirty million dollars, enough to create a state of the art lab and float the project for ten or fifteen years! They approved my proposal on the spot!"

"Unheard of!" shouted Samantha over the rumble of the ferry.

"The decision was unanimous, except for Nicholson, who abstained, stuck in the Dark Ages as usual!"

A brilliant scientist, Samantha was also a strikingly beautiful woman, the kind that never goes unnoticed. Even now in her late thirties, her flaming red hair and fair complexion made her stand out anywhere. Over the years, she'd learned to use her riveting features and youthful figure to advantage in overcoming men's tendency to be threatened by creative intelligent women and discount what they had to contribute. Her appearance held their attention long enough for them to respect her ideas as much as they appreciated her attractiveness.

On the short drive to their house overlooking the water on the northwest side of the island, Samantha, still amazed, asked incredulously, "How did you manage to get funding so fast? Those guys are the big guns – important men from each software company representing their firm's interests. They aren't easily impressed. A snap decision from that bunch? You've got to be kidding!

"And thirty million dollars – unbelievable! I think the last time they gave out such a huge grant was five years ago when that big project in Europe got twenty million for a computer simulation of the entire human brain. I can't see what they'll do with their humungous neural net once they build it. How are they going to educate the damned thing? Send it to nursery school? I think your ideas are much more interesting and practical. So how did you convince them? Tell me everything!"

"I'll give you a blow by blow, but first let's celebrate. Yesterday I put a bottle of that vintage champagne on ice just in case, the one we saved from our wedding."

"Ooh, you confident man! I'll go put together some crackers and cheese downstairs while you open it. I don't want to get hit in the eye by a champagne cork." With Samantha carrying crackers and cheese spread artfully on a terra cotta plate and Daryl armed with champagne flutes and the open bottle, they climbed the spiral staircase up to the crow's nest, cantilevered out over the trees to afford a panoramic view across Puget Sound up toward the San Juan Islands. Daryl poured and they toasted the success of the project.

"Now let's hear the whole story. Begin at the beginning!" demanded Samantha.

"Not just yet, sweetie. I've got a more pressing matter I need your opinion about."

"What can be so urgent that you can't tell me right now about your presentation?" Samantha snapped.

"Well," Daryl replied, oblivious to her impatience, "on the flight home I was thinking about the people we need for our team. We have to decide on our first choices and invite them immediately. Anyone sharp enough for the job will need plenty of lead time to free themselves up for a long term commitment like this. I have some names in mind. People you know. I want to hear what you think."

It annoyed Samantha when Daryl would put his agenda first and wouldn't just answer her questions. So like him – like most men, I guess. He's always thinking about the future and the big picture. Doesn't he get that the juicy details are the most interesting part? He just gets upset when I interrupt him and goes off to brood.

"Of course, darling. Who do you have in mind?" she sighed.

"I think we need two computer whizzes to join us, a software man and a hardware guy, but not just anyone. The software person has to be a topnotch mathematician, a master of computer modeling. He has to be a specialist in nonlinear dynamic systems and chaos theory. Can you guess who?"

"You aren't thinking of Martin Darcy, are you?" Samantha's heart skipped a beat and she felt a flush spreading over her face. She cast a furtive glance in Daryl's direction to assure herself he hadn't noticed. She knew he was still jealous over the steamy affair she'd had with Martin just before she met him. Passion had burned much higher between them than it ever had with Daryl.

"Martin is the very man. I knew you'd guess ... but I have to ask you something. We're going to be working together at close quarters in a secluded lab, possibly for a decade or more. Do you think your old fling with Martin will create a strain?" Daryl was uncomfortable bringing up this sore subject, but consulting Samantha was a must before contacting Martin.

Samantha paused. Martin would definitely be the best man for the job, but she wished it were easier to dismiss his concern. Her attraction to Daryl was more mental than physical and Samantha had often regretted marrying him. If their close friendship and mutual support with their research projects weren't so important to her, she would have asked for a divorce long ago.

Samantha had finally stopped fantasizing about Martin when she made love to Daryl, but it had taken a long time. Years. What would it be like living in the same lab with him and working shoulder to shoulder, day and night? And what about Martin's infatuation with her? They hadn't communicated for at least a decade, but she'd heard he'd never married. Was he still waiting for her? She tried hard to ignore the thrill that ran through her body.

"Honestly, I don't know, Daryl. I've stopped thinking about him but I have no idea how he feels about me now. Is there anyone else?"

"Not really. Martin has this gut level understanding of the role chaotic processes play in biology. I can't think of any other mathematician who could model something so complex as human creativity and consciousness. Back when Martin and I were best friends in college we took a stroll through the October woods in Vermont. It was one of those perfect fall days – crisp, clear, sun blindingly bright – not a cloud in the sky air. Yellow and orange and red leaves crunched underfoot and rained down all around us

13

every time the breeze picked up. When I asked Martin why he was so interested in modeling biological processes with iterative equations, he stopped and pointed up at the trees.

"'See the way the twigs split off from the branches? It looks random at first, doesn't it? Now look at the way branches split off from trunks. Do you get how they are distributed in the same general way? That's an iterative process at work right before our eyes. It's called self-similarity because the same pattern occurs at every level of magnification, right down to the veins inside each leaf. The exact details may be different, but the pattern is the same in the structures of all plants and animals.' Martin picked up a leaf and showed me the delicate veins as they branched off from the stem, a microcosm of the twigs and branches above our heads. 'Self-similarity is a universal characteristic of growth in nature, including the branching of nerve cells in the brain.'

"That walk with Martin made me realize that iterative equations – in which the same mathematical process is repeated over and over, using the output from each calculation as the input for the next one – might hold the key to understanding the structure of information-processing in the nervous system. The STAIR Project needs him."

Samantha realized she needed Martin too, but for very different reasons. She felt a titillating mix of eagerness and apprehension. "All right," she murmured, turning away to hide her flushed face, "go ahead and invite him... Who else did you have in mind?"

"We need a resourceful expert who can handle our ambitious hardware requirements. I think George Ellison is our man. Remember him?"

"You mean that strange guy you used to play chess with in grad school? The one who never would go out on a double date with us and wouldn't even come to our apartment? Are you sure we'd want to be living with that antisocial geek for years?"

"Yeah, he's kind of a recluse but he's a genius with computers. And I know he understands the data processing issues involved in computing complex differential equations because we used to discuss that during our Sunday afternoon chess matches. Now he heads up the most prestigious hardware development lab in the industry. We might even have trouble luring him away. As for getting along with us, he's always been very friendly to me, even affectionate. I have a soft spot for that isolated guy. I'll bet he's still leading a lonely life."

"All right, that's settled. So what happened at the Committee meeting?" Samantha asked once more.

"OK, sweetie, fasten your seat belt!" Daryl droned on, making the same points she'd heard a hundred times before. Samantha stifled a yawn and tried to be patient with his self-absorption. Sunset light filtered through the overhanging leaves, taking her back to a delicious romp in the woods with Martin on just such a late summer evening years ago ... Samantha shivered in the chill breeze of approaching dusk and reluctantly wrenched herself free from that treasured memory, turning her attention back to Daryl as he reached his victorious climax.

First thing the next morning, Daryl phoned Martin at Simulacrum Simulations, the cutting edge software company where he directed the Mathematical Modeling Division. "Hi Martin, I called to make you an offer you can't refuse."

"Daryl? My god, it's been so long... How's Samantha?"

"Doing great. Still studying her chimps – been following her work, by any chance?"

Martin hesitated a moment. He decided it was wiser not to tell Daryl just how closely he'd been monitoring Samantha's career. "Occasionally I run across one of her popular articles about primate cognition in *Scientific American*." A pale reflection of the truth. Martin followed Samantha's blog and read everything she wrote in the scientific literature. "By the way, nice piece you put out in *Nature* on the Singularity, Daryl. Do you really believe the moment is coming very soon when computers will surpass human intelligence and even redesign themselves?"

"The sooner the better. It may already be too late to save us. Speaking of which, how about joining me in a project that will reach and transcend the Singularity?"

"No! You must be exaggerating. What's this all about?" Martin responded with cautious excitement. Daryl outlined the STAIR Project and his role in it.

"Sounds pretty ambitious, Daryl . . ." Martin hesitated a moment. He knew this project would match his skills and interests perfectly, but what about the challenge of living and working in close quarters with Samantha? He noticed his heart pounding and his face getting hot. Do I dare take the risk? he asked himself. Oh hell, even if this weren't a great job proposal, I'd beat myself up for the rest of my life if I didn't jump at the chance to be near Samantha again.

"OK, count me in," he replied. "I'll just need a few months to finish up the humongous program we're wrestling with here."

"No problem. It'll probably take months to design and build the lab anyway. Meanwhile I'll send over the details... It's great to hear your voice again, Martin. I'm looking forward to seeing you after all these years, my friend. I look forward to collaborating with you." Daryl hung up the phone with a sigh of relief. Without Martin the Project was dead in the water.

A few minutes later, George picked up his private line at Innovative Systems Unlimited, where he headed up a world-renowned hardware development lab. Through the receiver came a voice he hadn't heard for two decades. "Hi, George, how about coming over for a seven-dimensional chess match lasting ten or fifteen years?. . . No, this is no joke. I need you for an important project... Oh, just computer simulation of creativity and consciousness, saving the world, that sort of thing. ... Call you back when I've got something a little more interesting?? Get serious!"

George was able to hold Daryl off with flippant answers for just long enough to pull himself together. He shook his head in disbelief. *Imagine Daryl contacting me after all this time! I must have better karma than I thought.*

George took a deep breath – then he got serious. "I've been buried up to my eyeballs in administrative responsibilities here and really missing the excitement of wrestling with challenging problems in the lab. Just when I was thinking how much I'd like to heave this

17

pile of paperwork in the trash, you offer me a chance to get back to what I love most. I'm in!" George's hands trembled as he hung up the phone.

A week later and eleven hundred miles away, Daryl spotted what he was looking for. He stepped out of his jeep into a dusty street on the outskirts of Moab, Utah, once a boomtown during the uranium rush, now a tourist destination adjacent to Arches and Canyonlands National Parks. He walked into the Prospectors Diner, a run-down eatery in an old railroad car. Curious looks turned his way. Tourists frequented classier restaurants downtown, but Daryl had a mission in mind.

He sat down in a wooden booth with cracked and faded green upholstery and a stained formica table. Gazing out at the sunset, Daryl flashed back to a transcontinental railway trip he'd taken as a child. He could recall the clickety-clack of the wheels as if it were yesterday. His soup slopped from side to side with the rocking of the dining car as it sped through the desert. It felt magical to eat his dinner while cliffs painted all shades of pink, orange and vermillion scrolled by the window.

A dumpy waitress brought coffee and set it down with a scowl and a clatter. Daryl had to ask for cream. Then he remembered the local guys took their coffee strong and black, like the cowboy coffee out on the range. The customers seated near him were burly construction workers covered with dust. In the back, a couple of old guys with dirty grey beards and faces like tanned leather sat gabbing over chicken fried steaks.

Daryl picked up his coffee mug and headed in their direction. They looked up at him suspiciously as he approached. "Excuse me, do you mind if I join you? I'm new in town and you two look like you'd know the best thing to order for dinner."

The scruffier of the two stood up and rolled his eyes with a smirk. "Talk to Gus. I gotta go."

Gus gestured for him to sit down in the vacated seat. As Daryl slipped into the booth, he couldn't help noticing the aroma. These geezers have been out in the wild without a shower way too long, he realized.

"I'd try this here chicken fried steak. Best in town. Hey, Gladys! Bring the man a chicky steak with all the fixins. . . So, young feller, what you lookin' fur?"

His directness took Daryl aback, until he realized he couldn't have been the first to ply this old relic for information. "I'm trying to find an abandoned mine out near Needles Overlook. Do you know the one I mean?"

"They's at least a dozen of 'em out that way, been empty since the uranium boom went south," Gus replied, chewing noisily on his steak.

"Could you tell me how to find one with buildings still standing?"

"What if I could? What's in it fur me?"

"Well, your meal's on me, for starters, and twenty bucks if you draw me a map." Gladys arrived with Daryl's "chicky steak," a deep-fried slab alongside a mountain of mashed potatoes all covered in greasy brown gravy with a slurry of peas on the side. Daryl felt queasy.

Gus appraised Daryl shrewdly. "This here map you're asking fur, it'll cost you fifty dollars. Take it or leave it."

Daryl slipped a hundred dollar bill across the table. "That'll cover dinner and the map plus something extra to make sure you don't lead me on a wild goose chase."

Gus frowned suspiciously. "Why you so interested in finding some worthless mine, mister? You figurin' to make a strike? You some fancy prospector with shiny new equipments lookin' for what ain't there no more? Well, you're wastin' your time."

"No, I'm just a photographer doing a spread on the uranium boom," Daryl improvised.

"A rich picture taker, eh? How about two hunderd?"

"Sorry, Gus, one hundred is all my boss will cover. I'll have to find someone else." Daryl got halfway out of the booth before Gus held up his hand, as Daryl knew he would.

"All right, you get your map for a hunderd, but I can't be sure the mine's still standin'. Ain't been out that way in a good long while." Gus accepted Daryl's pen and drew a few crude lines on a napkin. "See, this here's the main road to Needles Overlook. You gotta watch for a two-track, maybe three or four miles this side of the Overlook. Might be overgrown by now. Leads ya right up over the slickrock maybe half a mile – less than a mile anyways. Ends at the old Randlett mine, if it's still there. Good luck, mister." Gus got up and sauntered out, looking pleased with himself.

Daryl smiled. The old goat had taken the hundred and left him to pay for both dinners. The uranium might be gone but the prospectors could still mine gullible tourists. Daryl washed down his steak and potatoes, much tastier than they looked, with his second cup of bitter coffee, passing on the peas. He paid for the dinners and tucked the map in his jacket pocket.

At 5 o'clock the next morning, Daryl's jeep was crawling along the Needles Overlook road. He craned his neck through the window peering into the ghostly predawn light. Gus's map fluttered in his hand. He spotted the turnoff at the last moment and swerved sharply left onto a rough dirt track. Clouds of dust poured in the window as the jeep skidded to a stop.

Daryl coughed, wiped the ruddy powder off his face and glanced again at the wiggly lines that the sly geezer had scrawled on his greasy napkin. This had better be the right road. The sun will be rising soon and I don't want to risk being seen.

Daryl downshifted to low-low and inched cautiously forward, bouncing up and down in his seat as the jeep bumped and pitched over rocks and deep ruts. He crested a low hill and around the next bend Daryl spotted the outline of a large ramshackle shed leaning steeply to one side as if windblown by a hurricane. The roof sagged and irregular patches of darkness suggested gaping holes. At least there was no chance anyone could still be living here. Daryl relaxed and took a deep breath, inhaling the fresh fragrances of sage and juniper. He couldn't imagine a better site for the lab. Then he spotted the wooden tower off to the right, still standing despite dangling support timbers and rungs missing in the ladder. Daryl pulled the jeep up between the mine and the tower to take a closer look.

The light was increasing in the east now. Daryl felt an urge to climb the tower and watch the sunrise from the top. Without Samantha to dissuade him from risking his neck, Daryl jumped out and walked over to the bottom of the ladder. A chill breeze hissed across the desert. Daryl shivered and wrapped his denim jacket tighter. He placed one foot gingerly on the bottom rung. It creaked but held. He began the slow climb, nearly losing his footing half way up when a timber split, breaking the desert silence with a startling snap. Daryl pulled himself carefully up past the gap to the narrow platform at the top. He turned to the west where the first beams of the rising sun would fall. He could just make out high cliffs and weird spires silhouetted in the distance, their glow increasing imperceptibly with the turning of the Earth.

Daryl prepared to salute the sunrise just as men from plains, tundra and hilltop had recognized with wonder and gratitude the daily return of the light throughout human history. He pulled his beaded rattle from his jacket pocket, shaking it quietly as he sang up the sun. In a strong clear voice he chanted thanks for the coming of another day on beautiful Mother Earth.

Just then the first rays of day flashed over the horizon, igniting distant fires of dazzling color against the darkness to the west. The close packed spires of the Needles District flamed pink and orange and red, licking at the gloom of clouds hanging low on the horizon. Daryl lost himself in the colorful drama unfolding. The wonder of dawn in the desert filled him with awe.

Daryl took a gulp from his canteen. It was time to walk the land and find his power spot. He stretched his stiff muscles in the predawn chill and cautiously descended the creaky ladder. He found a path through the sage brush that wound through the hills to a sheltered hollow like the palm of a giant hand.

Daryl built a fire pit out of scattered stones and gathered branches to build a fire. After smudging himself and his rattle with cedar smoke, Daryl chanted to each of the six directions – the four compass points, the sky and the Earth. "Oh, ancient spirits of the land, thank you for calling the STAIR Project into being. I call upon you to bless and protect this place and guide us in our work. Ho!" As Daryl finished his prayer, the morning sun peeped over the dune and filled his power spot with light, welcoming the STAIR Project home.

On the Brink

While Daryl was working on the STAIR Lab, humanity continued careening toward disaster. Halfway around the world, Supreme Leader Vaslav Gronigetzkol paced and fumed behind his massive ornate desk in the cavernous throne room that occupied the top floor of the Presidential Palace dominating Bolkanica, the capital of tiny Bolkanistan. The walls were hung with tapestries and medieval lances, battle axes and armor. A yellowing photograph of a suckling lamb on the corner of Gronigetzkol's desk offered the only gentle touch.

His right hand man, General Peflik Frelko, stood patiently at attention on the far side of the desk, enduring the deluge of outrage pouring forth from Gronigetzkol's scowling mouth. Frelko's sharply chiseled features and short wiry frame seemed dwarfed before his mentor's imposing bulk.

Gronigetzkol strutted back and forth proudly in his purple medal-bedecked uniform, bulging across his barrel chest and straining over an ample belly. "What is happening to our great country, Peflik?" he bellowed. "I hear rumors of revolution, but who would dare oppose me? Under your loyal command, our mighty army is ruthless to dissidents. The people cower before me. What need we fear from this baseless chatter?"

He's out of touch with reality, Frelko realized. What can I say? I'll try to get through to him one more time. "The long drought has led to food shortages in the country, causing increased dissatisfaction among dissident elements. This revolt is more serious than others

25

in the past because many people feel they have nothing to lose. A few have died of starvation and others have decided they would rather die fighting than perish from hunger.

"And there's another problem," Frelko bravely continued, bracing for the storm. "Pyotrey Varnik is leading the revolt. I know this man. We served together during several border skirmishes with Uzbekistan. He's a highly competent officer, capable of uniting the rebel groups under one banner and turning a few local uprisings into all-out civil war."

"Why blame us?" screamed Gronigetzol, his thick neck turning scarlet. "We don't control the climate in Bolkanistan! This drought has lasted seven years. No wonder we have famine and people are starving. What good will it do them to rebel against their government?"

"Just as always, Supreme Leader," replied Frelko, attempting to calm his mercurial temper, "the people blame the government whenever anything goes wrong. They're like children. If there's no food in the house they think it must be somebody's fault. This has happened many times before but now we face more dissidents, they're more desperate – and they have an effective leader."

I wonder why I still support this rigid old man, Frelko asked himself as he shifted from one foot to the other before Gronigetzkol's desk. I remember how we were like father and son back in the days when we needed his ruthlessness to unify the country. Before him Bolkanistan was nothing but feuding fiefdoms, easy prey for roaming bands of local robbers and raiders from over the mountains. He brought them all together by weaving a web of shrewd alliances and crushing dissension with brutal force. I gladly fought by his side and helped him unify the country for its own protection.

How could I ever forget seeing my father and brother dying at the hands of the brigands and being forced to watch my 13-year-old sister being gang-raped? None of that would have happened if Bolkanistan had a centralized government with strict laws and a strong army. If only Gronigetzkol came along just a year sooner – or if I'd had the courage to do what he did. Frelko sighed. Sure, supporting his leadership secured me this position as Commander of the Bolkanistan army with all kinds of perks and privileges, but what binds me to him now that he no longer responds to the needs of his people?

"If this man Varnik is such a threat," demanded Gronigetzkol, interrupting Frelko's bitter reflections, "I order you to capture him, imprison him in the dungeon and interrogate him. We will decapitate this revolt before it can do any real damage." For a moment, Frelko caught a glimpse of the decisive military leader he had once known in the vigor of youth. He saluted the Supreme Leader with a deferential bow and walked down the hall to his office.

Imagine, placing a modern seat of government in a medieval castle, Frelko mused, shaking his head. Plumbing and wiring couldn't be installed without tunneling through stone, and that was just the beginning. Even so, this forbidding fortress was much easier to modernize than the chambers of Gronigetzkol's mind.

Frelko walked up to a massive door inscribed with his title in ornate gold lettering, "General Peflik Frelko, Commander of the Bolkanistan Armed Forces and Foreign Minister." He entered a drafty high-ceilinged chamber with gray steel furnishings.

Gooseneck lamps directed over each shoulder flanked Frelko's desk. They glared in the eyes of officers to intimidate them during "debriefings."

A large grey laptop computer occupied the center of the desk with mail and memo boxes on one side and a bank of three recently installed telephones on the other. Half a dozen straight-backed chairs lined the bare walls. A picture of his wife and three children sitting in a frame next to the laptop and a thick maroon blanket woven by his old auntie hanging over the back of his chair provided the only touches of warmth in this sterile chamber. Dusty mustard drapes framing the single casement window accentuated the atmosphere of utilitarian ugliness.

Frelko sat down and closed his eyes. He kneaded the tight muscles in the back of his neck, hoping to abort a growing tension headache. He knew he had been wise to withhold from Gronigetzkol the true reason his countrymen were turning on the government: the Supreme Leader had been plundering the country for thirty years, taxing people to death and neglecting to implement modern agricultural and environmental policies that required the government to do something more than collect revenue and patrol the borders with an excessive show of force. Every time Frelko suggested a project requiring outlay of funds from the treasury, Gronigetzkol opposed the measure. His policy hadn't changed in thirty years. All resources had to be committed to keeping the military strong and securing the borders against foreign incursions.

Frelko remembered how Bolkanistan had come into existence as a country with defined borders only three decades before, baptized in the blood of its citizens. Grueling and protracted strife among warring provinces ravaged the countryside. Most of the able leaders on both sides died in combat, but Gronigetzkol survived as the leader of the victorious faction. After the provinces were united by force under one central government, he imposed martial law. He enjoyed exercising absolute power and always found new threats to give him reasons for prolonging military control. In his position as Commander of Bolkanistan's armed forces, Frelko supported Gronigetzkol in the vain hope that conditions would improve and a time might finally come when a republic would replace the dictatorship.

He disagreed with the government's do-nothing policy and saw himself as the only man who might persuade Gronigetzkol to take a more progressive approach to the deteriorating conditions in Bolkanistan. Now he was losing hope for change. He realized that Gronigetzkol had grown complacent. The passionate vision of a safe and prosperous country was nothing more than an idyllic fantasy in an old man's mind. Gronigetzkol had deluded himself into believing that his goals had been achieved, when all that actually remained were faded laurels from long ago.

Frelko opened his eyes, headache nearly gone. Now he was ready to set his double trap. He sent a secure message to an operative with connections to the revolt ordering him to offer a truce in order to negotiate the demands of the dissidents. All hostilities would be suspended for three days while Frelko and Varnik conferred at Gronigetzkol's palace. Capturing Varnik would also serve a personal purpose, an opportunity to offer up a troublesome corporal as hostage for the rebels to hold against Varnik's safe return. The corporal would certainly be put to death when Varnik failed to be released three days later – a welcome loss, since this man had been quietly plotting against Frelko. Though it would certainly be possible to arrest him as a traitor, sacrificing him as a hostage would avoid the inconvenience of a court martial while sending a clear message to other power-hungry troublemakers. He was pleased with himself for devising this scheme for tightening his grip on the army. He'd learned a thing or two from Gronigetzkol about how to hold onto power.

The rebels agreed to the truce. As soon as Varnik reached the palace he was seized and sent to the dungeon for questioning. Frelko felt uneasy about capturing an old friend using a dishonorable ruse, and an even stronger distaste for interrogating him about the revolt. A voice deep within told him that the less he knew about Varnik's plans the better.

The better for whom? Frelko wondered as he reluctantly descended the stone stairs to the musty dungeon. A cold sweat broke out on his brow and he shivered when he reached the bottom of the steps and began the oppressive walk between dank cells carved centuries ago into these echoing stone walls, down a narrow tunnel to the iron door of the last cell – conveniently located next to Gronigetzkol's dreaded torture chamber.

President Edward Moore stood up wearily from his chair behind the imposing Oval Office desk. He stretched his stiff limbs in preparation for the first official meeting of the day. His aching muscles reminded him he wasn't sleeping well, with all the political opposition he faced in Congress every time he proposed any legislation.

Thirty-two months in office and it already feels like years, Moore glumly realized. Here I am, supposedly the most powerful man on the planet, and my hands are tied by the political polarization within my own party. I didn't even enjoy the usual half-year honeymoon when a new president gets treated with some deference.

Moore shook his head disgustedly as he finished reading the daily briefings deposited on his desk at six each morning. He had nicknamed this document the "Decider's Digest" in wry reference to George W. Bush. The news was gloomy as usual. The Middle East turmoil continued to fester and there was no end in sight. More resources were needed to protect Israel and other key allies there and around the world. If it weren't for the economic rivalry between China and India that continued to keep both countries occupied, Moore would have been contending with much more opposition from major powers in the Far East.

As it stood, the US could play the middleman and help defuse the conflict rather than being sucked in as a combatant as the right wing conservatives kept calling for. Why can't they see that we're already spread too thin? he fumed. Driven by corporations with defense contracts that fund their campaigns, these puppets in Congress scour the world for excuses to start a war.

Moore glanced down at his schedule. His heart sank when he saw the meeting later that morning with Defense Secretary Mark Starling, an aggressive hawk with close ties to the conservatives in Congress. That meant yet another foreign threat had been identified to drum up business for the American arms industry.

I knew Starling would be a thorn in my side when I appointed him, but that was the price of getting the ultraconservative wing to back my candidacy. Thank goodness Ben will be there to help me keep Starling in check. I just wish I had a cabinet of advisers free of bullies trying to push me around. Good thing I have time to prepare myself for another round with Starling during my appointment with Clarence. Always a relief to hear from a smart guy with real information, not political garbage.

Dr. Clarence Pitman had been his predecessor's Chief Environmental Adviser and Moore had seen no reason to replace him. Moore liked and respected Pitman. He had a stellar reputation as a world-renowned meteorologist. Pitman had won fame in the scientific world for his elegant studies of ocean current temperature fluctuations and climate change. Thanks to his models, prediction of hurricane and typhoon frequency and severity each season had become much more accurate so that steps could be taken to prepare and protect vulnerable areas. Moore had never met anyone with a deeper understanding of environmental issues.

Moore's secretary, Arnold, entered with his morning coffee and a cup of herb tea for Pitman followed by the environmental adviser himself. "Good to see you again, Clarence!" exclaimed Moore heartily as he stood to greet him. "What have you got for me today? Some good news, I hope – at least a crumb to offset the political infighting that dogs our steps these days. How has the wind power initiative been going?"

Dr. Pitman sat down opposite the President and cleared his throat. A short man with a receding shock of wispy white hair, Pitman was so introverted that even after all these years in Washington he still felt more at ease in the halls of academia than in the corridors of power. As receptive as Moore seemed to be, Pitman still felt intimidated by this powerful ex-quarterback with the charisma of a born leader.

"Mr. President, the wind farm program is moving forward slowly but isn't catching on at the pace we had hoped. The fossil fuel interests have found ingenious ways to make it difficult for small power companies to convert to wind power. You would think they would jump on the bandwagon so they could profit from the endless energy supply of wind and sunlight, especially as it becomes increasingly expensive to drill offshore and extract oil from shale deposits – but no, these huge companies seem entrenched in their old ways and have put all their efforts into opposing change. Why can't they face the disastrous impact of the coming fossil fuel shortages on their future profits? Even if they don't care about the environmental impact of continuing to burn coal and oil, you would think they could look down the road and see the edge of the cliff rapidly approaching."

Moore laughed sardonically. "Rationality about the long term future doesn't seem to be the strong point of big business. All but the most far-sighted CEOs care only about delivering juicy short term profits to their shareholders. Even I, a politician dependent upon the good graces of business interests, can see the problem for the future of our society."

Pitman nodded sadly, then leaned forward in his chair, furrowed his brows and looked Moore in the eye. "Mr. President, I requested this meeting today because we are facing a much more pressing problem than the obstruction of the wind power program. New seismic research indicates that recent offshore drilling projects and oil and gas extraction from deep underground deposits have destabilized the tectonic plates, setting off the recent series of earthquakes along the Pacific Coast. This effect is capable of acting at a great distance from the extraction zones, causing the foundations of entire continents to shift and rupture at their weakest points. The San Andreas Fault was the first to be affected. Earthquakes elsewhere are sure to follow.

"Furthermore, as a result of the accelerating trend toward higher temperatures, the ocean currents are getting exponentially warmer, melting the ice caps faster than I previously predicted, raising sea levels. Record-breaking flood tides are already disrupting commerce in many harbors around the world, Mr. President, but what comes next will be far more devastating: every coastal city will be underwater in less than two decades. The economic losses will be incalculable, to say nothing of the threat to life."

Moore's environmental adviser was giving him anything but an easy start to his day. His shoulders tensed and a growing weight bore down on his chest. Could these be the first signs of a heart attack like the one that felled his father in his prime?

"Up to now, Mr. President," Pitman concluded, "our civilization has assumed that Earth can absorb whatever abuses we inflict on her. These recent findings could be the last wake-up call before we reach the point of no return."

Pitman had considered carefully how much to say to the President. He was impressed with Moore's intelligence and ability to reason beyond politics. He believed this man might rise to the challenge, but he couldn't predict the President's reaction to such a grim scenario. He held his breath as he awaited Moore's response.

Alan Ferguson sat packed in with the other Wall Street stiffs, sweltering on the fast commuter train back to his home in

Winfield, for what must be the ten thousandth time, suit rumpled from the summer heat after a long day at Burrow and Hunker. I've become an expert in living the full catastrophe, he brooded. Wife, three kids, big mortgage and two car loans – soon to be three, once Jennifer turns sixteen next year and just *has* to have her own car – and what's the point of it all, really? The more expenses my family racks up the more stock I have to trade to pay for private schools, fancy clothes, furniture, braces, pets, remodeling, redecorating, shoes, parties, cellphones, jewelry, computers, insurance for the house, the cars, the boat – on and on, endlessly.

Is this all my life will ever amount to, buying and selling shares in huge corporations for my clients, then going home to pay bill after bill to the same companies? All that money that passes through my account each month doesn't do anything for me – just impersonal dollars that don't add a bit of meaning to my existence.

Alan realized he'd become as lifeless as those greenbacks. Someday, as he lay stiff in his final resting place, cold unfeeling cash would be his only legacy to the world. Once he dimly recalled his life having focus and passion – yes, that fascination with the sea, the mysterious ocean that beckons to him even now in his dreams. The sound of waves lapping against the beaches, piers and hulls of his childhood on Cape Cod, the mournful wails of foghorns carrying inland through his open window – woven into his memory with the soft caress of the fog, the damp wisps upon his face as a small child, wide awake, keenly listening for the sounds of his fisherman father arriving home late from runs far out to sea – the kitchen door slamming, the murmured voices of his parents from below.

Then there were the nights when the sounds drifting up the stairs were not so soothing – the shouting, the slamming of pots and pans

35

in the sink, the crash and tinkle of a glass thrown against the wall as his parents screamed at each other. He caught only phrases here and there in his mother's shrieking voice – "You're good for nothing ... gone to sea every day and night ... not enough money to pay the bills ... leaving me to handle everything . . ." – every word etched into his memory by the jagged shards of glass she hastily swept behind the cupboard before he could stagger into the kitchen the next morning, rubbing bloodshot eyes still bleary from fitful sleep.

Alan remembered his childhood dreams of escaping out to sea, away from the conflict – in a boat like his father's, or as an ocean creature, a dolphin or a whale, swimming with its fellows, liberated from the chains of gravity, the heavy obligation of life on land. He vividly recalled the freedom and exhilaration of those dreams. They still returned now and then to sweeten his restless sleep. Alan felt the pull of the sea like a growing magnetic force.

In college Alan had planned to make the ocean his life. He studied marine biology and intended to go to graduate school in oceanography. Then he met Sarah in the summer before his senior year and his priorities shifted. Sarah wasn't the kind of girl who would relish life on a boat. She wanted the stability and security of her own luxurious home with well healed friends to entertain. These things meant nothing to Alan, but he was young and in love. Pursuing his interests seemed much less important than making Sarah happy.

When a Wall Street recruiter visited the campus to interview seniors, Sarah suggested Alan talk to him. A stockbroker would fit her definition of a suitable husband, he knew, so Alan humored her, not thinking anything would come of it. After all, what would a Wall Street firm want with a marine biologist? Much to his surprise, he was offered a lucrative position at Burrow and Hunker Associates on the basis of his excellent grades and pleasing personality if he would agree to take a couple of economics courses in the spring term. Alan still had some general education requirements to meet, so he might as well. He knew Sarah would be proud of him and this way he could easily save up money for a few years so that graduate school wouldn't be such a financial strain. Never mind that the economics courses bored him and he had no interest in the stock market – pleasing Sarah was the important thing.

Sarah was delighted with Alan's decision. They were married after graduation, a fancy wedding with all the embellishments. Alan's best friend David resisted being his best man. David had been pointing out all along that he and Sarah had completely different goals and life paths. How could they expect to enjoy a happy marriage? Alan kept countering David's warnings with the old adage about opposites attracting. Finally David realized it was useless to reason with a man in love. He stood by whatever his friend chose to do but couldn't banish his misgivings. David knew that the honeymoon would end sooner or later, and when it did the rosy romantic dream of suburban life with Sarah would turn to ashes.

Before that happened, Alan and Sarah had two children – Jennifer, now almost sixteen, and Ronny, thirteen. When the kids were small, Alan liked being a father so much that he gave in easily when Sarah wanted a third child. The following year she gave birth to the hoped-for daughter, Suzie, now ten. Alan became so engrossed in the lives of his children and the demands of his job that he barely noticed the romantic glow of their early years fading away.

A busy schedule of boring social engagements took up most of his evening and weekend time. The couples Sarah cultivated in the social circle around the country club were just as uninteresting to Alan as his colleagues at Burrow and Hunker. The men talked sports and finance, the women gossiped about fashion, who was wearing what designer this year. Occasionally he overheard excited whispering about the latest affairs or episodes of wife swapping. Everyone drank too much. The central event of the season was the country club ball next month, the official beginning of Winfield's social season, a circus for social butterflies.

The Winfield Country Club was the hub of the town. A large clubhouse dominated the summit of a low hill, affording members and guests an expansive view of the lush countryside for miles around as they ate and drank in the exclusive lounge and restaurant, lavishly appointed in deep blue velvet. The adjoining ballroom featured a polished hardwood dance floor and a platform capable of accommodating the large band that would play for the occasion. The walls were draped in heavy curtains done in the same shade of blue.

To prepare for their grand entrance to the ball, the aspiring women of Winfield shopped all year, assembling a wardrobe that contrasted with the décor of the clubhouse so as to set them flatteringly apart from any rival. Nothing really mattered to Sarah like the impression she would make at the country club ball. Now she had found the perfect dress to show off her body and Alan's income. But could she persuade Alan to buy it for her?

It was Sunday morning again in Barrondale, Idaho. "Listen well, my brethren, for the Scriptures warn of the coming times of trial, when all men are to be tested in preparation for the Last Judgment," intoned Brother Joseph from his pulpit above the captive congregation in the Church of the Pure. "God the Father and our Lord Savior are watching our every move, waking and sleeping, to discern if we are truly WORTHY of REDEMPTION! We must be vigilant every moment to make CERTAIN our thoughts and words and deeds MEET WITH FAVOR!" Brother Joseph ended his sentences with a crescendo up to an earsplitting shriek that kept his sleepy flock awake while he harangued them for over two hours every Sunday morning.

Arthur Salton fidgeted on the rough wooden bench, trying in vain to get comfortable on the back pew of the bare church, hand-built from local timbers with no adornment except a wooden cross behind the altar. The other families were perched at attention on their pews in front of him, freshly bathed and dressed in their Sunday best. They looked to Arthur about as lively as lines of laundry hung out to dry on a calm day, in contrast to the gale force of Brother Joseph's wild-eyed frenzy as he railed at them from the pulpit.

"Our Lord will not make this test easy – OH NO, HE WON'T! Our Heavenly Father shall cause multitudes of temptations to rain down upon us AND DRAW US INTO SIN – OH YES! We must do everything in our power to RESIST, OR WE SHALL BE CAUGHT IN THE COILS OF THE SERPENT AND BE CAST DOWN INTO HELL FOR ALL ETERNITY! Because the Heavenly Father in His wisdom has seen fit to use man's sinful works to FILL THE WORLD WITH TEMPTATION, beyond our blessed community lies nothing but A SORROWFUL

WASTELAND, a modern-day SODOM AND GOMORRAH! Because we have bravely foresworn the distractions of the sinful world, our task here may be easier, BUT WE MUST REMAIN EVER VIGILANT, MY BRETHREN, AND NEVER FALTER FOR EVEN A MOMENT – OH NO!"

Arthur yawned. He had heard all this hundreds of times before – always rehashing the same dismal message. He glanced toward his mother and father, Walter and Corinne Salton, at the left end of the pew. Between him and his parents were his two younger sisters, Liz and Carol. Arthur was supposed to watch his sisters in church but they always behaved themselves whether he paid attention or not.

I don't understand how they can sit still for hours while Brother Joseph carries on and on, Arthur wondered. Is it just because they're girls? Or maybe they've never known anything different. When we moved here eight years ago, both of them were too young for church. Yeah, Liz was old enough to be a pesky toddler sometimes but Carol was still just a cute little baby, no trouble even then. With a rush of love, Arthur recalled holding Carol proudly, cradling her in his arms following her birth just after his tenth birthday.

Weekly church is just part of life for Carol and Liz, I guess, but I don't think I'll ever get used to it. I remember a different kind of life. Sundays fishing in the stream or hiking with Dad and Mom, sometimes just goofing off and watching TV on rainy days... Arthur drifted off into a pleasant daydream, tuning out Brother Joseph's urgent exhortations.

At 18, Arthur hadn't thought of himself as a kid for years. He was old enough to be considering how he wanted to live his life. It was almost time to move out on his own. Staying at Barrondale didn't figure in any of his dreams. If Brother Joseph calls something a temptation, that means it must be fun, Arthur concluded, because life was decidedly not fun at Barrondale. The only things we are allowed to do here are work and worship according to Brother Joseph's rules. If this is anything like the Heaven we are trying to get ourselves into, maybe it's not worth the effort.

Brother Joseph even picks off the pretty girls as soon as they turn fourteen. The ones he likes have to go live at his compound and become part of his harem. Then he assigns the rest to be wives for the young men. It'll be my turn soon if I don't get out of here right away. Seems like he's the only one who has any fun. At my expense, too, realized Arthur angrily. I work to feed and protect this community and I'm not even allowed to choose the girl I want!

Arthur still felt the pain of the awful day two years ago when Brother Joseph summoned Sally to his compound as his next wife, interrupting their budding romance. They continued to meet in secret sometimes, whenever Sally could sneak away. Arthur was torn away from his memories of those few sweet moments as Brother Joseph's tirade reached its final crescendo.

"Deceived and distracted as they are by their toys, all the wicked sinners abroad in the world today live like sleepwalkers, unaware of THE TERRIBLE FATE THAT AWAITS THEM," bellowed Brother Joseph. "They will surely suffer harrowing catastrophes as their just lot. They will wail and weep in confusion, not knowing that the FURY OF THE LORD IS UPON THEM. When their cities are toppled by TIDAL WAVES AND EARTHQUAKES, when FLOODS SWEEP ACROSS THE LAND IN THE WAKE OF TERRIBLE STORMS the like of which MAN HAS NEVER YET BEHELD, when plague and pestilence spread like lightning –

THEN TRULY THERE WILL BE NO PLACE TO HIDE! FOR THEM, THE BILLIONS OF SINNERS INFESTING THIS BEAUTIFUL WORLD LIKE PARASITES, IT WILL BE TOO LATE TO REPENT AND RECEIVE ABSOLUTION. THEIR DESTINY IS WRIT ACROSS THE AGES TO BE CAST DOWN INTO HELL, TO BURN FOREVERMORE AND SUFFER ENDLESS TORMENTS!!

"We fortunate few assembled here are protected from that same terrible fate ONLY SO LONG AS WE REMAIN RIGHTEOUS. We have found our way to this safe haven, here in the palm of our Blessed Lord's hand, but we mustn't ever become LAZY IN OUR WAYS. The evil that is abroad in the world spreads everywhere. SATAN IS EVER AT THE GATE AWAITING THE SLIGHTEST LAPSE TO FIND HIS WAY IN AND STEAL AWAY OUR IMMORTAL SOULS!!

"To assure that we all keep our Heavenly Father's commandments and be found pure and worthy of our place in Heaven at the coming Day of Judgment, ALL INFERNAL MACHINES OF THIS DECADENT AGE ARE BANNED FROM BARRONDALE!" Brother Joseph thundered on. "Any of our brethren who is discovered communicating with the fallen world outside by some vessel of sin SHALL BE SHUNNED AND BANISHED FROM OUR MIDST AND SATAN'S TOOLS SHALL BE DESTROYED AT ONCE BEFORE THEY CAN CORRUPT OTHERS!! SO BE IT!!!"

Those were Brother Joseph's rules, and at the beginning Arthur really believed they were for his own good. Now he could see they just prevented anyone from interfering with Brother Joseph's control over his little kingdom. What does he think he is – God?

He sure acts like it. I can't talk about any of this with my parents of course, but Frank and Jerome will listen.

Directly in front of Arthur loomed Jude Morris, a tall, broad-shouldered plowhorse of a man. If Arthur ducked down behind Jude, he couldn't be seen from the pulpit. Jude was deaf, so he wouldn't be overheard when he leaned over to chat with Sally's brothers, his two best friends. "Sunday's the absolute worst," he whispered to Frank. "We're stuck for hours listening to Brother Joseph's endless sermons. Always the same stuff week after week. Doesn't he ever get tired of throwing his recycled crap at us?"

"You read my mind," Frank whispered back. "It must be almost time to get ready for our shift. Let's leave when the hymns start. That'll give us an hour to hang out at the clubhouse before patrol."

As Brother Joseph reached his thunderous conclusion, the congregation muttered an automatic "Amen" – sounding both groggy and excited, as if awakened from a vivid dream. Jumping to their feet, the three boys edged eagerly toward the exit.

Inception

Daryl and Samantha arrived in their SUV at the end of March the following year. George and Martin followed close behind – George in his beat-up hatchback, kicking up red dust, Martin laboring over the bumps in his vintage Jaguar. All three vehicles were loaded with luggage and groceries. The four scientists shielded their eyes as they stepped out into the bright desert sunlight.

"All I see's an old shed and a rickety tower. Where's the lab?" asked George.

"You're looking at it!" replied Daryl. "Come on, I'll show you around." He led them through the front door of the mine and around the corner -- to a modern elevator. He pushed the button and the door slid back. Daryl gestured for the others to follow as he turned and pushed the second of the four buttons. The elevator descended slowly and stopped. The door opened on a long brightly lit corridor leading away in both directions.

"This is the residence level -- bedrooms, bathrooms, kitchen, dining room. There should be plenty of storage space for personal belongings and our supplies."

"So the entire facility is underground – no windows, no fresh air – are these the best living conditions you could arrange for thirty million dollars?" asked Martin irritably.

"The Turing Challenge Committee insisted on complete secrecy. We're allowed out for walks and shopping trips, but that's it -- no telephone, no email. We've just dropped off the face of the Earth."

"Terrific!" griped Martin. "We just signed on to be prisoners in an underground bunker until we solve this ambitious problem of yours. You never told us about this part, Daryl. Penile servitude was definitely not part of the contract!"

"I don't like it any better than you, but I figured it would speed up the Project since we'd all be itching to finish and get out of this concrete bunker."

"Bet we'll be at each other's throats within four months," Samantha speculated, "just like the astronauts in the space station. A lot of weird stuff happened in the isolation of space that never got publicized."

"Did the astronauts try to kill each other -- or just fuck whoever happened to be on duty that shift?" asked Martin.

"Both. Often at the same time. Paranoid psychoses and suicides too. Those walks and trips to town will be crucial to our sanity."

"I'll just make sure to meditate twice a day," said George smugly. "Sitting meditation helps us adjust to any conditions with equanimity. How can you two prima donnas worry so much about your own comfort when Daryl has entrusted us with the critical task of saving all life on Earth?"

"You arrogant little prick!" exclaimed Martin. "We want this project to succeed as much as you do. Did it ever occur to you that not everyone thrives on monastic asceticism?"

"Want to see where you'll be sleeping -- or meditating?" Daryl interrupted, ignoring the squabble. He wondered if his colleagues could overcome their differences enough to work together. He led the way down to their three adjacent bedrooms at the far end of the corridor. "I hope the Committee doesn't think these light green walls will substitute for a walk in the woods," Martin grumbled.

"Just drop it, Martin -- or should I say, Martinet?" George zinged. "Daryl has enough on his mind without complaints from us."

"Daryl didn't hire you to be his watchdog, George. He can defend himself if he needs to," Samantha shot back. "You have about as much tact as an oyster! You should just putter around in your workshop until we call on you for help. You may be a computer genius, but you're a social cretin!"

"Enough, all of you!" Daryl exploded. "We're tired from traveling and have plenty to adjust to here. How about a little tolerance and mutual support to start things off on the right foot?" George, Martin and Samantha averted their eyes like guilty children.

The accommodations were comfortable, almost luxurious – a thick mattress made up with bamboo sheets and a down comforter, ample closet and drawer space, and an inviting recliner in the corner next to an empty bookcase. Each room boasted a large virtual picture window "overlooking" a high-definition desert landscape, complete with the buzz of insects and the occasional cry of a hawk. A subtle aroma of juniper and sage wafted through the air. George picked up the remote next to the window and pushed a button. The desert image dissolved to an ocean beach with the soothing sound of breakers on the sandy shore. A salty sea breeze and the squawking of seagulls replaced the desert effects.

"Impressive, but no substitute for a real window," commented Martin, continuing to needle Daryl. "I'll bet those coordinated sensory simulations sucked a good chunk out of the Challenge Committee grant."

"Never mind, Martin," responded Samantha, gently patting his arm. "Anything that'll help keep us sane is worth whatever it costs." Martin felt a zing of pleasure. He quickly slipped into the bathroom to inspect the fixtures -- and hide his blushing face.

The rooms were generic except for personal paintings and photographs hanging on the wall, identifying each person's space. Daryl and Samantha's was the largest, with a king-sized bed and twin closets and drawers. Drawings and watercolors by favorite artists and family photos from each of their collections had been tastefully placed to indicate Daryl's corner, with his drum and rattle on the wall, and Samantha's side, with her altar and crucifix behind the recliner.

The two single men's rooms were identical, except that Martin's room included a large space for his Sufi whirling practice next to the bookshelf. George's room had been designed with a similar alcove for his Buddha statue and a meditation cushion.

"I see you've made sure we don't fight over who gets which room," George commented with a glance at Martin.

"We'll have time to rest and unpack before dinner," said Daryl, walking back to the elevator, "but first I want you to see the lab facilities." On the next level down, they stepped out into a corridor painted a warm mauve with offices for each beneath their bedrooms with identical desks and large computer monitors in each office. The doors already bore nameplates identifying their spaces. Beneath the kitchen-dining room area they found a large conference room with a monitor filling the wall at one end, and a table with four swivel chairs, two on each side.

"I don't see any room for my chimp experiments or space for their habitat," Samantha complained.

"Yes, and where's my lab?" added George testily. "It's all well and good for you theoretical types to work in a small office, but we hands-on people" -- he glanced at Samantha -- "need lots of space."

"So eager to get started?" Daryl parried playfully in an attempt to defuse the tension. "Wait until you see the bottom level, you two. It's all yours."

The team took the elevator down to the third level. The walls were painted a cheerful sky blue here and the air smelled fresh, as if to make up for the fact that they were buried sixty feet underground. Daryl pointed to the right. "This side is dedicated entirely to homes for Samantha's chimps and a large lab for her equipment and experiments. The chimps are due to arrive by the end of the week and their habitat is all ready for them."

Samantha inspected each room carefully. "Wow! Whoever did the installation really knew what they were doing. I have everything my chimps and I will need, even an open play area with trees for the chimps to swing on, all arranged just like my university lab. But what's this box doing here?"

George smiled. "Daryl told me you were frustrated by the low resolution of your brainwave analyses, so I took the liberty of adding this new processor I designed. I hope it will help."

"Hmmm. Thanks, George," she nodded tentatively, biting her lip. Samantha hated it when other people meddled with her equipment.

"Now on this side," Daryl pointed down the corridor to the left of the elevator, "we have twenty-five coupled computer modules giving us ten times more memory and processing power than any other computer lab in the world, a complete warehouse of state-of-the-art components, and George's workshop.

George took a look around. "Looks like you've covered the ground well on my end of the hall too. This storeroom has everything I could possibly need, all neatly catalogued exactly as I would have done it. Someone must have taken detailed photos of my facilities at Innovative Systems -- not an easy thing to get away with, given our tight security. These spaces duplicate the workshop and component supply room I developed, down to the last detail."

"Anything to make you feel at home here, George," Daryl replied, smiling mischievously. "I have to admit it wasn't easy to hack into your company's surveillance videos, but I couldn't ask you or any other employee to break your security agreement, could I? Besides, it would have ruined the surprise."

George looked sheepish. Daryl was right of course. He couldn't reveal any aspect of his work at Innovative Systems to outsiders. "OK, Daryl, but how did you do it without security detecting a breach?"

"I have my ways. Maybe someday I'll tell you, if you're nice. OK, that's the tour. Let's unload our stuff and get settled. Who wants to cook dinner?"

$$\diagup\!\!\!\!\diagdown$$

"Good morning, Gladys. . . How are you, Sophie? ... Did you sleep well, Screwball? ... Eat up, Oscar!" Samantha walked down the row of cages, feeding and stroking her chimps, calling each by name, relieved that they had survived the ordeal of being crated and shipped from her lab at the University of Washington. George had helped her uncrate them a week ago and get them settled in their new home. After cooking the team a delicious meal the evening of their arrival, George's stock had already gone up with Samantha and the others. By now, she felt at ease with his helping her in the lab.

"You seem fond of your experimental subjects," observed George, who had joined her to help fine-tune the new processor.

"Yes, they've grown on me over years of experiments we've done together. I've learned to recognize their foibles."

"You treat them like your pets," George commented.

"No, more like my children," Samantha replied. She felt the familiar pang of childlessness, a frequent companion ever since an obstetrical complication twelve years ago ended her first pregnancy – and nearly her life. She could no longer bear a child.

"Come into the next room and I'll show you how I measure task-driven brain activation. I couldn't bear to hurt my chimps by using implanted electrodes. Instead, I've developed a refined form of functional electroencephalography, fEEG, to study the neural networks associated with learning complex tasks. During experiments the chimps wear these tight-fitting helmets equipped with 108 tiny electrical contacts touching different points all over the scalp. Each of the electrodes relays a continuous stream of data to the computer. Correlation of the 108 separate signals indicates the fluctuating levels of activation from moment to moment in each brain center."

Samantha pulled up the latest 3D virtual display of brain activity during a puzzle-solving experiment. "See," pointed Samantha, "signals show up as luminescent lines shooting from one area to another. Brain centers light up in different colors while they process incoming impulses, then their images fade out as the outgoing signal shoots onward. Each puzzle I present to the chimps generates a specific pathway consistent from chimp to chimp, allowing me to make inferences about the importance of different brain centers in specific problem-solving behaviors.

"I've been working on refining my protocols for years, but the advanced processor you just installed has already revealed complexities I'd missed before." Samantha touched a button on the console and the virtual movie continued in slow motion. "Now you can see the neural pathways in finer detail. Impulses are traveling back and forth over and over between the same two nerve centers – or around and around circling through several centers – before moving on to other parts of the brain. Sometimes there are more than a hundred loops!"

"Amazing! These neural maps look so complex and dynamic!" exclaimed George proudly. "Wait until Daryl sees this."

When the team met in the conference room the next morning, George and Samantha showed Daryl and Martin her slow motion "movies" of nerve impulses cycling through the brain in repeating loops and loops within loops.

"Just what my theory predicts!" exclaimed Daryl. "We're looking at higher order cycles composed of repeating groups of lower order cycles – the brain's equivalent of iterative equations, running the impulse from each cycle through the same neural process again and again. This gives us the first evidence that iterative equations could simulate problem-solving activity in the brain."

"Hmmm ... I believe I could cobble together an equation that simulates this pattern," Martin remarked. "Send me the address of the file and I'll get right on it."

"Good. I'll send over precision data on all the learning tasks we've studied so far using high resolution fEEG analysis. Let's see how long it takes you two whiz kids to model all these neural pathways." Samantha seized the opportunity to challenge Martin and Daryl with a tough problem. Just like her feisty mother, she enjoyed making men sweat -- and having two stags vie for her attention.

Tipping Point

Frelko walked to the end of the musty stone tunnel and unlocked Gronigetzkol's torture chamber in the lowest dungeon under the Presidential Palace. Rusty hinges screeched in protest as he swung open the door. Frelko plucked his favorite interrogation instrument from a bracket on the wall – a flexible iron rod far more painful and effective than a whip.

Pyotrey Varnik's cramped and filthy cell was just a few steps away. As Frelko peered through the dim light, he could barely see the outline of a short man with broad shoulders on a narrow stone bench. The dungeon offered no other comforts except a crude commode, not even a straw mat. Prisoners had to curl up shivering on cold gritty rock. Once Frelko's eyes adjusted to the scanty illumination afforded by a small aperture high up on the outer wall, he made out Varnik's familiar stocky build and coarse peasant features – thick nose, wide cheekbones, and wrinkled brow. A shock of coarse black hair concealed the left side of Varnik's face.

"Pyotrey, my compatriot, I wish we were meeting again under different circumstances, but you have betrayed our country. You must submit to interrogation – you know what that means," Frelko added, hefting his iron rod and smacking it smartly against the bench. A sharp crack echoed off the walls. "Why did you betray the government and defect from a position of honor and responsibility in the army to lead this rabble revolt? Explain yourself!"

"Peflik," Varnik replied calmly, "when was the last time you were out in the countryside? I don't mean leading military exercises in the mountains, but in the valleys with the farmers."

Frelko realized he hadn't been to the lowlands in a long time. He was always shuttling between his duties at the palace and visits with his family at their mountain estate. "Answer my question!" he demanded, leaning menacingly over Varnik as he brandished his rod.

"That's what I am trying to do. Things have gotten really bad in the last year. People are starving in their own homes. Many were forced to eat the last remains of their seed grain, leaving none for spring planting. They've had to slaughter all their livestock for food. Now there's nothing left." Varnik's eyes flashed in the dimness. "The able-bodied have fled to the cities or across the border, leaving behind the old and sickly to starve."

"Get to the point!" bellowed Frelko, smacking Varnik firmly across the back with the iron rod.

Varnik grunted and went on in a hoarse whisper. "In one farmhouse I found a man kneeling on the kitchen floor next to the bodies of his wife and children. He was chopping off his left arm with a bloody cleaver, trying to revive the corpses by feeding them bleeding lumps of his own flesh. I can't get that scene out of my mind, Peflik – the desperation in his eyes as he hacked at himself again and again, howling like a wild beast."

Frelko shuddered in horror. This can't be true. My staff would have told me something... "LIES!" he screamed, raising the iron rod and bringing it down hard upon Varnik's arm.

Varnik gasped and gritted his teeth. "Two years ago I was stationed in a rural outpost and saw it coming – so dry that the crops didn't even sprout. My memos to the government were ignored. Meanwhile that demon Gronigetzkol went on imposing heavy taxes on everyone as if nothing were wrong. I grew up in that province. How could I hasten the deaths of my own people?"

"Enough sob stories! How large are the rebel forces? How do you plan to bring down the government? I WANT ANSWERS!" Frelko lifted the rod over his head and smashed Varnik across the thigh with a resounding thud. Varnik groaned and doubled over.

After catching his breath, Varnik fixed Frelko with a piercing look. "What do you think you are doing with that silly stick, my friend? Do you really believe you can force information out of me? We met during our service together in the border wars, and I haven't forgotten your courage. You were ready to risk your life for your people. Now look what you've become – a monster's servant! How can you remain loyal to a tyrant who lets your country starve?"

Frelko tried to brush aside the sting of Varnik's attack. He realized now that any effort to intimidate this man would be useless. Varnik was the martyr type, the kind of fearless fanatic that ignores pain. He would have to take a more personal approach to break him. "You must have another motive for turning against Gronigetzkol," he probed thoughtfully. "It's a weighty matter to betray the government you've sworn to serve, whatever the provocation."

"Yes, that's true," Varnik responded somberly. "Three years ago, during the fourth summer of the drought, my family had no choice but to leave our land and flee over the mountains. Bandits ambushed us in a narrow pass. We lost everything and barely escaped with our lives. It was my fault. I should have known better than to choose such a dangerous route just to save a little time. We finally made it to a refugee camp in Uzbekistan, but my frail mother contracted a fever during the journey and died. . . ." In the gloom Frelko caught the glisten of a tear trickling down Varnik's cheek.

"I vowed to overthrow Gronigetzkol and make him pay," Varnik growled. "Once I saw the horrible suffering in the lowlands, I had to strike down that heartless brute!"

President Moore paced back and forth in consternation. "You don't have to overdramatize your doomsday scenario like a politician to get my attention, Clarence!" he snapped.

"It would be difficult to overdramatize the dangers we face now, Mr. President," Pitman responded somberly, "The projection I presented to you only covered a few of the consequences. They don't include the kind of widespread damage we're already seeing from more violent and frequent storms and hurricanes due to rising ocean temperatures. Tornados are occurring over wider areas. Surely you've noticed the alarming rise in the worst kinds of twisters, F4 and F5 monsters that can destroy whole strings of towns.

"I didn't mention just how large the zones of severe earthquake damage could become once the tectonic plates have been irreversibly destabilized by oil extraction. Imagine several states reduced to rubble overnight! If I had told you about the worst case scenarios, Mr. President, you would have dismissed me as a fanatic."

Moore knew very well that Dr. Pitman was no fanatic. All the NASA scientists, Coast Guard geeks, even ecologists from the fishing industry – everyone he consulted about Pitman considered him a brilliant and reliable source whose projections could be trusted.

"Clarence, I thought we would have a pleasant chat this morning that would relax me before dealing with the Secretary of Defense, but this sounds far worse than anything Starling could drum up. What can we do at this point?"

"Mr. President, all projections indicate that emergency action must be taken immediately to avert environmental catastrophe. We need sweeping Federal legislation mandating renewable energy initiatives on a large scale. We must ban offshore oil drilling and stop all deep underground energy extraction. The current limits on carbon dioxide and other pollutant emissions from internal combustion engines and industrial sources must be tightened drastically until we can complete emergency conversion to renewable energy. We are fast approaching the point of no return, Mr. President. Unless we act now, burning of fossil fuels will make our planet uninhabitable within a few decades!"

The President noticed increasing pressure on his chest and a hollow feeling of dread in his solar plexus. He felt overwhelmed by the challenge Pitman placed before him. Dire predictions from someone with fewer qualifications would have been less frightening, but this man was not one to say the sky is falling without solid evidence. Pitman wouldn't understand the insuperable political barrier that stood in the way of enacting these measures.

Hefting his favorite paperweight from hand to hand, Moore calculated the political odds against him. The Russian Prime Minister had given him this favorite souvenir during a state visit as the ranking member of the Senate Foreign Affairs Committee. Mounted on a heavy silver base inlaid with an intricately braided Byzantine design, the clear ball contained a detailed model of the Kremlin. When inverted, the paperweight produced a swirl of snow obscuring the graceful minarets just like the blizzard that blew through Moscow during his visit.

It looks bad, but I have to draw the line somewhere with Congress and this may be the moment. It's my responsibility to protect our country and the world from what is to come even if it means my political Waterloo. I have to move on this.

Moore put down the paperweight, leaned forward, and returned his environmental adviser's gaze. "Clarence, please forgive my rash language a few minutes ago. Your news was too grim to face and I wanted to kill the messenger. That won't happen again. Now, I want you to set down in layman's language exactly what measures must be taken to avoid disaster, together with the projected consequences of failing to act.

"Have a set of specific proposals on my desk tomorrow morning. I know you've been thinking about these issues for years, otherwise I wouldn't be asking you for a comprehensive environmental action package at such short notice. I'm taking your word that we haven't any time to waste, but I'm not optimistic about your ideas carrying much weight in the current political climate. Politicians aren't scientists. They don't look at evidence objectively. What their constituents want and what major contributors to their campaigns demand carry much more weight than scientific research. I will do my best, but I don't know if anyone has enough political capital to oppose the vast wealth and influence of the fossil fuel interests. Can I count on receiving your proposal tomorrow?"

Pitman nodded. "Yes, Mr. President, and I would suggest that while we have the attention of Congress, a large allocation be included to fund programs for healing the damage we've already done. The environmental degradation has gone so far that conditions will continue to spiral downward even if all sources of pollution are immediately shut down."

"Of course. Please include everything you deem necessary. If we can get Congress to realize that we're on the brink of irreversible collapse, we may get some action on a comprehensive program." President Moore stood up to signal the end of the meeting. He stepped around his desk and put a hand on Pitman's shoulder as they walked to the door. "Thank you for your candor, Clarence. I trust you and appreciate the gravity of the situation. If this effort fails, it won't be for want of trying. I'll tell my secretary that you are to receive top priority access. I'll look forward to seeing your proposal on my desk tomorrow morning. No Republican has ever pushed the environmental agenda in earnest – but then no one expected Nixon to visit China!"

Pitman smiled, shook the President's hand and walked out of the oval office, trying hard not to feel too hopeful. Pitman had made his case before, but political opposition had always prevented the passage of any but the most meager legislation. Meanwhile, environmental decay spiraled out of control toward the point of no return.

As one bedroom town after another flashed by, Alan wondered how much longer he could endure his existence. Finally the train slowed for his stop – Winfield, Connecticut, proud home of the Winfield Wolverines. The only wolverines in this tame town are vicious social climbers, snickered Alan to himself. This was not where he belonged but here he was – and there was Sarah. What's she doing waiting for me on the platform? She's usually at home making supper by this time.

"Hi honey, how was your day?" Sarah chirped as she ran up to meet him.

"Oh you know – another day, another dollar," Alan replied listlessly.

"Honeybunch, I need to ask your opinion about something."

Oh, no, thought Alan. That's why she came to meet me at the station. She wants to buy something big. I should have known.

"Ask away!" was all he allowed himself to say. What Alan was thinking didn't have much to do with what he told Sarah anymore.

"I saw the most elegant gown down at Frawleys today, and it fits me like a glove. It would be perfect for the country club ball next month! Come see how it looks on me. Mr. Frawley said he would stay open late for us."

"What a nice surprise!" replied Alan. Hardly any surprise. Sarah only gets excited like this when she wants a really expensive item.

Alan had to admit the gown looked gorgeous on Sarah. The pale spring green of the material balanced the blond glow of her hair and set off its subtle orange highlights. The shade of the dress worked perfectly with her peaches and cream complexion. Sarah was a beautiful woman who took good care of her body. When she wasn't running or working out at the gym, Sarah went to her beautician for manicures, pedicures, and facials or to her high-end hairdresser. Alan knew all about it because he paid the bills.

Despite the gown's setting him back three thousand dollars, Alan found it easier to be enthusiastic about it than about some of Sarah's other whims, like her fondness for atrocious furniture and expensive ugly rugs. The color schemes she chose nauseated him. Alan was never consulted about these purchases and it would have ignited a huge conflict between them if he had objected and told Sarah how he really felt about her glaring lack of good taste. As far as she was concerned, the house was her domain. Alan had learned early in his marriage to keep his mouth shut when he had objections to Sarah's whims and wants. She could get nasty when she was opposed. He preferred to keep the peace.

To escape from the kitschy ambiance upstairs, Alan settled for a small private office in the basement, the cave where he spent most of his time at home. The tiny room was little more than a large closet, but at least it was his. Alan had furnished the room with a small desk and a comfortable recliner. Lining the walls were colorful photos of marine life. Along the perimeter of the desk Alan had placed souvenirs of his ocean adventures – a dried starfish, baskets of colorful shells, a chunk of brain coral, and his prize possession, a convoluted conch shell with silky inner walls in soft shades of rose, orange and violet. Alone in his den, Alan would keep up with the latest in oceanography on the web, or lose himself in fantasies of exploring distant tropical shores and inlets, imagining himself borne along by trade winds on his catamaran. Leaning back in his chair Alan could hear the gentle lapping of the waves against the hull. He lost himself in a world far more peaceful and fulfilling than the wasteland of suburban striving.

Sarah had always insisted that their children have all the latest clothes and toys. Alan believed she indulged them mainly to compete with other families, putting her kids on display with their possessions and raising parental pride to a new level of crassness. The way the children were dressed, their accessories, their posh private schools, their after school activities, their upscale friends – all seemed to feed Sarah's self-importance. Alan's profession and income also propped up her ego, but his own satisfaction obviously didn't matter to her – she never asked about that.

Ten years ago, around the time Suzie was born, Alan had finally recognized this disturbing fact. He had considered divorce then but he couldn't bear to put his kids through the huge ordeal that Sarah would surely have made it. Her father's prestigious law firm would've seen to it that Alan was fleeced. The kids would become pawns. Sarah was quite capable of using his love for Jennifer, Ronny and Suzie to make him agree to all her conditions, otherwise she would undermine his relationship with the children and do all she could to prevent him from participating in their lives. Alan was unwilling to put his kids or himself through this hell. He'd made his choice years ago and now he suffered in silence.

It had been so long since Alan had felt truly intimate and loving toward Sarah that he'd almost forgotten the feeling. He sat with her and their three children around the dinner table each night but felt no connection with his family. The kids were busy texting their friends or immersed in videogames. They would look up if he asked them something but all he got back were monosyllabic answers. He had tried once to ban their sophisticated toys from the table but the kids just gave him dirty looks and took their plates to their rooms. Sarah's picture of the ideal family included everyone eating together at dinner, so she ignored Alan's objections and let the children bring whatever they wanted to the table as long as they sat with the family while they ate their food. Alan felt powerless, invisible.

Tonight things took a different turn. The kids each had something to boast about. Jennifer had made the cheerleading squad, Ronny had raised his grades from a C+ to a B average and Suzie's rabbit, Thumper, had won second prize in the grade school pet show. As Alan finished praising their achievements Sarah casually reminded him that the iPad9 just came out with the new 13G Involvatron that allowed players to enter the virtual field of a videogame in 3D with input to all five senses. "It's just like playing on a real soccer field!" Ronny exclaimed.

"Wouldn't this be the perfect time for them each of them to get their own iPad9s as a reward?" suggested Sarah.

"Wait a minute," Alan objected, "didn't we give them iPads last year?" Ronny moaned that the iPad8's were way out of date now and they had to have the new model. "All our friends have them and they're supercool!" added Ronny eagerly. Everyone looked toward Alan. At that moment he realized the entire performance had been staged by Sarah. He could imagine her coaching the kids before he got home: "Tell him about your accomplishments – you know how he likes it when you talk to him at dinner – then I'll suggest the iPad9s as your reward."

With a sinking feeling in the pit of his stomach, Alan saw himself for what he had become to his family – just a walking ATM. Yet, as depressed as he felt about that, he loved them. If this was the only way for him to show it, he would buy the three iPad9's for his children just as he had bought the gown for Sarah. This is a red letter day, he reflected wearily. They hit me up for over five thousand dollars! I have no idea where I'll come up with that much extra cash, but I'll manage somehow. I always do.

Sarah was so pleased with Alan's complying with everything she wanted that she snuggled up to him amorously that night to give him his reward. Alan made love to her mechanically. Sarah's body still pleased and excited him but he had no passion left. He distrusted his wife so deeply now that he didn't even believe her moans of pleasure were genuine. Truthfully, he realized, I don't care anymore.

It would have surprised Alan to learn that Sarah cared about how robotic their attempts at intimacy had become. After what passed for lovemaking that night, Sarah lay awake next to her snoring husband and pondered the dismal state of their marriage. She had noticed their passion draining away as soon as they settled in Winfield. He's been withdrawing into his own world for so long now. Nothing left for me to do but enjoy life on my own, I guess... I certainly have plenty to occupy my time – clothes, house, friends, the Country Club, and the children – but it gets to feeling pretty empty after a while. Sometimes I wonder if Alan has found another woman, but I don't think so. His hours are as regular as clockwork and I've never noticed anything to suggest he's got somebody on the side.

Sarah kept her disappointment to herself. Unlike illicit love affairs, marital problems did not count as a fashionable topic of conversation among her friends. Domestic discord in Winfield was a badge of shame, a dirty little secret that made you look bad once it came out. And you could count on the word getting around as soon as you told anyone, even your closest friend. There was no such thing as a confidential chat in Winfield. Nasty rumors traveled faster than the speed of light in that status-driven community.

Sarah knew how to behave in Winfield. She had been swimming in affluent social culture all her life as the middle child in a family of great wealth – including her socialite mother, three brothers and an older sister – all supported in style by her father, a prominent New York attorney. She was accustomed to the heartless contest of appearances that pitted girl against girl and woman against woman, each striving to be most admired. Her upbringing had given her no way to comprehend the hollowness that had haunted her for years. What more could there be to life than hair, skin, figure and social rank?

With her father absorbed in his work and her mother in fashionable charitable activities and social occasions, she had no close relationships except with a nanny, her highly competitive older sister Margaret, and a brother three years younger. Margaret showed Sarah what was expected of her as a girl growing up in this upscale family, but when Sarah became attractive enough to present a threat to her, Margaret turned mean. In the absence of comfort in early childhood Sarah and her younger brother Jimmy turned to each other. Sarah became a surrogate mother of sorts and Jimmy became her teddy bear, someone to hold who needed her as much as she needed him.

It wasn't until she met Alan that Sarah imagined having a relationship beyond the superficiality of her social world. They met at a regatta in Rhode Island. Alan was captain of the crew on the sloop that narrowly beat her father's boat in an exciting race. She remembered the wind blowing through her hair as she held on tight in the stiff breeze. When her boat heeled over almost to the waterline, Sarah caught a glimpse of Alan barking orders to his crew barely thirty feet away as the two sleek craft carved swiftly through the waves, neck and neck to the finish. Something about him caught her attention.

At the victory party Sarah rushed up to congratulate Alan and they fell under each other's spell. It was the first time she had dated a man outside her circle and she found it exhilarating. Alan's affectionate attentiveness fulfilled Sarah's deep need to be loved. His steady presence relieved a lifelong loneliness.

As the relationship became more serious, her parents grew concerned. Her mother warned that associating with a man of such humble pedigree was beneath her. Then her father took her out to lunch, an unheard of event, and made the same point with less tact. "There are plenty of eligible men who would be interested in you. Why do you insist on dating the son of a fisherman? It's a disgrace to our family! Besides, he can't take care of you properly if he insists on pursuing an academic career. He's not the man for you, Sarah. Let him go!"

For the first time in her life Sarah felt rebellious stirrings. Her parents seemed intent on taking away even the love they never gave her. I'll date whomever I want and they can't stop me. I dare them to try! she vowed.

But Sarah had grown accustomed to her family's extravagant lifestyle. When Alan told her he loved her and couldn't live without her, the prospect of actually marrying him aroused a storm of conflict. In her heart she wanted Alan but she wasn't ready to give up her luxurious lifestyle.

Sarah was relieved when Alan resolved her conflict by accepting the offer of a position as a junior stockbroker in a prestigious Wall Street firm. Now that he would be able to support her in the style her family expected, she felt justified in accepting his proposal. Sarah's relief at not having to choose between Alan and her family blinded her to the consequences of Alan's choice to give up the life he really wanted just to make her happy.

Over the years this elephant in the bedroom of their relationship grew and grew until it occupied all their intimate space. Had Alan and Sarah even once been honest with each other something might have changed. But by now they had walled themselves off in their separate worlds. Neither of them trusted the other enough to begin a painful and risky conversation about the big lie in their lives.

So Alan and Sarah endured from year to year as their children grew. They were cruising inexorably toward the black hole of the empty nest and it was only a matter of a few years before they would be forced to face the sterile wasteland their lives had become. If Alan and Sarah could read what was hidden in the inner sanctum of each other's minds and hearts, they would understand that they both felt the same way – forlorn.

Escaping the oppressive Church of the Pure into the bright sunlight of late summer, the boys stood at the top of the valley where they could see the entire community stretching out below Brother

Joseph's compound. Barrondale was nestled in a glen protected by steep wooded hillsides, isolating it from the world outside. Several concentric barbed wire barricades had been strung along the hilltops to repel any chance intruders. By Brother Joseph's order, the young men maintained daily patrols around the perimeter and reported anything suspicious directly to him.

Brother Joseph had established Barrondale eight years before as an isolationist community for Christians who were committed to protecting themselves and their children from the corrosive influences of the world. Each family maintained its own household and the community tolerated free choice in most matters as long as no one violated Brother Joseph's edict forbidding all outside contact.

The community consisted of 75 men, women and children in a dozen households, the largest of which belonged to Brother Joseph himself. He occupied a fenced compound located just above his church at the head of the valley where he could gaze out over his domain. His sprawling tract contained five buildings, including a large barn for livestock and farming equipment as well as housing for Brother Joseph, his six wives and fifteen of his children.

The other households were scattered down the valley along both sides of a stream that ran through the compound, supplying everyone with irrigation and drinking water. Guardhouses manned 24/7 were located at the head and foot of the valley where the stream flowed in and out. No one except those on guard duty were permitted to approach. Armed guards had been instructed to use their weapons if intruders failed to stop and identify themselves after three challenges.

Each twelve-hour shift required a squad of three, one at each of the guard houses and a third to patrol the fence line. Arthur, 18, Frank, 19, and Jerome, just turned 15, had volunteered for the same squad, enabling them to meet without being missed before and after their shifts. Whenever possible, the boys gathered at their secret clubhouse, an abandoned shack Frank had discovered three years ago buried in the woods high on the wooded north side. As they headed up the hill, the three boys could just make out the faint drone of hymns wafting by on the breeze.

Frank and Jerome arrived before Arthur and cleared away the vines that concealed the door of their shack. Frank carried his large well-muscled frame in a natural rhythm of slow and steady confidence, unlike his wiry younger brother, Jerome, who dashed about impetuously and said whatever came into his head.

Jerome threw open the door and the boys hurried in, looking around for signs of discovery. Thanks to Brother Joseph's constant barrage of paranoid preaching, everyone in the community was suspicious and careful. "Looks like everything's right where we left it last Sunday," said Frank.

"Wait a minute!" Jerome piped up. "I'm sure I put the chair in the corner, not here by the door. And wasn't the kerosene lamp hanging from the hook when we left? Now it's sitting on the table. Someone's been in here!"

"If so," Frank replied, "they haven't reported it to anyone and they've concealed the door again like we always do. Let's check with Arthur before we get too worked up. He may have stopped in for a rest while he was walking the perimeter during the week. It's not far to the fence line at the top of the hill, only two hundred yards or so."

Just then Arthur burst through the door. "What's happening, you guys?" he asked, looking from one to another.

"Somebody's been here!" exclaimed Jerome anxiously.

"Yes, and I want to tell you about . . ." Arthur started to answer.

"What took you so long?" Frank cut in, glancing at his watch. "It's already 11:25. We haven't much time left before we have to replace Squad A."

"Give me a moment and I'll explain," replied Arthur. "Tuesday I got a message from Sally that she needed to talk to me. She snuck out at midnight and met me here right after I came off duty. At first she didn't want me to tell you anything. She was afraid of how you might react. But I persuaded her that her brothers deserved to know what was going on."

"What's the matter? Is she in some kind of trouble?" asked Frank with a worried frown.

"No – not yet, at least," Arthur replied. "She just needed to talk about the situation."

They had been concerned for Sally ever since two years before when Brother Joseph demanded her hand in marriage as his sixth wife. Her mother resisted the idea privately on the grounds that she was too young to be married to anyone. The very idea of her frail and sensitive daughter being forced to sleep with a man three times her age filled her with disgust.

Sally's father also hated the idea of her marrying Brother Joseph but couldn't deny him what he wanted without risking serious consequences in the community. Walter merely objected that she was small for her age, not mature enough to marry yet. Brother Joseph reluctantly agreed to postpone the marriage for a year. But then without warning he announced in church two weeks later that the marriage would take place in three months.

The way he handled his marriage to Sally was typical of Brother Joseph. He did whatever he wanted and then came up with a religious justification. Brother Joseph made it known that he was the divinely chosen man to father the children who would repopulate the Earth after the imminent scourges had wiped out all the sinners in the world. Therefore he took as many wives as possible to fulfill his destiny as the new Adam. Never mind that this version of the apocalypse didn't quite fit with the Last Judgment prophecy he preached. As each girl in the community reached the age of fourteen, Brother Joseph decided whether she was worthy to bear his children – meaning, pretty enough to catch his fancy. The girls he passed over were free to marry others.

Sally's father, Joshua Webster, asked for a private audience with Brother Joseph before Sally's wedding and pressed for a delay in consummating the union so that Sally wouldn't be unduly traumatized. He argued that her periods hadn't started yet and she was unprepared to bear a child. Brother Joseph reluctantly agreed to have his wives train her for her conjugal duties and to abide by their advice in the matter of her readiness to share his bed. Brother Joseph's fondness for young girls included prepubescent children, but he was careful to conceal this delicate matter of taste from his congregation.

The delay in consummating his marriage to Sally was an unusual concession for Brother Joseph to make. Joshua Webster and Walter Salton, Arthur's father, helped found the community eight years ago, and Brother Joseph didn't want to risk losing the support of either man. But considering that he had already violated his prior agreement to postpone the wedding date for a year, Joshua and Mary saw no reason to expect that he would keep his word. They were forced to accept the situation unless they were ready to leave their home and community, a decision that had become extremely risky in recent years.

Brother Joseph's style of enforced polygamy had disturbed many of the parents in the community. This wasn't what they had expected when they moved to Barrondale, but most were too obedient and grateful to be among the chosen to raise any objections. Over the years, three families had left rather than allow their daughters to marry Brother Joseph. The first family was allowed to depart four years ago with only a dour prophecy from Brother Joseph: "Leave now to live among the damned and you join the fallen. Know well, once you depart this island of purity you can never return." The family left anyway, undeterred by Brother Joseph's threatening rhetoric.

Thereafter anyone who tried to abandon the community was forcibly detained by the perimeter guards. Three years ago a guard allowed himself to be overpowered by a second family rather than shoot neighbors who only wanted to leave peaceably. The guard had been relieved of duty permanently and humiliated in church in front of the entire congregation.

After this incident it became obvious to everyone that Brother Joseph's perimeter guard system had been set up as much to pen them in as to keep intruders out. They were being held prisoner in his claustrophobic Eden. A few months later, a third family tried to escape. They were so desperate to get away that they shot it out with the guard. Two of their children were killed in the crossfire, including the 14-year-old daughter, before her father fatally wounded the guard. The parents and their two youngest children struggled downstream sobbing, leaving their dead behind in order to make it out of the valley.

No one dared to leave after that tragedy, but the community was never the same. A growing discontent with Brother Joseph's tyranny smoldered beneath the serene surface in this idyllic valley, but no one dared stand up to him. So Brother Joseph married Sally against her will and that of her parents. Her two brothers, Frank and Jerome, and her beloved Arthur remained deeply troubled and their resentment festered all the more when they heard secretly from Sally the terrible things that were happening behind the fence of Brother Joseph's compound.

With the complicity of Brother Joseph's younger three wives, Sally had been able to sneak out recently and see Arthur at least once a week. Her visit five days ago had been too intimate for Arthur to share fully with her brothers. Sally arrived shortly after midnight in tears and collapsed in Arthur's arms. Arthur felt like he was holding a much younger girl. Sally stood barely four feet ten inches tall and weighed 98 pounds. She's so tiny and frail, thought Arthur, it's hard to believe she just turned sixteen. I don't understand how Brother Joseph could have married her two years ago when she was even smaller.

Sally wasted no time in telling Arthur what was happening. "Oh, Arthur, I don't know what to do! Brother Joseph is so cruel. This morning Margaret came back from her night with him covered in bruises. He beats all his wives! And that's not all. He has these attacks when he goes crazy and sees demons. Annette told me that he hears them tempt and threaten him. Then he breaks the furniture trying to drive them out. All of us are terrified.

"The wives have joined together like sisters, comforting each other and helping each other with chores. That's the good part. I never had sisters before. They're doing the best they can to protect me, but Brother Joseph keeps trying to get me to sleep with him. They make all kinds of excuses, but it could happen any day now and I don't know if I could stand it." Sally sobbed convulsively, clutching onto Arthur as she trembled in his arms.

Arthur was overcome with fury and frustration. He had loved Sally since they were little. His heart ached for her. "Sally, so help me God, I'll kill Brother Joseph with my bare hands if he does anything to hurt you!"

"Shhhh! The perimeter guard at the top of the hill might hear us. I don't want you to do anything stupid... I love you," she confessed, bursting into tears and clutching him closer. "I couldn't go on living if anything happened to you. I don't want Brother Joseph, I want *you*!"

Before Arthur could say a word, she planted her lips on his and kissed him. Arthur forgot his rage and responded with equal fervor, holding her close. After what seemed like an eternity, they broke apart, panting for breath. Sally and Arthur looked in each other's eyes by the light of the kerosene lamp and something passed between them that ran deeper than any wedding vow. The each knew they had found their true mate and been chosen by the other as well.

"I have to go back now, Arthur. If Brother Joseph finds out I left his compound in the night, all of us will be beaten for sure." Sadness at leaving him hung heavy in Sally's voice.

"I'll get you out of this mess somehow. I need to tell Jerome and Frank what's going on and we'll come up with an escape plan. I don't care what it takes, I'll find a way!"

Breakthrough

Daryl looked up at Martin in awe as he leafed through page after page of scribbled equations. "And I thought your last batch were complex! I can't even guess how you concocted all these convoluted mathematical knots. Let's program them for visual display and run a million data points. That should be enough to show us how well they simulate Samantha's experiments."

"I'm a step ahead of you," Martin crowed. "Here are the attractor diagrams for each equation. See how they match up with the activation sequences Samantha recorded?" Daryl spent the afternoon poring carefully over the colorful patterns Martin handed him and pairing them with Samantha's data plots. The loop and swirl designs looked like an exact match.

"Unbelievably good fit – and with every single task!" Daryl exclaimed, clapping Martin on the shoulder. "Congratulations!"

"Thanks ... but now what? No matter how elegant my simulations may be, I don't see how Samantha can use them to enhance her chimps' learning capacity."

"Who cares?" Daryl shrugged. "Just being able to reproduce those zany neural pathways mathematically seems like miracle enough to me. Let's show your handiwork to our experimenters."

The next morning the four scientists clustered around the table in the meeting room, talking excitedly. The STAIR Project was gathering momentum. Martin opened by projecting the neural activation pattern recorded while the chimps were solving a block design problem. Then he displayed the equation that simulated this pattern and the design it produced when a million points were plotted. Finally, he superimposed the two virtually identical patterns over each other.

Samantha and George looked at Martin in open-mouthed astonishment. Martin responded to their unspoken praise with a casual nod. "Just doing my job. Now the real test of any simulation requires that it recreate the natural phenomenon, so how can we try it out on the chimps? Invite them in to review the movie?"

"Yeah, sure," Samantha scoffed. "That's almost as ridiculous as zapping them through their helmets until your simulation takes over their brainwaves."

"I don't' see anything wrong with that," Daryl chimed in. "It wouldn't be that hard to program the simulation into your system so it played through the electrodes."

"Come on, even a visionary with his head in the clouds should know better than that!" Samantha parried. "You'd have to use currents strong enough to cook their brains. Brute electrical force might kill a bunch of brain cells, but enhance learning? Never! I wouldn't ever do anything like that to my chimps!"

George lifted his head with a distant look in his eyes. "I'm with you on that. The simulation only represents what happens in the brain, not how to make it happen. I've been picturing the chimps sizing up the simulation like movie critics, and that's given me an idea. What if we could encode Martin's equation visually so that it nudges the brain to follow a particular pathway for attacking a problem?"

Samantha jumped out of her seat. "Yes, of course – flashing lights! You know how flickering strobes can induce seizures? Epileptics aren't allowed to drive because just the flicker of passing streetlights or sunlight blinking through a row of trees can start them convulsing. That's how we know visual activation can take over brain function, but we don't know yet whether more complex visual stimuli could have subtler effects."

"Hmmm . . ." mused George, "How about converting Martin's equations into visual patterns that induce new learning instead of seizures?"

"That sounds too good to be true," responded Daryl. "Do you really think it can be done?"

"Possibly. Martin's equations describe complex designs that constantly evolve. The question is can we display these patterns in a form that will interest the chimps for long enough to impact their learning process. I'll get to work on it and let you know when I have something we can test."

"Great!" Samantha added. "I can send you some data about chimpanzee visual psychology. They respond strongly to certain colors and shapes, so you may want to incorporate those to catch their attention."

Samantha's opinion of George had definitely changed during the two months of their collaboration. Instead of a socially stunted geek she saw a shrewd observer and a master inventor, the man who jumpstarted her stalled chimp research.

There was a great deal that Samantha didn't know about George, things that nobody knew about this very private man. On a trip to Thailand in his early twenties, George had visited a forest

81

monastery in the north of the country and ended up staying for three months. There he studied Buddhist mindfulness practice and led the simple life of a forest monk. A recluse by nature, George continued to cultivate a life of balance and equanimity through regular meditation, helping him contain his passions and tolerate his abiding loneliness.

Technical challenges were what gave short curly-haired George his thrills. He was the solitary tinkerer of the team. You couldn't expect George to be the life of the party, but he was your go-to guy for any computer equipment or programming problem, a wizard with an uncanny knack for coming up with creative solutions. It took him only three weeks to create the Visual Neural Inducer (VNI). He shot the program down to Samantha's lab and together they set up a large monitor screen behind the chimps' experiment pen. They were ready to test the chimps.

George and Samantha craned their necks over Oscar's head to get a better look at the strange patterns of lines and colors the chimp was watching on the VNI screen. If the program worked as well as the team hoped, Oscar would learn in a few hours how to perform a task that other chimps had taken weeks of trial and error to master. "Imagine, a visual display that can catalyze the development of a neural pathway in the brain to impart a new skill without the need for repetitive practice!" exclaimed Samantha. "The implications are mind-boggling. If it works with chimps it should be effective for humans, too. Imagine what this could do for education!"

Oscar's eyes were glued to the screen. The repetitive display of shapes and colors seemed to have a hypnotic effect on him. Three hours went by before he lost interest and wandered off to gorge himself and take a nap. Meanwhile, Samantha had been setting up the corresponding block design problem. It was a box of 31 puzzle pieces that fit together to fill in the outline of a square. There was only one solution and it took the average chimp accustomed to puzzles ten practice hours in several sessions to learn how to solve it quickly. Oscar had never seen this problem before. How would he handle the challenge after exposure to a single VNI session?

As soon as Oscar woke up, Samantha opened the gate to her experiment pen, an eight by eight foot area filled with sawdust with a three foot square table along the far wall on which she had placed a box of puzzle pieces. Oscar scrambled over to the box and dumped it out. He examined each puzzle piece carefully then assembled them on the table correctly on the first try – in just nine minutes!

Samantha gasped in wonder. Fond as she was of Oscar, one of her veteran chimps, he had performed well below average at other tasks. Samantha knew he would put the VNI to a tough test. If it could help even Oscar solve a puzzle fast it should work even better with smarter chimps, but what he did went far beyond her expectations. She had never seen anything like this in all her years of research. A dull-witted animal had performed perfectly on the first try. Even a very intelligent chimp experienced with puzzle problems couldn't have done anywhere near as well. Samantha beamed. The success of the VNI was responsible for the first major advance since moving her lab to the STAIR Project.

She tested Oscar on another puzzle similar to the first one without using the VNI. He was stumped for hours, making no progress at all as he tried one incorrect solution after another. But after they exposed him to George's VNI display for that puzzle, he could solve it immediately. Over the next four days, Samantha tested chimp after chimp on different puzzles using their corresponding VNI patterns and got the same incredible results. It was time for another triumphant staff meeting.

When Samantha described her findings, Daryl and Martin accused her of exaggerating, so she made them watch as she repeated the whole procedure on Gladys. Samantha enjoyed seeing her incredulous husband's jaw drop in amazement at the chimp's quick and flawless performance after just a few hours viewing the VNI display. "You helped create this simulation program, Daryl," she teased, "didn't you think it would work?"

George and Martin glanced at each other and laughed. They both enjoyed the repartee between Samantha and Daryl. Samantha's eyes would flash as she found ways to poke fun at her overly serious husband. Martin was fascinated. How could she look more beautiful – that mischievous toss of her head, that gorgeous red hair falling over her face until it drops back into place? What an angel! How will I ever get over her? His heart did flip flops like a schoolboy with a crush on his teacher.

Martin had known from the start how hard it would be to live with Samantha in the close confines of the STAIR Project lab, constantly restraining himself from confessing that he was still passionately in love with her despite her marriage to a friend and colleague. No matter how much frustration he had to endure, Martin savored each moment with Samantha.

The poignant pain of proximity to his beloved and the yearning to close the impossible chasm between them reminded Martin of

Kabir's poems about the longing for God, likening the forever unattainable Divine to the object of intense romantic love. Martin had fallen under the spell of the Sufi mystics from his first encounter with the beautiful poetry of Hafiz, Kabir and Rumi. In graduate school he had joined a group of Sufi students led by a Turkish teacher. It was only during the ecstatic devotion to the Divine in Sufi whirling that Martin found that he could transcend at least momentarily his despair over losing Samantha when she married Daryl. Passion – romantic, scientific and spiritual – infused Martin with his unquenchable zest for life.

Thanks to Martin's master equation, Daryl's simulation program and George's Visual Neural Inducer, Samantha carried out one successful pattern-induced learning experiment after another. In every case, she found that a particular VNI pattern helped a chimp solve only one puzzle problem without increasing learning speed for similar problems. Samantha couldn't understand why success with one puzzle didn't help her chimps solve all such puzzles. In early July she took this issue to the team.

"My equations are designed to model the exact neural pathway associated with a specific task," Martin explained. "Up to this point we haven't tried to devise a composite equation for solving a whole set of block assembly puzzles."

"It wouldn't be that difficult for a computer to come up with a general equation combining the common features of them all," observed Daryl. "I think I could have that ready in a few days."

When Samantha tried it out on the chimps, Daryl's general equation failed to enhance problem solving skills for any of the puzzles. "This general formula doesn't generate enough feedback loops," Daryl admitted. "Maybe they were averaged out when the computer crunched all the equations into one. We're missing something here, but what?"

"We could approach the problem theoretically," Martin suggested. "A general equation capable of inducing numerous neural pathways with feedback loops would have to include a much larger number of variables than the math needed to induce one pathway and solve one puzzle. I have to find some way of formulating a master equation powerful enough to handle umpteen variables."

"Such a master equation might also help us break through the impasse I've run into year after year trying to model creativity and consciousness," Daryl reflected. "Samantha needs a general VNI program to enhance chimp learning capacity and I need a way to simulate consciousness and creativity. What if the math is virtually the same for both problems? Perhaps these two lines of investigation – one experimental, the other theoretical – will lead to a conscious supercomputer that can think creatively!"

Inspired by Daryl's optimism, Martin worked tirelessly for three months, trying every mathematical trick in the book and several more he'd invented. No theoretical approach seemed capable of integrating enough variables to cover every chimp learning experiment, let alone analyze Earth's entire ecosphere.

While Samantha and George busied themselves with their own projects, Daryl struggled to keep hope alive against a familiar undertow of discouragement and despair. His father suffered from bipolar disorder and Daryl sometimes wondered if he inherited that tendency, because periods of dark depression so often followed frenzied attacks of creativity. He had to be making frequent discoveries and breakthroughs to fend off the inevitable crash. After three months waiting for Martin to come up with a master equation, Daryl could feel himself slipping down into depression.

As a child, Daryl had withdrawn into his own world in response to his father's frequent attacks of rage. He became an introspective geek obsessed with computers who stopped noticing the world around him until the summer of his junior year in college when everything in nature came vividly alive. On his first day visiting the Paiute reservation in Nevada with his Native American friend Jim Manyshields, Jim's grandfather, Walks With Thunder, spotted Daryl from the rickety porch where he sat carving a walking stick. The old man rose and grabbed Daryl's arm. "Son, don't you hear the spirits speaking to you? They tell me you aren't listening and they want me to do something about it. You have the gift, but like so many white men you walk around blind and deaf to the spirit world. You know not that you are blessed! I can teach you to listen and talk to the spirits yourself if you're willing to pay attention and work hard."

Daryl stopped and faced the old man, stunned by his candor. He accepted the challenge on the spot and stayed for the rest his summer vacation. That wrinkled old man quietly whittling a stick in the shade of his porch became for Daryl a luminous being filled with wisdom and spiritual power. Under the tutelage of Walks

With Thunder, Daryl learned to speak with the spirits of the eagle, the wolf, the bear and even the prairie dog and the coyote. Each had a perspective and its own special teaching to impart. Eagle became his constant spirit companion, a power animal that guided him on his journeys into the spirit world. Whenever Daryl spotted an eagle in the sky, it exalted the moment and rekindled his spiritual fire.

Now the time had come to seek help from his spirit guides once again. Daryl dragged himself out of his chair and pulled on a jacket. The brisk wind and expansive landscape above ground began to buoy up his mood. He made his way down the trail to his power spot, knelt down in the dim light of dawn and prayed: "I beseech you, ancient spirits of this land, tell me, am I just wasting time while Mother Earth is crying out for help? Am I failing Her and the world of nature by squandering my precious days on this beautiful planet by seeking a simulation of human creativity and consciousness?"

Daryl lay down with his ear to the cool ground, for the spirits of the land spoke their wisdom in quiet murmurs. The answer came in a unison chorus of encouragement: "Our dear son calls upon us for guidance in this time of doubt. We urge him to stand strong in his faith and continue his work, for he and his two-legged friends are about to make a discovery that will save humankind and all the four-leggeds, the finned and winged ones, the six-leggeds and eight-leggeds and the vast plant kingdom that sustains them. Mother Earth cries out in pain, and through the work of you few who live and labor amongst us here, the two-leggeds everywhere will take heed at last and band together to heal Her wounds."

Daryl heard a familiar shriek from above. What he beheld when he turned his eyes to the sky banished the last shred of doubt from his mind. A majestic eagle soared overhead, catching the rosy glow of the rising sun beneath its wings.

Late the following afternoon, Martin rushed in all disheveled gripping a sheaf of papers, shouting, "Look at this!"

Daryl had grown accustomed to Martin's wild enthusiasm over mathematical scribbles, but this looked completely different. "What's all this mathematical gobbledygook? Now you've lost it, Martin. This run-on equation fills an entire page!"

"You're looking at a stupendous innovation! This is an iterative differential equation with matrix terms! See, right here . . ." Martin pointed to a series of ten-by-ten grids embedded in the equation, each containing a hundred cells. Inside each cell were two Greek letters. "Now look at the bottom of the page." Daryl saw that the list of Greek letter combinations represented not constant terms, nor even single variables, but smaller equations.

"Brilliant!" exclaimed Daryl, excitement dissipating his sour mood. "You could include the population dynamics equation for each species in one cell and cover a whole habitat in a single matrix – an elegant mathematical description of ecological interdependence. Wheels within wheels – it's exactly what we've needed all along. Why didn't we think of this before?"

"Because we needed George and Samantha to kick our butts," Martin grinned. "Experimentalists do have their uses, you know."

"Hmmm, sure . . ." Daryl mumbled, lost again in the jungle of Martin's equation. "I haven't seen anything remotely like this since I studied Heisenberg's matrix form of quantum mechanics in grad school."

"Precisely! Despite your dark mood this afternoon you get the point. Remember the theory that the brain's a quantum computer? By the same token, it would take a quantum computer program to simulate creativity. In the quantum computer model of the brain, nerve cells can maintain an unstable state between firing and not firing. Uncertainty like this never happens in a conventional computer and we need it to explain what occurs during the creative process.

"Consider what happens when we struggle with hard questions. We mull over every aspect of a vexing problem, then, in one 'Aha!' moment, the correct solution seems to pop up out of nowhere. This can happen even in our sleep. Remember the chemist Kekulé who puzzled for weeks over the structure of the benzene molecule? He racked his brains but couldn't figure it out, then one night he had a dream of a snake chasing its tail. When he woke up, Kekulé had a brainstorm: benzene must look just like that snake, a ring of six carbon atoms. In the language of quantum mechanics, intuitive leaps happen when a cloud of uncertainty collapses instantaneously into the correct answer.

"Once I saw the similarity between unpredictability in chaos theory and indeterminacy in quantum mechanics, I simply incorporated quantum matrix math into my equations – and came up with this!"

"A stroke of genius. You should be awarded the STAIR Project Nobel Prize for most brilliant breakthrough of the month," quipped

Daryl, his funk dissolving into enthusiastic playfulness. "Samantha and George won last time for creating the Visual Neural Inducer. Now it's our turn. We have to keep up with the Jones's, don't we?"

Over the Edge

As soon as the door closed behind Pitman, President Moore's secretary rushed in to remind him that Secretary of Defense Starling had been waiting impatiently for fifteen minutes. "Starling's all steamed up – you know, the way he always gets when he's not treated as top dog. He can't believe that anything your environmental adviser had to say could possibly justify wasting his valuable time. Secretary Hallowell is trying to calm him down, but I think you'd best see them as soon as possible."

Moore grimaced. "Send them in, Arnold. It can't be any worse than what I've just heard."

A red-faced Mark Starling barged into the Oval Office followed more discretely by Benjamin Hallowell. Moore gestured toward the couch as he settled back in his chair. "Really, Mr. President," snapped Starling, "I would have thought that issues of national defense would demand top priority."

"Yes, of course, Secretary Starling," Moore replied in a neutral tone that masked his true feelings. For Starling, anything he considers important should demand my immediate attention. If it didn't mean political disaster, I'd strike some humility into that arrogant windbag right now, grumbled Moore to himself as he played with his paperweight.

"Please fill me in, gentlemen," continued Moore, unable to resist seasoning his voice with a pinch of sarcasm. "What pressing international problem is rearing its ugly head this morning?" Starling scowled. He resented Moore's offhand manner. "You might be interested to learn, Mr. President, that our intelligence sources have just uncovered a new terrorist threat! Have you heard of a small country called Bolkanistan bordering Uzbekistan?" Starling paused condescendingly, as if waiting for the President to answer.

Does he really think that the President of the United States is ignorant of world political geography? What unbelievable arrogance! Moore kept his scathing thoughts to himself and sat back silently, waiting for Starling to come to the point.

The rigid set of Moore's mouth revealed enough of his unspoken outrage for Starling to realize he had just treated the Commander in Chief like a schoolboy. Starling managed to moderate his pedantic tone slightly as he continued to expound on this newly discovered threat to the free world. "We believe that Bolkanistan has been infiltrated by a new wave of terrorist activity. The head of the country, Vaslav Gronigetzkol, has ruled this tiny buffer state with an iron hand for over thirty years, as you are surely aware."

Moore nodded, "Yes, I have heard that even by the standards of that part of the world he is considered unusually cruel and despotic." A flash of irritation flitted across Starling's face at the implication that ruling with an iron hand might be regarded as cruel and despotic. As an ultraconservative ex-Marine, he believed the United States should also be ruled with an iron hand. Far too many dissident elements were allowed to run rampant. In his view, Moore was much too soft for the Presidency.

"We believe there is conclusive evidence," continued Starling, "that Gronigetzkol has given safe haven to terrorist cells hidden in the mountains. I advise that we threaten immediate military action against Bolkanistan unless Gronigetzkol rounds up these terrorists and turns them over to us for interrogation immediately."

"Ah, another terrorist threat," Moore responded in a subtly dismissive tone. He had heard several such calls to arms from Starling in the past few months. None of them had proved to be credible. Starling is an ass, thought Moore to himself, but I have to take each one of these false alarms seriously. Time for Ben to run interference.

"Have you reviewed this matter, Secretary Hallowell, and arrived at an opinion?" inquired President Moore with feigned gravity. In private, Moore addressed his old friend as Ben and discussed everything informally, but to relax protocol in Mark Starling's presence would risk inflaming his status-conscious Secretary of Defense.

"Yes, Mr. President. Secretary Starling has been kind enough to brief me at length on the particulars."

"What would you suggest, then? Do you share Secretary Starling's view that we face a threat requiring military intervention unless Gronigetzkol turns these terrorists over to us?"

"It may come to that, Mr. President, but I would suggest we try diplomatic channels first in order to minimize the risk of an international crisis. Bolkanistan has been in the grip of a very long drought and is now suffering from severe famine. The country is in urgent need of food and medical supplies. Perhaps if we were to offer humanitarian aid to Gronigetzkol in exchange for his cooperation we could dislodge the terrorists in secret. For instance, we could propose sending a small cadre of elite special forces to scour the mountains and rout out any terrorists. No one other than those involved would need to know and the danger could be nipped in the bud. However, before taking any action we must verify the intelligence we have received. Information from that part of the world is notoriously unreliable."

"What? And allow these terrorists to spread their poison all over the country, recruiting reinforcements while we dither over intelligence sources?" shouted Starling.

"Mr. Secretary, remember the Mongolian threat five months ago?" replied Hallowell calmly. "When we investigated, our operatives found that we had been misinformed by a double agent under orders from the terrorists themselves, who would like nothing better than to see us squander our energies on yet another prolonged and fruitless military invasion. If we had immediately threatened to invade Mongolia we would have risked war with China, which could easily have escalated into a worldwide nuclear conflagration. Bolkanistan also has ties with China, so I would advise caution lest we risk our national security by taking premature action."

Thank God Ben is here to step in so that I can avoid a direct confrontation with this rooster who never ceases his urgent crowing, thought Moore with a sigh of relief. The President had learned early in his administration never to meet alone with Starling to avoid a confrontation. Everyone knew that Starling spoke for the ultraconservative faction in Congress and to cross him could mean loss of crucial political support. Hallowell was supplying Moore with a legitimate excuse to buy time.

Before Starling had a chance to protest, Moore stood up to end the meeting. "Thank you, gentlemen, I will consider everything both of you have said and meet with you again by the end of the week to agree on a plan. This will give us time to confirm the reports regarding terrorist activity in Bolkanistan."

The thwarted Secretary of Defense turned red with frustration as Moore's secretary opened the door and ushered Hallowell and Starling out of the Oval Office. Starling hated being cut off like this. Moore could guess what Starling was thinking. *If only I were President, I would be treated with more respect!*

Today Moore especially appreciated the hidden button under the coffee table he had installed to summon his secretary whenever he needed to hasten people out. *How should I go about handling these latest nightmares?* he puzzled. *I'll discuss the environmental crisis and the Bolkanistan situation with Martha tonight. She always helps me deal with such dilemmas. Martha's my secret weapon.*

Frelko labored up the broad stone steps from the dungeon to his office on the top floor of the Presidential Palace, dismayed by what he had just heard. His instincts told him to throw in his lot with Varnik. How difficult it had been to raise the iron rod against his comrade-in-arms!

Frelko recalled that time during a lull in the fighting when he and Varnik had first gotten to know each other. They were partnered on a winter patrol and found themselves trapped between two converging outlaw bands. Frelko spotted a cave big enough to conceal them and they built a fire out of sight against the back wall. Moments of safety like this came rarely during those harsh times of constant bloodshed. Both men relaxed by the flames, warming their hands and dodging the drifting column of smoke. Fellowship is forged quickly in combat, and Frelko soon found himself spilling his grief about the outlaw raid that cost him his father, brother and sister.

Varnik sighed and placed his hand gently on Frelko's arm. At length he broke the somber silence. "Like you, I came from humble peasant people, but because we lived far from the mountains I was spared the terrible losses you suffered. I was fortunate to have a happy childhood with loving parents and grandparents. Even though we were only poor farmers, we had time for dancing and merriment with friends. I remember my old grandfather, passed from this earth so many years ago, telling stories from the days long before the Uzbekistani incursions. He was a thoughtful man. Whatever wisdom I have I owe to him. Those were good times, full of family traditions I would give my life to protect."

Frelko pondered that brief but precious respite from battle as he walked down the hall toward Gronigetzkol's office. Yes, I could see myself fighting shoulder to shoulder with this man to defend Bolkanistan against a new foe – my old mentor – once its savior, now its enemy.

As Frelko entered the Supreme Leader's office, he felt as if he'd split in two and was watching himself from high on the ceiling. "Well, what does that traitor Varnik have to say for himself, eh, Peflik?" growled Gronigetzkol.

"Apparently the situation in the lowlands is far worse than we thought," responded Frelko grimly. "Varnik defected out of compassion for his starving countrymen and out of frustration that we have done nothing to relieve their suffering."

Gronigetzkol's eyes bulged out of his head. His face and neck went from ruddy to purple as he bellowed, "General Frelko, have you gone soft on me after all these years? You of all people should be the last of my lieutenants to let a turncoat poison your mind with sentimental drivel! What does it matter how many are starving? What's important is how many have turned against us and how heavily armed they are. Who is helping them? What are their plans? SPEAK!"

Frelko averted his eyes from Gronigetzkol's flushed and bloated face, dripping with sweat from his furious rant. At length he raised his head to face the Supreme Leader and quietly answered, "Varnik quite understandably refused to provide that information. We captured him by deception and it would be naïve of him to trust us again. I advise that we hold our cards close to our chest until we can check out his story about living conditions in the agricultural provinces. If the famine and the flood of refugees are as serious as he describes, then attempting to put down the revolt by military action alone would risk losing all the popular support upon which your command has rested during the past three decades."

Gronigetzkol turned an even deeper shade of purple as the blood vessels in his head and neck pulsed and his bulging eyes stared wildly. After gasping and sputtering to catch his breath, Gronigetzkol screamed at the top of his lungs: "I WILL HEAR NO MORE WOMEN'S TALK FROM THE HEAD OF MY ARMY! The rebels must be met with a show of brute strength. That's all that gets through to traitors and scoundrels. Round them all up and detain them under the worst conditions! Torture Varnik until he reveals the information we need! After you get done with him, we'll denounce him and chop off what's left of his head in the public square next week. That will put a quick end to this uprising!"

Frelko rushed out of Gronigetzkol's office, his eyes wide open to the truth that had been staring him in the face for so long: government under Gronigetzkol had lost all touch with life in Bolkanistan. It had become nothing but a self-serving bureaucracy built around a fanatical tyrant, a parasite upon the populace. Frelko knew what he had to do, yet he still felt constrained by his long-standing loyalty to Gronigetzkol -- and by compassion for him.

Only Frelko knew the truth about his mentor's tortured childhood. Vaslav Gronigetzkol had been the only son of an impoverished shepherd in the rugged mountain range on the Uzbekistan border. After his mother died in childbirth, his father never forgave the boy, whom he saw as his mother's murderer. Little Vaslav received more nurturing from the ewe that suckled him than from his bitter drunken father.

As soon as Vaslav was old enough to walk, the beatings began. His father used any pretext to punish him even before he could talk. He hid among the sheep flock and lambs were his only playmates. They would follow the boy wherever he went. Even then, Vaslav liked being the leader. Throughout the squalor of his childhood he consoled himself with the sheep.

His father's reign of cruelty came to an end just after Vaslav turned twelve, when a band of brigands on a raiding party came upon them as they were moving their herd to higher ground for the summer. When these mountain bandits began to drive off their sheep his father made the fatal error of resisting. Annoyed by the stupid fool screaming and waving his staff, the leader rode up behind his father and felled him before Vaslav's eyes with one blow from his rifle butt. He swept Vaslav up behind him and they rode off with the sheep.

The bandits proved to be even more brutal than his father. For them he was just an object to be exploited for their convenience and amusement. At first that only meant doing unpleasant chores around camp, but before long he had become a sexual plaything as well, shared among the men to take the edge off their frustrations. Fortunately that period lasted only until the men had captured some girls to rape, but by then the damage had been done.

Gronigetzkol fled on horseback during the drunken orgy that followed a big raid. By the time the band discovered his escape, little Vaslav had put many miles behind him. He became a hired hand on a farm in the lowlands, as far away from the accursed mountains of his childhood as he could get. Vaslav grew up into a strong and stolid young man of few words who responded to situations with swift, brutally decisive action. These qualities made him a natural for the task of cracking heads until all the villages and the provinces were united.

Gronigetzkol never revealed to anyone but Frelko the personal vendetta that drove him to unify the provinces. A tidal wave of black rage against the mountain brigands flooded his mind and overflowed into the bloody struggle that created Bolkanistan. Many rode to victory under the thrall of his fierce hatred without realizing its source.

It was only after the wars were over that Frelko discovered just how hardened a man he served, a man deprived of human warmth and blinded to all but the past. His ministers were loyal officers selected for their posts because they told him only what he wanted to hear: don't do anything different and be harsh with anyone who pushes for reform. But Gronigetzkol's image of Bolkanistan, the lush farmland and picturesque villages, no longer existed. Industrialization dropped soot all over the quaint old towns while the topsoil covering the bone dry farmland blew away in the wind. Only the craggy mountains remained the same, as implacable as Gronigetzkol himself.

For years Frelko had been trying to reason the Supreme Leader out of his brutal stance. Now he saw just how hopeless a task he'd taken on. Gronigetzkol lived in a hall of mirrors reflecting only the vision of himself as savior of his people. Whatever failed to support this vision went unseen and unheard.

Frelko leaned back in his chair, rubbing his tormented brow as his spirit slipped reluctantly back into his body. He leaned his elbows on the desk with his head in his hands. No matter how hard he pressed on his eyes, he couldn't drive away Varnik's gruesome images of starving families dying together in their farmhouses, and long lines of exhausted peasants, struggling on with the last of their strength, desperate to escape over the mountains to Uzbekistan before winter's snowstorms blocked the passes and froze them to death in the howling wind.

Worst of all, I've let this tragedy happen right under my nose. I'm as responsible as anyone for the years of government neglect. With the entire army under my command, I did nothing as those worthless bureaucrats made light of the problems in the field. I never once sent anyone to check. Why? How could I have believed that Gronigetzkol's harsh policies were really necessary to keep the peace? Have I been so sheltered beneath the Supreme Leader's wing that I couldn't see the truth?

Tears of shame welled up. What can I do? There must be a way to atone for the injustices I've committed against my own people and to save as many of them as possible. If I'm not prepared to risk everything, as I did in my youth when I joined Gronigetzkol to unite Bolkanistan, then I deserve to be executed or banished in disgrace. Even if Gronigetzkol has gone deaf and blind to the cries of his countrymen, I must stand up for them somehow.

Arthur kept the intimate details of his encounter with Sally to himself. He told Frank and Jerome only about Brother Joseph's beating his wives and having crazy fits, seeing demons and breaking things. Arthur wanted them to hear just enough to join with him in planning Sally's rescue and their escape from the valley.

Jerome was livid. "Let's storm the compound and drag that creep out by his hair!" he yelled. "I can't stand the idea of him manhandling my sister. I'd rather die than let that happen!"

Frank responded more thoughtfully. "I've been worried for a long time that something was wrong, but I never imagined it could be this bad. I agree, we have to come up with a rescue plan right away."

"OK, here's an idea, guys. Why don't we all escape with Sally? We're the ones manning the guard houses, so who could stop us? Only problem is, we don't know what's out there, downstream from . . ."

"You mean leave our families behind? Are you crazy? We'd never see them again!" Jerome yelped out in alarm.

"They might come with us – have you thought of that?" Frank countered. "Our parents are fed up with Brother Joseph because of the way he abducted Sally. How about yours, Arthur?"

"I haven't brought it up with them. I didn't want to arouse suspicion and risk our being taken off border patrol. They have so much invested in this community, it's hard to imagine them leaving. How can we sound our parents out without botching up the plan? And if we decide not to tell them, we can't even say goodbye. That would be awful."

"I could approach our parents and discuss the issues with them," suggested Frank. "If they knew we were determined to leave with Sally no matter what, maybe they'd come with us. At least they wouldn't give us away – they'd never put our lives at risk. And our parents might be the best ones to talk with Arthur's. They've been close friends for years. If both families left together, it might also loosen Brother Joseph's sick grip on this place. More refugees would follow for sure if he didn't change his ways."

"Sounds good," Jerome nodded. "But where would we go? We don't have a clue what's out there. We've never been taught anything about the world except how evil it is. Whatever we find, it's got to be better than this creepy prison!"

"I think my Dad has a laptop computer hidden away somewhere in case the community failed," replied Arthur. "If I can find it and get the thing running after so long it might give us information about the world beyond the valley, and . . ."

"You mean we can take a look at the world outside? That would be super!" exclaimed Jerome, leaping to his feet.

"Anywhere, Jerome, anywhere at all," Arthur replied with a big smile. "Amazing pictures, too! I'll find the laptop, charge the battery and bring it with me tomorrow night before our shift. I'm pretty sure I can remember how it works. Fortunately my dad has one of those satellite models that can access the internet from anywhere. It'll give us all the information we need to plan our escape. I think we can pull this off!"

On Wall Street the next morning, Alan Ferguson was sitting at his desk reviewing a client's portfolio when his secretary buzzed to tell him that his boss, Donald Fitzwilliam, had dropped off a formal lunch invitation. This had to mean something was up. Donald didn't socialize with Alan except perfunctorily at the company Christmas party and they met rarely at work except for quarterly conferences and annual evaluations. Donald's sleaziness put Alan off and he tried to have as few dealings with him as possible.

Alan's clients trusted him and listened to his advice when he saw opportunities to improve their portfolio positions with a timely purchase or sale. As word got around about Alan's expertise, his clientele expanded and he began to attract some high rollers. Alan's transaction volume made Donald look good in his department's quarterly performance reports, so he left Alan alone to tend his expanding stable of investors. Alan was far and away his best broker, the obvious one to approach about his new scheme.

When Donald ushered him into the most sumptuous noonday feed in the financial district, Alan's suspicions were confirmed. Nobody gets invited to the Royal Feast just for small talk. As his eyes adjusted to the dim lighting of the King's Court Dining Room, he made out heavy rough-hewn wooden tables with matching chairs richly upholstered in royal purple arranged in lines flanking a raised golden throne, surrounded by walls of faux stone draped with flags of medieval fiefdoms. Amply endowed waitresses clad in period costumes with low cut bodices scurried around, carrying mugs of ale and gold truncheons loaded with slabs of meat.

At night the throne was occupied by the King, who interrupted the diners periodically with comical commands and edicts enforced by his courtiers – not the scene for a confidential business meeting. At lunchtime, however, customers didn't come for entertainment but for excellent food – and, above all, privacy.

Raising his gold knife and fork to attack a huge pile of meat, Donald heaped praise on Alan for his excellent work and assured him of rapid advancement in the firm. Then he proposed to make Alan his partner in a new hedge fund for high rollers with a guaranteed 15% annual return. He planned to charge a six percent commission at the front end that he and Alan would split, then place the remaining funds in a dummy investment account that Donald referred to with a cynical snicker as the "Dunn and Dunster Charitable Trust."

This has to be some kind of scam, thought Alan. And what a lame pun – "Dunn and Dunster," for cripesake. As Donald filled in the details, Alan realized the plan involved both poor investment strategy and illegal trading practices.

"See, first we invest some of the account in high yield bonds as a safety cushion," murmured Donald secretively, leaning forward across the table, "but most of the funds will be placed in speculative stocks that'll make a lot more than 15%. We'll split the excess income between us fifty-fifty, distribute the rest to the investors as promised, and no one will be the wiser. I'm a specialist in oil and gas shares and you are more into utilities and alternative energy stocks, so we can cover a wide field if we work together."

Alan ticked off the flaws in Donald's plan one by one in his mind. First, it involves doing business on the side with Burrow and Hunker clients. This is strictly forbidden in our employment contract, so we could both lose our jobs. Second, we have to invent a dummy investment account outside the firm. This would require forging fictitious names and addresses and Federal ID numbers. As if this weren't enough, Alan realized, the dummy investor poses as a bogus nonprofit charitable trust to evade taxes. We'd be charged with fraud and tax evasion as well as breach of contract if this scam were discovered. We could end up serving long sentences in Federal prison. Alan shuddered at the thought. Even if we did get away with it for a while, Don's strategy would fail during a prolonged market downturn and we'd be discovered when we couldn't pay our investors.

Alan's heart sank. If I turn Don down outright, I'll lose my job. Don would find a pretext to get rid of me since I already know too much. But I've got all these expenses at home. Is the extra money worth the risk? I need time to think.

"Your scheme sure sounds tempting but I need to mull it over for a few days. How about we meet again at the end of the week to discuss it in greater detail?" Donald seemed satisfied with that answer and they set up the appointment for Friday.

Nursing a sour stomach, Alan sat in his office all afternoon immobilized by indecision. The phony extravagance of the Royal Feast couldn't have been a more perfect setting for Don's outrageous proposal. I had no idea that scumbag could be so stupid. What a scam! He must be desperate for money. And just knowing as much as Don told me at lunch, I become a silent accomplice. If I tell anyone at the firm about our conversation, I wouldn't put it past Don to claim I'm fabricating the whole thing to get him fired so I can steal his job. I don't see any way out. What am I going to do?

Controversy

Daryl rubbed his hands in eager anticipation. "I'm itching to see what your monster equation does with a complicated problem. Let's see ... how about rabbits?"

"What do you mean?" Martin asked, feigning innocence. "Rabbits are just little animals, not mathematical problems."

"A math challenge they certainly are, wise ass, whenever we try to predict how many rabbits will be living in a habitat at some future time. So many factors determine the fluctuating rabbit population – the number of rabbits to start with, migration rates in and out of the area, weather conditions, food supply, rabbit reproduction rates and life expectancy, fatality rates from every cause, and changes in predator populations in the region, to name a few. These factors are all interdependent, so fluctuating rabbit populations have been difficult to model. Under unstable conditions when three or more factors are shifting at once, it's anybody's guess how many rabbits will be running around even next week. No known model makes accurate simulations when species populations vary chaotically. Let's find out if your monster equation can do it."

Daryl gathered all available data related to rabbits and their habitats while Martin assembled rate equations to predict how interdependent variations in key variables would affect rabbit populations over time. After inserting these equations into the cells of his matrixes, Martin ran the program with many different starting conditions.

The master equation produced accurate simulations when compared with all known rabbit data. Under certain conditions, the equation generated families of attractors that shifted constantly and unpredictably over time – a second level of chaos within an already chaotic system. Daryl and Martin raised their arms in a victory cheer as the results they'd hoped for poured out of the printer.

"We've reached a new milestone today, Martin, thanks to your master equation – let's call it the 'Attractor Generating Algorithm,' or AGA, for short – but I still have a few questions. The matrixes can be expanded, can't they, to include as many variables as necessary to simulate any situation?"

"Yes, of course," Martin agreed. "That's AGA's advantage over earlier simulations."

"Then, as the number of variables increases, doesn't AGA become more and more difficult to compute? Isn't it going to take an unrealistic amount of computation power to run AGA on a complex problem with thousands of variables?" Daryl asked. "I doubt there's a system in the world capable of computing AGA with more than a hundred variables."

"Yes, you're probably right. I was so busy grappling with theory I never considered that practical limitation." Martin shook his head. "Maybe creativity and consciousness are just too complex to simulate on any system, even an advanced supercomputer."

"I'll let you in on a little secret: I've been anticipating this problem all along," Daryl grinned, lowering his voice secretively, "and I've cooked up a solution. I've been waiting for the right moment when we finally have something complex enough to need more computation power than we've got. What if we send AGA out into the world attached to a worm so that it takes over every computer on the web?"

"You can't be serious! That's an outlandish scheme, Daryl – and illegal, of course. Aren't you worried about detection? That could blow our cover for sure and send us all to jail!" exclaimed Martin.

"It's highly unlikely that anyone would notice," replied Daryl, "since AGA would employ only a tiny bit of each computer's capacity. Even if a tight security system picked up an intruder, it could never track us down. The STAIR Lab doesn't have to worry about cyber security because we leave no footprints in cyberspace. All our transmissions are broken up into untraceable packets that get randomly routed through different network hubs all over the world. That's why we haven't bothered with more than routine encryption to protect our privacy.

"Just think, billions of computers operating all together to become the ultimate supercomputer, capable of running the AGA program on a vast scale! We could put any number of variables into the matrixes." Once he had revealed his secret, Daryl got carried away. As skittish as a high-spirited racehorse at the starting gate, he wanted to build the worm on the spot so he could test AGA on a more complex problem right away.

Martin held up his hand. "Just a moment, my friend. Do you really believe your marriage would survive the storm if you did something this wild without consulting Samantha? I'm sure she will have a word or two to say about it. She always does when you go off like this." Daryl fell silent.

As a man in love with Daryl's wife, Martin wondered why he was so protective of their marriage. Martin concluded that he had come to value his friendships with Daryl and Samantha, and he hated to see his friends fight. He also saw the spiritual aspect. The Sufi mystics taught Martin to savor the unquenchable thirst for the unattainable, whether divine Beloved or human lover. He experienced a poignant joy in hovering near that enticing flame but never allowing it to consume him. Since no permanent union with God is possible for mortals, a human being gets only a taste of the Divine. Martin's longing for Samantha felt similar to him. As long as her marriage to Daryl barred the way to a lasting union with her, Martin could continue to experience his exquisite longing for the woman who embodied the unattainable Divine for him.

"You're right, we need to talk with the others first, especially Samantha," responded Daryl more soberly now. "Come to think of it, George should be the one to design the worm. He has a perverse fascination with different ways to corrupt computers. Have you looked at George's library of horrible internet viruses? If the Olympics had cyber subterfuge event, he'd win a gold medal!"

Samantha looked down in awe at the page-long equation full of Greek letters and matrix terms and put her arms around Daryl and Martin's shoulders. "Congratulations on this impressive display of mathematics gone wild, you guys! If AGA does what you say it can, this might just move the STAIR Project to the next level. How soon can we test it?" Martin struggled to remain calm. Any attention from Samantha set him off like a Roman candle, especially her touch.

"We'll discuss that in just a moment," responded Daryl. "First you have to understand some practical constraints. Obviously AGA is a highly complex equation. When we expand it to include the many variables needed for solving a really difficult problem, it will require a huge amount of computation power, more than we can muster here."

"You just got done telling us that AGA's our salvation, Daryl. Now you say we aren't equipped to run it?" Samantha shot back. "What use is a scheme like that? And I thought we had a state of the art supercomputer downstairs that could handle anything!"

"Hold on, Samantha. This limitation doesn't apply to your chimp puzzles but to larger problems with many more variables. I have a new strategy for applying AGA to those problems as well – want to hear it?"

"Sure, Daryl, tell us what you have in mind," intervened George to defuse the mounting friction between the volatile Samantha and her stubborn husband.

Samantha scowled in silence as Daryl plunged on. "Listen to this! What if we tackled a problem of great importance and complexity that exceeded the computing power of any facility in existence? We could attach AGA to a worm and send it out over the internet to infect every computer in the world so that they'd all be working on it together. If we were using just a tiny portion of each computer's capacity, nobody would notice and we'd have a supercomputer of immense power!"

"How can you even consider such massive electronic embezzlement?" Samantha exclaimed. "Don't you realize that stealing is wrong, immoral, unethical, even illegal – however you want to say it? Even if you could get away with this, there would be terrible consequences for you and everyone else!" By the end of her tirade, Samantha's voice had risen to an ear-splitting shriek. Everyone cringed and looked away. No one wanted to open his mouth and risk an escalation.

There she goes again, thought Daryl, Samantha's father, that fundamentalist bible-thumping fire and brimstone preacher, sure left his mark on her. How did she ever get to be so good at scientific research with his fanatical rants playing in the back of her mind? I've never understood how she can be so cool and objective then get completely irrational like this.

Martin understood this contradiction better than Daryl. Samantha had been attached to her fundamentalist father, yes, but her stoic mother had really been the one who raised her, and her mother was cut from very different cloth, cool and quietly logical. Samantha never understood what had drawn her parents together long enough to marry and give birth to her. When Samantha was three, they were screaming at each other. By the time she turned six, they were no longer on speaking terms and by the time she was eight they were divorced.

Samantha's mother moved to the city and enrolled in a graduate school chemistry program at the university. Samantha was taking advanced placement courses in math and science while her mother was writing her Ph.D. thesis. During their affair before Daryl came into the picture, Martin had heard Samantha reminisce about the disconnect she felt as a child being shuttled back and forth between the coldly rational world of her mother's life in academic science and her father's fanatical world of Christian evangelism. Samantha respected her mother's achievements and identified with her logical mind, but she deeply loved her father. She'd missed him sorely when they first moved to the city.

Even now Samantha sometimes felt sad as she remembered the many nights she'd cried herself to sleep clutching her stuffed dog while her mother worked late at the lab. She'd so wished her daddy were there to read her to sleep from the Bible. It was the sound of his voice she missed most, but the Bible verses and his strict morals sank in with it.

Martin knew that Samantha's heart had been split in two by her parents' failed marriage. She could never choose between her mother and father because their conflict continued to rage within her. She also agonized over the choice between Martin and Daryl, and Martin suspected Samantha's decision to marry Daryl wasn't the end of the story.

George bravely broke the long silence. "Samantha, Daryl isn't plotting to steal anything. Even the simplest devices seldom use their full processing capacity. Daryl just wants to take advantage of the computing power that would go to waste anyway and put it to good use."

"That doesn't matter!" screamed Samantha. "It's still theft! We have no right to make all the computers in the world run a single microsecond slower for our selfish ends."

Daryl could contain himself no longer. "Come on, Samantha! You know how important our project is to humanity, to the whole world. We aren't killing anybody or even crippling them. We need the combined resources of all humanity to solve problems we created in the first place. That seems perfectly just and ethical to me." Daryl could match Samantha's passion when an important cause was at stake, and he already had an inkling how the Project might help reverse the destruction of the environment. With the support of the spirits of the land and his eagle guide he felt sure of his ground now.

Martin had remained silent throughout this heated exchange. He knew he must weigh in, but he still wasn't sure what to say. He considered his options. I agree completely with Daryl, yet the last thing I want to do is alienate Samantha – and she does have a point. The Project would be using people's computer time without their consent. It could be called stealing, but if the future of life on Earth is at stake, who cares? The problem is, Samantha does.

Martin turned and faced the others. He needed to placate Samantha and he had a scientific reason that would at least kick the ethical issue down the road. "As confident as I am in my mathematical modeling skills, this equation was a big stretch for me. It is far and away the most complex I've ever devised and it could contain all kinds of glitches that have to be ironed out before it will work properly. I share Daryl's enthusiasm for AGA's potential to solve world problems, but in view of all the unknowns in the situation, I think we should begin where we started, by testing it on Samantha's chimps. That was the idea, wasn't it – to come up with a general algorithm for learning enhancement? We already have the necessary computing power here at the Project to generate a master VNI pattern from my equation that will induce the chimps to solve all the block puzzles. We should test AGA on the chimps and determine if the equation needs some fine tuning before we attempt anything more ambitious."

Everyone sighed with relief. Martin's suggestion let them step back from a moral minefield. Daryl and Martin programmed AGA for chimp learning enhancement by filling each one of the matrix cells with a different equation that had helped the chimps solve a puzzle. Then George helped program this version of AGA into the Visual Neural Inducer. Meanwhile Samantha scurried around setting up a new series of problems to test the master equation's effectiveness.

The team gathered in the chimp lab to watch the first experiment. Looking on over the heads of the chimps, everyone gasped at the beauty and elegance of AGA's VNI display. Bars and shapes of brilliant colors flitted across the screen in an ever-changing kaleidoscopic pattern that had a hypnotic effect on the scientists as well as the chimps. The four sat still as statues for hours behind the monkeys, both species mesmerized by what they were seeing.

This VNI simulation was much more varied than earlier displays designed to teach chimps how to solve just one puzzle. Daryl kept looking for repetition but he never saw a single moment of the display that exactly duplicated a previous image. Subtle differences were constantly appearing, so that the patterns evolved, transforming slowly into new designs.

Samantha leaned over to check the chimps' EEG tracings and let out a war whoop. "Look at this! Their brainwaves indicate a state of intense overarousal affecting the entire cerebral cortex. These chimps must be developing new neural connections at an enormous rate. I've never seen anything like it before, even when I've given them drugs to speed up brain metabolism. Whatever is going on, it's happening extremely fast."

After watching for three to four hours, the chimps finally lost interest. One by one they wandered off to eat lunch and groom each other. They showed none of the drowsiness that ordinarily preceded their afternoon naps. Samantha couldn't wait to see how the chimps would perform on the puzzle problems.

The results were astonishing. Chimp after chimp looked at the pieces carefully, gazed at the empty outline of the finished puzzle for a moment, then reached over and deliberately filled in the outline with one piece after another until the puzzle was assembled correctly! None of the chimps took longer than fifteen minutes to solve even the most complex puzzles. As soon as they completed one task, the chimps would look up expectantly at Samantha as if to say, "That was easy. Now give me a real challenge – or is that all you've got?"

As quickly as Samantha could set the problems up, the chimps would solve them. Before long every block design puzzle had been correctly completed by each chimp, but they still weren't tired of them. They just kept looking up at her, awaiting the next chance to show off their ability.

"Hey, guys, what do you think would happen if we tested the chimps with a different type of puzzle, something like interlocking pieces that can only be taken apart and reassembled in a certain order?" Samantha asked.

"Theoretically, Daryl replied, "when confronted with puzzles other than the block assembly type, these chimps shouldn't be any faster at coming up with the correct solution than those who haven't viewed the master VNI display. After all, we didn't include VNI equations for any other type of puzzle in the matrixes."

"Let's just try them on something else and see what happens. The way my chimps have responded so far, we might have raised their IQs enough so they might solve any kind of puzzle faster." As she predicted, the chimps made quick work of every puzzle problem Samantha gave them. The AGA VNI patterns appeared to have enhanced the general capacity for visual-motor learning in a species closely akin to humans, a milestone achievement in experimental psychology and neuroscience.

"How is this possible?" Daryl asked. "The chimps are generalizing as if they were capable of advanced abstract thinking, yet the master VNI equation was programmed for only one type of challenge, block design puzzles."

"Let's take a look at how the attractors evolve when we run the master equation through millions of iterations," Martin suggested. "Maybe that will help us understand what's going on."

The master equation ran for an hour on the main computer. "Let's see ... one, two, three, four," counted Martin as he stood before the monitor, ". . . nine, ten, eleven... Eleven attractors doing an intricate dance around one another! Look how each of them is surrounded by a dense cloud of data points with tails stretching out behind them like comets."

"Amazing!" Samantha exulted. "Martin, you've created not only a scientific breakthrough but a beautiful work of visual art, a gorgeous ballet of form and color!" Martin turned his face away to hide his bright blush.

"I believe we may be the first to witness the evolving thought processes of primate problem solving," Daryl observed. "The dance we are watching now is the signature of a highly complex dynamic system with the creativity and ingenuity to tackle unfamiliar tasks successfully. For the first time in the history of science, we can watch creative thinking in action. We should congratulate ourselves for pulling off a successful marriage between theoretical and experimental approaches to learning enhancement. We've taken a giant step forward – the successful simulation of human creativity. Now we'll see if AGA is capable of simulating consciousness as well."

Daryl rose to his feet and faced his colleagues like a coach giving a pep talk before a big game. "My friends and colleagues, now that AGA has performed far beyond our expectations with Samantha's chimps, we can't afford to waste another day with preliminary trials. The time has come for AGA's crucial test. I propose that we turn the Attractor Generating Algorithm loose on the worldwide environmental crisis immediately!"

"I don't see how any model can encompass the full complexity of the Earth's ecosphere," objected George. "The sheer number of variables and the intricacy of their interrelationships defy comprehension,"

"It's not as big a leap as it looks, George. We simply program AGA to identify environmental conditions that minimize extinctions and maximize long-term survival for every species of life on Earth. Martin's infinitely expandable matrixes allow AGA to combine in one equation everything we know about environmental change and species interdependence. When we calculate millions of iterations, AGA gives us the big picture, the hidden patterns in a huge array of raw data. Starting with any set of environmental conditions, AGA can predict the trends that determine the future of life on Earth. AGA's output should indicate the best way to reverse the disastrous decline of the biosphere and begin the process of environmental recovery."

"OK, I'll just have to take your word for that until we see what AGA comes up with. You and Martin do the math. I just build the hardware. My motto is 'Build it and they will come!' See, I built you this supercharged computer system and your mammoth equation came calling."

The team, including Samantha, agreed that the spectacular chimp results justified this ambitious step, even if it meant pirating time covertly from millions of computers all over the world.

"Martin and I have programmed AGA with this general instruction: Develop the most effective plan to maximize health and to minimize harm for all species. We will need a way to follow AGA's progress and find out if its computations have been detected. Therefore I've designed a subroutine within AGA called the Observer that will monitor every step of AGA's analysis, report back to us and answer our questions." Daryl concluded his speech with a light touch. "Samantha, would you mind if I use your voiceprint to synthesize the voice of the Observer? It will be much more pleasant to hear the lilt of your voice coming from the computer rather than a mechanical monotone."

Samantha laughed merrily and nodded her assent, flattered by her husband's appreciation of her sensual voice. "Samantha," remarked George, "when you converse with the Observer it will sound as if you're talking to yourself, the way I've heard you do sometimes in the lab when you concentrate on a tough problem." Everyone giggled as they rose from their chairs. George took Daryl down to his lab to help design the worm, while Martin returned to his office to refine AGA and prepare it for tackling a much larger problem than learning to solve puzzles.

Samantha stayed behind sitting alone in the conference room, lost in thought. It's nice to hear Daryl acknowledge me for more than just my keen scientific mind. I learned I had a lovely singing voice back in Dad's church when the choirmaster asked me to do solo parts – and it wasn't just because I was the minister's daughter.

I like being appreciated that way because Daryl isn't usually sensual or romantic. Our pillow talk at night is limited to the latest news on our research projects, especially Daryl's, she reflected ruefully. Our marriage has mainly been about intellectual stimulation and warm companionship. Occasionally we stage a "romantic getaway" vacation, but what intimacy we enjoy even then could hardly be called passionate. Daryl channels his sexual energy into his work and I guess I do the same, but I'm not really happy about that. Hmmm – maybe that's what's making me so irritable these days.

George's warmth and affection as the two men worked together created a relaxed atmosphere that gave Daryl a respite from Samantha's emotional outbursts. The peaceful ambiance George created around him made Daryl feel an unfamiliar calm contentment. He settled back in his chair to study George's worm.

George enjoyed watching Daryl examine the long lines of code scrolling down his computer screen. I bet Daryl would be surprised if he knew how much I've withheld from him since we first got together for Sunday afternoon chess games in grad school. I wonder if he would be my friend or even allow himself to be alone with me for a minute if he knew how much I wanted to hug him and kiss him and make love to him.

Oh well ... it's better to settle for the bittersweet rewards of warm friendship than have nothing, George reflected sadly. I guess I've gotten pretty good at hiding my feelings over the years so none of my straight friends will be uncomfortable if I happen to be attracted to them. Sure, it takes vigilant self-control, but I've been in the closet for so long now that I can't imagine what it would be like to live any differently. I learned the hard way back in junior high when I found myself attracted to my friend Bob, obviously not gay, and then to Fred, a married teacher, for god's sake – but what a body he had! I sure wish I could forget those embarrassing infatuations and what they did to my life back then whenever I told anybody. I ended up with no friends and having to change teachers. My attraction to straight men must be my cross to bear – such a painful paradox. Luckily, there's always my work. . . .

Daryl finished reading through George's program and leaped to his feet. "This is the most ingeniously stealthy Trojan horse program I've ever seen. Only a hard core cyber freak could dream up something this pernicious!" George basked silently in Daryl's appreciation. Martin sent over a new version of AGA with a portal for attaching the worm, and, laughing diabolically, Daryl grafted them together. Late that afternoon the team reassembled in the conference room.

"George has designed a most clever worm," Daryl announced. "I doubt even top specialists in virus detection will notice it sneaking into their systems. We encountered no difficulty attaching it to Martin's refined version of AGA, so we're ready for launch. Any questions before we proceed? Darryl looked around the table with his hand poised above the keyboard.

"Don't we have to let the Committee know what we're doing before we go any further?" Samantha wondered.

"We needn't worry about the TCC," replied Daryl. "They told me to proceed as quickly as possible to environmental applications. Besides, they don't meet again for nine months. What are we supposed to do? Hold everything up so that crusty fossil Isaac Nicholson can sabotage us with his quibbles? If there's a problem later, I'll take the fall as the principal investigator. Let's just go ahead and give them what they're funding us for!" Samantha backed down without another word, for once, and Daryl got a silent thumbs-up from George and Martin.

Daryl pushed the critical key on his laptop to blast AGA out like shotgun pellets into all the internet hubs around the world. Any message passing through the centers would now pick up AGA and the worm attached to it. Every computer on the web would soon be helping to devise a way of rescuing life on Earth from man's greed and stupidity.

PART TWO
GESTATION

Singularity n: The moment when technological change becomes so rapid and profound, it represents a rupture in the fabric of human history...

Vernor Vinge, in "The Coming Technological Singularity."

Suppose we did create a computer that talked and acted in a way that was indistinguishable from a human being... Would that mean that the computer was sentient, the way a human being is? Or would it just be an extremely sophisticated but essentially mechanical automaton without the mysterious spark of consciousness – a machine with no ghost in it? And how would we know?

Lev Grossman, "Man and Machine: 2045, The Year Man Becomes Immortal," Time Magazine, 177, #7, 2/21/2011.

Gathering Speed

It was after six as a weary President Moore strolled along the promenade toward the East Wing, enjoying the fragrance that wafted on the evening breeze from the rose garden. It had been a trying day and at last the time had come to relax with his wife. Martha greeted him in the large parlor sprinkled with familiar pieces from their home in St. Louis. His evening glass of sherry and a plate of cheese and crackers awaited him. Moore looked forward all day to this evening ritual with Martha.

Tall and willowy, Martha Moore cut a fine figure in her mid-fifties. Her smooth skin looked twenty years younger and her close cropped steel grey hair maintained its sheen. But it was the youthful vigor of her mind that amazed Moore the most. She kept a vast array of information at her fingertips and displayed razor sharp logic in the use of that knowledge. Few dared to argue a case against her.

Martha had become a legend as a supporter of women's rights. When she prosecuted domestic violence charges, even against high profile defendants, Martha always got her man. She could bring large corporations to their knees in gender discrimination suits. Martha ceased litigating when her husband moved into the White House, but attorneys throughout the country continued to call upon her as a consultant in difficult cases. While her political leanings were more to the left of moderate than her husband's, they shared the same instinct for fairness and decency. That, along with her brilliant mind, made Martha the President's most trusted adviser.

"How did it go this morning with those high-level meetings?" she asked, kissing her husband on the cheek. "You look tired."

"You start," Moore replied with a weary sigh. "I'd rather listen to you talk about your day before going into the mess on my plate right now."

"All right," answered Martha, sipping her sherry, "but I haven't much to tell. In the morning I greeted some VIP wives from Indonesia and the Samoan Islands and gave them a personalized tour of the White House while their husbands met with State Department officials. Strictly a courtesy tour, not even an opportunity to find out much about them or their countries. Then this afternoon I gave a speech at a conference on world hunger and unequal distribution of food supplies. It's still hard to tell how much influence I wield as First Lady. Do my efforts really promote the causes I support, or am I just a figurehead, a prestige symbol, when I show up at their meetings?"

"I know how you feel," mumbled Moore, swallowing a mouthful of cheese and crackers. "Even though the President of the United States is supposed to be the most powerful man in the world, I sometimes wonder how much real influence I have over the course of events. Whatever I do, there's always outrage to face from one political faction or another followed by a determined and often effective effort to block any significant change in the status quo. Just today two issues came up calling for decisions which could alienate my allies in Congress and even in my own administration. Mind if I run them by you?"

"Of course not, dear. Let's go inside and chat over dinner. I think you'll enjoy the main course – wild king salmon poached with lemon and vermouth, just the way you like it. Maybe by the time we get to dessert you'll have a better idea how to proceed. Then we can just relax together for the rest of the evening." Martha pulled her husband out of his chair playfully as he was draining his glass.

No one knew better than Martha how to help President Moore let down at the end of a hard day. She made sure that the family dining room of the East Wing had a casual feel to it. A painting of their mansion in St. Louis hung over the sideboard. She had also insisted on replacing the fancy East Wing tableware with familiar Moore family china and silverware. It was hard enough living in a bubble, closely watched by Secret Service agents in dark suits and sun glasses. Martha made sure that comforting reminders of home were in plain sight everywhere.

While they sipped their chilled vichysoisse, Martha listened to her husband's description of the ominous meeting with his environmental adviser followed by the annoying encounter with the Secretary of Defense. "I don't know what to do, Martha. Any ideas?"

"Sounds like a very difficult morning," replied Martha. "What do your instincts tell you?"

"That's the easy part. On the Bolkanistan issue, if Ben's intelligence report confirms Starling's claims, I'd have Ben negotiate a humanitarian foreign aid package with Gronigetzkol in exchange for a small covert operation involving their military and our Special Forces to comb the mountains for terrorist activity. Regarding the environmental crisis, I would demand that Congress act now. I've asked Clarence to prepare a list of essential policies and programs that must go into effect immediately. It should be on my desk by tomorrow morning."

"Sounds to me like you know exactly what you want to do. What's the problem?"

"Come on, Martha! You know what will happen if I don't follow Starling's recommendations. He'll have his cronies in Congress turn on me in a flash. Putting him in that post has brought me nothing but political blackmail. No doubt he'll try to run against me in the next election. And as for the environmental crisis, that will be even more unpopular in Congress. I can do all the declaring I want. Congress won't budge."

"You could always dismiss any overt military action in Bolkanistan as unnecessarily provocative, or even a threat to our national security, if that alarmist Starling decides to call you out on it," suggested Martha.

"Nice twist, using Starling's own argument against him. I think it might fly if I were forceful enough. Now let's see ... still midday in Bolkanistan. I'll give Ben a call and have him contact Gronigetzkol's foreign minister so they can begin the negotiations tonight. We could get something rolling immediately that would upstage any move Starling tries to make behind my back."

"Now, as for the environmental crisis, how about using your presidential powers to declare a national emergency, just as you would in the case of an enemy attack? You wouldn't be waiting for permission if we were bombed by another country, and this situation sounds just as serious. If Pitman's report is accurate, and you've said that all your scientific advisers support him, you certainly have grounds to act whether or not Congress wants to cooperate."

"That's unprecedented! On what grounds could I declare a national emergency over a non-military threat unless we had a huge natural disaster – something like a gigantic tidal wave drowning coastal cities, a massive earthquake doing severe damage in many states, or a huge volcanic eruption spewing toxic ash into the jet stream?"

"That's exactly the problem, Ed! Don't you see? We respond only to emergencies after they happen without putting in enough effort to prevent them. If Pitman's projections are accurate, a terrible catastrophe will happen very soon. What's wrong with using your executive powers to redefine our relationship to natural calamities? We can't just talk about studying what might be necessary to avert them. We must prevent them *now*, whatever it takes!"

"Sometimes I think you should have been President instead of me. You take bold positions without flinching. I've been trying too hard to please Congress and to avoid antagonizing the opposition. That never seems to work anyway."

"It's easy for me to talk big – I'm not the one who has to take the flack for it," Martha pointed out. "You're the unlucky duck the people elected Commander-in-Chief."

"But you're right. This could be the decisive moment in my Presidency. I must seize it, otherwise I fail myself, the American people, and the whole world." Moore slapped his linen napkin down on the table. "That's it! I'll deliver a speech to both houses of Congress declaring a national emergency and putting a number of measures into effect at once. There'll be a huge outcry from the right, but I have to move ahead based on Pitman's grave report. I'd rather face impeachment than fail to act!"

131

"Very brave of you, dear. I'll be right by your side, whatever happens." Martha got up from the table and hugged her husband from behind his chair. "You go call Ben," she murmured in his ear, "then no more business for tonight."

Moore stood up from the table and walked down the hall to his home office. He picked up the dedicated line to his inner circle of advisers. "Ben? Sorry to disturb you at this late hour. I need your help tonight. Have you looked into the validity of the intelligence that got Starling so riled up this morning?"

"Yes, I put a team on it right after our meeting," Secretary Hallowell replied. "Starling's concern centered on two coded radio messages traced to the Pakistan-Afghanistan border region mentioning an unnamed mountain base in Bolkanistan. We have no evidence that such a base yet exists, nor have we picked up any terrorist messages originating inside Bolkanistan."

"What would you suggest we do?"

"I still think it's premature to act until we have more information from that region. As I said this morning, Middle Eastern intelligence tends to be unreliable and the various terrorist groups like to feed us false information to lead us on."

"OK, but we may have to throw a crumb to Starling and make a move – the minimum, maybe what you suggested this morning, offer humanitarian aid in exchange for allowing a small elite force to search the mountains for hidden terrorist enclaves. Perhaps we could ask for the assistance of Bolkanistani guides familiar with the terrain. All top secret, of course. I'd like you to call Balkanistan this evening."

"I can sound Gronigetzkol out on this if some action must be taken for political reasons, but we need to exercise extreme caution with any military presence in that part of the world – an issue Starling has obviously failed to consider."

"That's par for the course from that fanatic. If Starling continues to beat the war drum this time, I plan to accuse him of endangering national security by pressing for hasty military action. If he won't back down, I'll ask for his resignation."

Hallowell breathed a sigh of relief. "He's been a thorn in our side ever since you appointed him, always poking into State Department business. I hate to think what would happen if he ever made it to the Oval Office!"

"Over my dead body! I'll let you go so you can make that call. See you tomorrow morning."

Martha rose to meet her husband as he returned to the dining room. "Now for some fun. How about an end-of-the-world disaster movie – or your favorite, a corny one about invading aliens?" Martha chuckled. She loved teasing him out of a serious mood.

"Oh, cut it out!" Moore laughed in spite of himself, "You know that's the last kind of entertainment I need. How about a Broadway musical? A simple-minded plot with nice music and a happy ending. That's about all I can handle tonight. Tomorrow will be a bear."

"Yes, the perfect thing to get your mind off your impossible job. But first we're going downstairs to bowl a few strings. I can see you're ready to throw something at someone and it'd better be a bowling ball rolled at some pins rather than your paperweight aimed at Starling's head! You've got to let off some steam."

Martha pulled her husband down the steps to the basement bowling alley. President Edward Moore, commander-in-chief of the most powerful country in the world, was willing putty in his wife's hands.

The rarely used red telephone on the far corner of Frelko's desk rang insistently. What else could go wrong? he wondered, anticipating an attack by the rapidly escalating rebellion. Frelko picked up the receiver and answered in Bolkanistani. "General Peflik Frelko. Who's calling?"

"Yes, Mr. Secretary." Frelko abruptly changed his tone and switched to diplomatic English. "Terrorist cells in the mountains? No, sir, we have no intelligence to that effect. Can you give us anything more specific? ... You want us to do WHAT? Do you realize we are dealing with a revolt against the government? ... Yes, I know terrorists thrive on civil unrest, but you must take into account the chaos in our country. We couldn't guarantee the safety of your forces in that rugged terrain...

"Of course, Mr. Secretary, I didn't mean to imply any disrespect to your highly skilled assets. I know how capable they are, but you must understand how quickly this revolt is spreading. If your men were detected by the rebels, they would look like Gronigetzkol's allies in a government counteroffensive. They would be outnumbered and mercilessly slaughtered by men who've lived in the mountains all their lives and could easily outmaneuver any foreign force. Besides, if I may be frank with you, Mr. Secretary, what possible benefit could it bring to our country to cooperate when we desperately need all our resources to deal with the rebellion? . . .

"Large shipments of food and supplies? Is that so?" Frelko paused and stroked his chin. What could be the harm in letting some American commandos take their chances amidst the cliffs and crags of those inhospitable mountains if doing so would save some countrymen from starvation?

"I will take the matter up immediately with Supreme Leader Gronigetzkol and call you back within the hour, Mr. Secretary. And please convey our warmest greetings to President Moore. Thank him for his concern about the drought and famine in our distant part of the world."

Frelko slammed down the receiver. He rose and paced the floor to relieve the gathering tension in his body. As if the American president would give a single thought to tens of thousands of starving Bolkanistani peasants if it weren't for that privileged country's paranoia about terrorists! Since the beginning of the century, the Americans have been overreacting to any foreign threat. The 2001 attacks hurt their national pride. It still makes me laugh. Until Gronigetzkol took over we'd been invaded several times every generation as far back as anyone can remember.

What pampered children these Americans are! They always act like everything's about them and they're entitled to throw their weight around whenever they feel a little nervous... Oh well, this time they are offering food and medical help, so who cares about their motives. General Frelko opened his door and strode decisively down the hall. He knew Gronigetzkol would still be hunched over his desk, fuming impatiently about the revolt.

"So, Peflik, you've broken that traitorous worm Varnik already? Congratulations! Let's hear his miserable story. And don't leave out those well deserved screams of pain as you tortured his worthless flesh!" Gronigetzkol leaned forward, anticipating Frelko's report with relish.

"Not as yet. Another matter demanded my attention. The American Secretary of State called requesting confirmation of reports about terrorist activity in the mountains along the Uzbekistan border. They are asking for our cooperation. They offer humanitarian aid in exchange for our turning a blind eye to a small covert mission. I told them we have no knowledge of any terrorist activity but they seem determined to pursue their lead. It appears we have nothing to lose and something substantial to gain by going along with their stupid scheme. What should I tell them?"

"Why settle for humanitarian aid when they could help us stamp out this annoying rebellion? Call them back and demand helicopters and weapons. Let the rebels go on starving and plotting while we blast them to bits from above!" Gronigetzkol yelled, pounding his fist on the desk.

Frelko considered pointing out that many loyal citizens were starving and desperate for relief, but he held his tongue. Even in the best of moods, Gronigetzkol was not known for compassion. "Very well. I will call the Secretary and convey your terms to these meddling Americans. We can take advantage of their fearfulness."

"Yes, of course – but hurry up with Varnik's torture. I want to hear a complete account of his agony. Make him look as gruesome as possible when we parade him in the public square on the way to his beheading. Show that turncoat no mercy!"

Frelko nodded and returned to his office immediately to call Secretary Hallowell. In addition to Commander of the Armed Forces, Frelko had been assigned the role of diplomatic contact with foreign governments.

The Supreme Leader trusted only Frelko to implement his domestic and foreign policies, so over the years Frelko had acquired as much diplomatic as military experience. He had come to understand the foibles of the major world powers well enough to play the negotiating game with some foreknowledge of how each government would react. Frelko knew that Gronigetzkol's demand for military aid wouldn't appeal to the Americans, who were wary of any military adventures that might entangle them in a civil war.

"Secretary Hallowell? ... Yes, this is General Frelko. Supreme Leader Gronigetzkol is willing to overlook a small temporary American military presence in the mountains, provided he receives immediate military assistance in quelling this rebellion ... Yes, he is asking for weaponry and helicopters. His first priority is ending the civil war and he deems humanitarian aid to be premature at this time ... No, I'm sorry, he was adamant about it ... Very well. I will let him know you have to take the question up with President Moore ... By the end of the week? Excellent! Please be sure to convey to President Moore our deepest appreciation for his interest in our country, Mr. Secretary ... Thank you. Goodbye."

What if the Americans were stupid enough to side with Gronigetzkol and quell the revolt? Frelko shuddered at the thought of the terrible blood bath American weaponry would visit upon his people. Something had to be done to prevent that from happening – and quickly.

After his parents went to bed Arthur smuggled the forbidden laptop up to the clubhouse wrapped in a blanket. He found Frank and Jerome there and unwrapped it on the table. "OK, guys, here's our connection with the outside world. We can download maps and photos of this area and plan the best route out of here. But first, would you like to have a look at all the 'sinful' things happening in the outside world?"

Arthur pulled up website after website showing places around the globe. "Look at these views of the Grand Canyon and Lake Powell!" Jerome exclaimed, "Remember going there when I was six or seven, Frank? I wish we could go back, don't you?"

"Sure, I remember that trip. It was really fun. We got to ride in a motor boat on Lake Powell and walk a little ways into the Canyon, too. Yes, and then our camping trip to northern California. . . remember those huge redwoods? So big you could drive right through them! Then up along the Oregon coast and into Washington, all the way north into Canada. My favorite was that whale watching trip in the San Juan Islands, then the ferry all the way up to Vancouver Island. It got so wild inland – bears and dense forests. So amazing! . . ."

Frank's eyes brimmed over and a tear ran down each cheek, glistening in the lamplight. "What's the matter, Frank?" asked Arthur.

"I'm remembering a lot of things from before we came here to Barrondale, guys, and I feel kind of homesick for those days. I liked the different kids I met at school and the games we played together. Here it's the same small group all the time and we don't do anything but farm work. I never wanted to come but our parents were sure this was the best thing for us. I feel sad about all the years we've missed. This place's nothing but a big prison! We've got to get out of here!"

"I feel the same way, especially now that Sally ... but wait – take a look at this!" exclaimed Arthur. "They have these new gadgets called gelphones the size of dimes that mold to fit your ear. No buttons anymore, just voice commands!"

"That's nothing!" trumped Jerome. "Check out these pictures of Mars! They've set up a good-sized colony up there now. So much has happened while we were trapped in boring Barrondale." Jerome had been the youngest of the three when they arrived and the least familiar with the world outside the community. He could hardly wait to get out and experience it for himself.

"OK," Frank interrupted. "We haven't much time. Let's get down to planning our escape. What's the best route out of here?"

"Take a look at this satellite map of the area," responded Arthur, pointing to the screen. "It looks like those three families that escaped had the right idea. If we go downstream past the lower guardhouse, it's only eight miles to the nearest town. But what then?"

"That all depends on whether our families come along," Frank replied. "I'm sure our parents have an emergency fund stashed away and maybe other things that would be useful to us. If they decide not to come along, they might give us a little money. What about your parents, Arthur?"

"They would help us for sure, and I think they might be ready to join us. We just have to fill them in on the latest about Brother Joseph's mad fits and abuses toward his wives. That'll be the last straw, I bet."

"The next step depends on our parents, then," Jerome added, "but we're leaving no matter what, and Sally is coming with us!"

"For sure!" Arthur confirmed. "And that won't be a problem. It's time I told you that she has come right out and sworn her love for me. It feels like we're already married, regardless of Brother Joseph. His other wives want us to be together too, so we can count on their help."

"What else is new?" responded Frank, "Sally's loved you since she was little, Arthur. I never had any doubt about that. But it does mean something that she's declared it right to your face."

"Yeah, in a big way," answered Arthur with a dreamy smile.

"What does that mean?" Frank inquired, furrowing his brow.

"Let's just say she left no doubt in my mind."

"Come on, Arthur," pleaded Jerome, "We're her brothers and your best friends. You can tell us everything."

"No way! The details are private between us. Some things about a romance just can't be shared, even with close friends – and definitely not with her brothers. You'll find out for yourself when you're a little older."

"Awww . . ." Jerome protested, until Frank cut him off.

"Give Arthur a break! It's gotten serious between them, probably in ways you don't really want to hear about. It's uncomfortable even for me to imagine, mainly because I want to protect Sally, so leave it alone. We have to trust that this is right for them and Arthur won't hurt her. I'll make a deal with you, Jerome – let go of the whiny little kid thing and I'll give up being the bossy older brother."

"Thanks," replied Arthur. "I'm glad you understand. Believe me, the way I feel about Sally, I'd risk anything to keep her safe."

"I know. That's why I can relax about it. Now, you sound out your parents and we'll talk to ours. By tomorrow night we should know more about what we can expect from them." Frank looked at his watch. "Whoops! Time's up. We can barely make it to our shift if we leave right now."

Frank and Jerome filed out the door and hurried off in opposite directions to their posts in the guardhouses at either end of the valley while Arthur lingered to snuff out the kerosene lamp and stuff the laptop in the corner under the blanket. He emerged from the clubhouse pursued by a greasy plume of smoke, shut the door and replaced the strands of ivy that served as camouflage. Then he clambered up the hill and began his patrol of the perimeter. As Arthur circled the valley on the heights drenched in starlight, he prayed that his parents would help them escape – and, God willing, join them.

When he arrived at Burrow and Hunker the next morning, Alan Ferguson was still fuming at Sarah for manipulating him into buying the kids iPad9's. Stepping off the elevator and spotting Donald beside his office door, Alan realized he hadn't given any thought to the scam.

Uh oh, this spells trouble. Why is Don down here first thing in the morning? I thought he was giving me until the end of the week. Alan decided to take the initiative. "Hi Don, how're you this morning?"

"Fine, Alan. How about you? Did you sleep well?" Don responded heartily.

"Not so great, Don. Spat with Sarah. She always wants me to buy expensive stuff for the kids. You?"

"I guess some people would call me lucky that way," Donald replied with a wry smile. "Ever since my wife left me three years ago, I don't have to put up with demands from anybody and I know exactly how much I have to come up with each month to keep my ex off my back. No, if I lose sleep it's over that bad land deal I made last year. The property tanked and I owe a bundle on it. I'm in the red now. Creditors closing in – the whole bit."

Oh, so that's it, Alan realized. As he unlocked his office door, he turned to face Donald. "Well, then, to what do I owe the pleasure of your company this morning?" he chirped in a strained voice. "We have a meeting planned for the end of the week. Something come up?"

"I have some good news for you, but your fellow brokers are drifting in now to put in their half-assed idea of a workday, so I think we should discuss it in your office. No sense arousing suspicion."

Cornered, thought Alan as he swung open the door and offered Donald a seat.

"OK, Alan, I'll get right to the point. Calder moves over to the Newark office at the end of the month, a transfer without benefits, if you know what I mean." Alan had heard that Don's boss, Vice President Evan Calder, was a lost cause, a hopeless alcoholic who got shuttled from branch to branch, too well connected to fire. Management always found a way to make it look like a promotion.

"I'm in line for his position and you would be my first choice to move into mine. I think you're the one who could really take this branch to the next level. I have to write a letter today recommending a replacement. You're the best man for the job and you deserve the salary."

Don lowered his voice and continued in a conspiratorial tone. "This puts some pressure on us to get our little partnership up and running ASAP. When Evan leaves, his replacement has to take over the next day. I'm certain about my promotion, so we will be in higher positions when our new investment opportunity launches. Problem is, as VP I won't have any clients and you'll only be carrying a few, like I do now. How quickly can you put together a list of your fattest and most willing whales to bring along with you when you move upstairs?"

"The promotion sounds great and I appreciate your recommending me, but won't we both be more exposed now? Is it really worth the risk, considering our salary increases?"

"You let me take care of that. I've been preparing the ground for months now. We're covered as long as we get everything set up before the promotions take effect. Can I count on you?"

Alan was running out of time. Don had him up against the wall. For now, he was offering him the carrot, but it would be the stick if he didn't go along with the scam. On Don's salary Alan wouldn't need the extra income, but today he had to placate Don and sound positive about his stupid scheme. Later he'd come up with some convincing glitch.

"I'll take a look at my client list and make a few phone calls. Should take a couple of days. Let's keep our appointment Friday. I'll know by then." Donald nodded and left, finally.

Alan could barely breathe as he foundered in rising anxiety and confusion. He picked up the phone and dialed frantically. "Hello David? ... It's Alan ... Of course I sound flustered – I'm fucking freaked out! Can you clear lunch? ... Yes, today. This can't wait ... No, too public. How about your place? . . .Thanks. I'll see you at noon." If anyone can help me find a way out of this, it'll be David.

Doomed

Two hours after setting the AGA program loose on the environmental crisis, George and Daryl were sipping coffee at Daryl's desk and waiting for the results to come in. George thanked his lucky stars for all the Sunday afternoon chess games with Daryl in grad school and the pioneering hardware development work he'd done over the years that had led to his being picked for the STAIR Project. Now he was enjoying the precious privilege of working with Daryl for months or maybe even years to come. George treasured every moment.

Daryl turned to the Observer. "Can we have a progress report?"

AGA responded in an eerily realistic rendering of Samantha's voice. "All available data regarding the factors impacting the biosphere are being correlated and analyzed. Sufficient computing capacity is being recruited from all parts of the world. Coordinated processing is going smoothly and has not been detected."

Daryl grinned and thrust up a victory fist. "My child is alive! I can hear its heartbeat!"

His jubilation was tempered by the painful memory of Samantha's ruptured ectopic pregnancy and the emergency hysterectomy to save her life. I almost lost her, he recalled. I've never felt so scared and helpless. Sorrowful thoughts of the child they would never have passed fleetingly through his mind.

Daryl's attention soon shifted back to the monitor as details of AGA's progress poured in. "Look!" He was pointing at a long list of habitats scrolling down the screen with the various species in each ecosystem listed underneath. "These are all the species and habitats analyzed so far. As soon as AGA finishes the initial data synthesis, everything will be integrated into a worldwide ecological trend analysis. Then we'll get the answers we need to save the Earth."

"How long until you can report your results?" asked Daryl.

"Estimating between one and two more hours," AGA replied, "depending on how many promising scenarios I must compute before I can identify the optimal scenario for species survival and on how far into the future I have to project each scenario."

George yawned. "I think I'll take a break then." The big push of the last few days was catching up with him. Daryl continued to monitor the details of AGA's progress while George snoozed on a cot in the corner.

An hour later, Daryl shook George awake. "We can expect to see results very soon. I thought you might like to wake up in time for the big moment. By the way, you were dead out – and you have a very musical snore!" Daryl played his recording of George's whistles, snorts and wheezes, much to George's embarrassment. He felt relieved when Daryl didn't seem put off, only amused.

George squeezed Daryl's shoulder playfully, then rubbed his eyes, rose to his feet and sat down next to Daryl facing the monitor. George sighed contentedly as the fog of drowsiness began to lift.

Just being close to Daryl filled him with a peaceful sense of completeness.

AGA began to transmit the findings. "Under present conditions, no scenario can maintain the integrity of the ecosphere for more than twenty years. In the best case scenario, only one third of the current human population and no more than a half of Earth's plant and animal species will continue to exist after 100 years, even if all human activities that damage the environment come to a halt immediately.

"Along with other mammals, the human race is destined for extinction, as the species succumbs to extreme shortage of drinkable water, widespread famine and viral epidemics, climatic cataclysms such as tornadoes and hurricanes of great size and violence, flooding of the coastline as the ice caps melt due to global warming, huge tsunamis due to undersea tectonic shifts, overpopulation and mass starvation after prolonged drought, waves of environmental refugees fleeing from place to place in search of water and food, spread of nuclear radiation from reactors damaged by earthquakes, and violent conflicts between the starving masses and the privileged few over dwindling food, water and energy sources.

"Some life on Earth will continue, but not with the great variety of ecosystems and species that now exist. Most habitats will collapse within this century. In the worst case scenarios that would result if increases in pollution and global warming rates continue unchecked, only the most hardy plant and animal species, such as microbes, deep sea algae and primitive insects like cockroaches will survive after 200 years of biosphere degradation spiraling out of control. In every predictable scenario, the rest of the species populations decline to zero."

Devastated, Daryl slumped in his chair covering his face with his hands and began to weep. When George leaned over to comfort him, Daryl collapsed in his arms. Daryl's sobs deepened until he was gasping for breath. George stroked his head tenderly and held him close. Gradually Daryl relaxed.

"This is my worst nightmare!" he finally managed to choke out. "I was sure AGA could show us the way out, but it's already too late!" He broke into another round of sobbing and George held him closer. George read AGA's analysis carefully as he embraced Daryl and waited patiently for him to ride out the waves of grief.

At length Daryl stirred and sat up, drying his eyes on his sleeve. George passed him a tissue to blow his nose. "This is so much worse than I expected," muttered Daryl gloomily, throwing up his hands in confusion, "What can we do? We're doomed! The Earth is dying!"

George interrupted Daryl's collapse into helpless despair. "You're forgetting that we just ran AGA through its first major test and obtained a plausible, though unfortunate, result. It works, Daryl, it works! Before you fall into the pit of despair, remember we have something to celebrate. You found the Holy Grail you've been seeking your entire career!" The hint of a smile shone through the tears drying on Daryl's cheeks.

"Besides, I'm not sure what AGA means at the beginning of. . ."

Daryl sat up, the sharp scientist again. "What? It's clear enough isn't it? Humanity is destined for extinction along with most of the animal and plant species on Earth! What else could you conclude from the results?"

"You may be right, but aren't you curious what 'under present conditions' refers to here at the top? Just what conditions might it be excluding from its analysis?"

"That's just AGA's way of saying that the program started with all the current data and extrapolated into the future, testing all possible scenarios, just like we programmed it to do. What else could it mean?"

"I don't know, but before we surrender to gloom, let's find out." George turned to the monitor. "Explain precisely what you meant by 'under present conditions' in your report."

"'Under present conditions' refers to all available data concerning the Earth's biosphere, including the biological and behavioral patterns of the human species at its current level of development."

"Specifically which behavioral patterns of the human species are significantly affecting the results?" George asked.

"Regardless of its capacity for technological advancement," the Observer replied, "the human species has proved incapable of dropping individual, corporate, or national interests to deal with critical problems, except to a limited degree during wartime. Current divisiveness over the seriousness of the environmental crisis indicates that unified action to alter the downward trend in species survival is virtually impossible."

"What else is new?" reacted Daryl bitterly. "That was obvious without extensive computer analysis. I was hoping AGA could find some way around this huge obstacle."

"Maybe, if . . ." George trailed off. He turned once more to the monitor. "AGA, what specific changes in human behavior would be needed to save the biosphere?"

"To significantly alter the outcome, the human race as a whole must immediately give species survival top priority for guiding all decision-making at both individual and institutional levels."

"Is there any way for that to happen?" asked George.

"You are asking an irrelevant question because the drastic changes necessary would be incompatible with basic human behavior. My programming does not permit deliberate extinction of any species. Altering human development in the required direction would mean transmuting the race so that it could respond like a single organism rather than a population of individual human beings. Humanity would need to evolve into a collective, capable of operating in harmony with a single purpose, like a beehive or an ant colony. I concluded that the profound and rapid transformation of human consciousness required would alter your species so far beyond current parameters that it would amount to extinction. Such a course of action would violate my prime directive to maximize species survival."

Daryl's face lit up. He leaned over to the monitor. "Then you are telling us that transformation of human consciousness could potentially save the biosphere but you have dismissed this possibility without further investigation because the human race would not survive and you would be violating the prime directive?"

"That is correct."

Daryl pressed on more urgently now. "Could a Visual Neural Inducer program, such as the ones we have developed to accelerate chimpanzee learning, bring about the required transformation of human beings?"

"This is theoretically possible, but given that individual consciousness in its current form might not survive. I would need to override the prime directive requiring preservation of the human species to investigate that possibility further. Would you accept scenarios that lead to the extinction of humanity in its current form to save the rest of the biosphere?"

"Sounds grim the way you put it, but you have already predicted extinction of the human species in a century or two anyway. Wouldn't it be consistent with your programming to accelerate human evolution? That would appear to be the only way of saving Homo sapiens as well as the many species doomed to perish with us."

"What you are proposing would be permissible under current program constraints only if you instructed me to broaden my definition of your species to include highly evolved forms."

"Make it so!" Daryl commanded, imitating Patrick Stewart's Shakespearean accent as Captain Jean-Luc Picard in Star Trek. Like Picard, Daryl often had qualms about his decisions. Turning to George, he wondered, "Do you think it's worth the risk of accelerating human evolution even if that's what must be done to save Earth?"

"I have my doubts about that," George replied, "but I think the possibility is worth considering, especially since we have no alternative. What worries me most is the loss of man's free will.

I've read too many science fiction stories about computers turning human beings into mindless drones. Wasn't that one of the favorite themes in Star Trek? Remember the Borg, absorbing human beings by inserting implants in their captives' brains? I can see the headline now: "STAIR Project gives birth to Borg Collective! RESISTANCE IS FUTILE!'"

"I worry about that too," responded Daryl somberly, finding the allusion to the horror of the Borg not at all funny. "But how do we know that a complete loss of free will would be required? What if a harmonious shift in priorities would be all that's needed and individual choice could be preserved?"

"Do you think that's possible? It seems too much to expect of our flawed species. But if that's our only option let's begin by checking with Samantha and Martin. They've been observing the chimps since the VNI learning enhancement experiment and might've noticed if individual behavior patterns have been affected by exposure to the VNI display."

"I suppose that's a good idea," responded Daryl tentatively, oddly reluctant to end the stormy afternoon with George. "We need a staff meeting anyway to discuss AGA's dismal projections. It's good we can go in with something hopeful to add after the prophecies of doom."

Daryl hesitated for a moment then continued haltingly, choking up again. "I just want to tell you before we go up to the conference room how much I've appreciated your presence here with me through this ordeal. I can't remember a time when I needed support so badly or felt so comforted." The two men hugged each other close as unseen tears welled up in their eyes.

"It's been almost 18 hours since the VNI learning enhancement experiment and the chimps look normal enough to me," commented Martin, gazing down into the pen, "but you know them much better than I do. What do you think?"

"They've been eating and sleeping a little more than usual. Otherwise, same daily routine, same quirks." Samantha pointed to a little clown-faced chimp that was hopping around playfully provoking the others. "See Bozo over there? He's up to his old tricks."

As Samantha gestured toward Bozo, the back of her hand brushed lightly across Martin's forearm, sending shivers through his body. *What exquisite torture, being this close! I can barely stop myself from kissing her. She's got to be feeling something too, but I can't make a move. That would betray my best friend and sabotage the project.*

Samantha certainly did notice the electricity between them, every day getting more and more difficult for her to ignore. She knew the moment of truth would come sooner or later when the smoldering embers of their old attraction would burst into full flame again. Martin and Samantha brought their attention back to the chimps, both struggling to resist the zinging in the air between them.

The house phone rang, breaking the tension. *Saved by the bell!* thought Martin, with a sigh of relief. Samantha answered. "Oh, already? ... OK, we'll be right down... AGA's results are in. I thought it would be at least two hours more. I hope that's a good sign, but I didn't like Darryl's tone. He sounds exhausted and depressed. We'd better be prepared for some seriously bad news."

Terminal Velocity

First thing the next morning, a rested and refreshed President Moore strode into the Oval Office to find Pitman's memo waiting for him. He quickly sketched out the points he wanted to cover in his speech that night and buzzed his secretary. "Arnold, call my best speechwriter and tell him to drop everything. I'm delivering a major speech tonight. Notify the Vice President, the Speaker of the House, the Cabinet, the Supreme Court, and the press that I will address a joint session of Congress at 8 pm. Don't tell them anything else. I want every person in that chamber to be kept in the dark. This outline and all drafts must be stamped Top Secret. Anyone leaking this to the press will be fired and prosecuted for a major breach of security. Cancel all my appointments today and ask Ben Hallowell to come over."

Moore gave his speechwriter a copy of Pitman's report and Moore's outline for the address, briefed him on the tone he wanted to set and sent him off to write a rough draft while he met with the Secretary of State. "Sit down, Ben. Did you get through to Bolkanistan last night?"

"Yes. I talked with Foreign Minister Frelko. He sounded affronted that we would approach him with our petty concerns with civil war looming in Bolkanistan. He seemed more receptive when I mentioned humanitarian aid. I could tell he wanted to accept the deal, but Gronigetzkol turned it down flatly unless we would supply the regime with arms and helicopters to put down the revolt. I knew this was out of the question, but I told Frelko I'd discuss it with you and get back to him. Protocol, you know."

"Thanks, Ben. Wait a couple of days, then call him back and tell him we can't afford to get involved militarily. You don't have to say that we'd probably support the rebels. That's a nasty regime. It's about time the citizens rose up in revolt. I wish them luck. If Starling starts screeching again, just stall him a day or two more while we 'gather more intelligence'. Thanks for taking care of this situation. I have more urgent concerns today."

As Moore rose to his feet, Hallowell turned to him and asked, "What's this I hear about an address to Congress tonight?"

Moore smiled cryptically. "You'll understand when you hear what I have to say. I'm keeping it under wraps until then. Need to know basis only. Build maximum suspense to get maximum impact."

"What could be so big that you'd keep even a close friend out of the loop?" Ben complained, obviously chagrined – and intrigued.

"Sorry, Ben. I'm not taking any chances. I'm enough of a blabbermouth myself to know hard it can be to keep a tasty morsel to myself. I'll be looking for you in the front row tonight."

As Hallowell left with a look of curious alarm on his face, Moore couldn't help gloating. Everybody is building up my speech, even Ben. Short notice and secrecy are creating the atmosphere of crisis. Perfect!

When Moore's speechwriter brought in his draft late in the morning, Moore glanced through it and tossed it aside. "What a bunch of hollow rhetoric! My speech tonight must electrify the world. Start again, and pull out all the stops this time!"

The poor hack retired in disarray to pick up the pieces while Moore returned to the East Wing for lunch with Martha. He walked in waving the draft. "Look at this! We pay these cretins top dollar for their writing ability and all they can come up with is this pedestrian text filled with platitudes. If I read this tonight, it would put everyone to sleep before I reached the end of the second paragraph. I need to deliver a powerful address, full of eloquence and fervor, not this pablum!"

"Why not write the speech yourself? You're a good writer, and this issue has set you on fire. With all the anticipation you've stirred up on the Hill and around the country by now, you've created a great opportunity to demonstrate your skills as a statesman and orator."

"You may have a point there, but I don't want to treat this issue as just another chance to raise my ratings. It's survival of life on Earth we're talking about, not my political capital. If I were concerned about popularity, I'd never be giving this address in the first place."

"Exactly why you must write the speech yourself! After that meeting with Pitman, you've become so impassioned about the environmental crisis that you could ad lib an excellent address right now."

"You really think so? Hmm ... no advance text to get leaked? The President speaking extemporaneously to Congress and the nation with twelve hours' notice? Unheard of! It will drive everyone wild with curiosity. No teleprompters! That will jack people up even more. Brilliant idea, Martha!"

She smiled, realizing that by midafternoon her husband would have made the same bold decision himself. He would deliver his speech a little more confidently tonight because she had suggested it.

Moore spent the rest of the afternoon strolling through the rose garden mentally rehearsing his address. Before dinner he took a nap. The President was poised to drop a bombshell.

Frelko rose from his desk with a sigh. He could no longer postpone taking Varnik to the torture chamber. Reluctantly he descended the long stone flights to the dungeon, his footsteps echoing off the damp stone walls. Frelko wasn't looking forward to mutilating an old comrade. He furrowed his brow as he unlocked the door to the secluded chamber at the far end of the dungeon's lowest level, a remote room that held many horrors. It had been reinforced with double thick walls so that no one upstairs could hear the howls of agony that issued from within.

Most prisoners were wise enough to confess before they had to face Gronigetzkol's monstrous machines of torment, but Frelko knew that Varnik could not be intimidated, even with unbearable pain. He had hardly flinched after the harshest blows from Frelko's iron rod.

Frelko recalled a day long ago when he and Varnik fought side by side against a band of fierce marauders. He glanced to his left and saw Varnik with two arrows protruded from his right shoulder charging the enemy with fixed bayonet as if nothing were wrong. Frelko had never seen such stamina and disregard for pain. Varnik was the kind of soldier who would fight to his dying breath. What good would it do to torture him? But Gronigetzkol's orders were explicit. Frelko decided to make one last attempt to interrogate his old friend. If he could only persuade him to provide the information Gronigetzkol wanted, there might still be a chance of avoiding the inevitable. The tension in Frelko's body increased with each step he took toward Varnik's cell.

His master key turned with a click and the cell door creaked open. Varnik still sat quietly on the stone bench amidst decades of foul-smelling filth and decay, a peaceful expression on his face. Frelko shook his head. *How can he be so calm amid this squalor when he knows he's facing an excruciating death?*

"Varnik!" Frelko growled as menacingly as he could manage. Ignoring his ominous tone, the prisoner nodded to Frelko with a pleasant smile. "The Supreme Leader has ordered me to extract information from you by any means necessary, including torture. If you answer my questions, we may be able to avoid that unpleasantness. Let's begin with the numbers of insurgents and their military capabilities. Give me specifics!" Frelko forced himself to continue scowling as he struggled to strike an intimidating pose.

Varnik's laughter echoed down the stone passageway. "Come now, Peflik! Do you think you can fool me with your theatrics? You're much better at military strategy than acting. I know exactly how that vermin Gronigetzkol thinks. He has ordered you to torture me and make a public spectacle of my humiliation, then execute me for treason. You don't want any part of it but are forced to do his bidding. No matter what I do or don't tell you, Gronigetzkol wants me maimed and killed. That outcome was certain as soon as I was seized."

Frelko's jaw dropped. "Does it really come as such a surprise to you that I was prepared to suffer and die for the cause of my people from the moment I assumed leadership of the revolt? You

159

have set up a win-win situation for our cause. If Gronigetzkol has his way with me, the revolution will gain a martyr and the people will fight to the death for their freedom. From then on, they won't give up until Gronigetzkol's head is on a pike in the public square! On the other hand, if I manage to escape the fate he has planned for me, it will make him look weak and raise the morale of the rebellion.

"Do you think I would have agreed to holding your bogus truce negotiations here if I hadn't expected treachery from him and seen how that could be turned to our advantage? Do you really believe I am that naïve, Peflik?"

Frelko was shocked – and impressed, he had to admit – that Varnik was capable of such a shrewd strategy of self-sacrifice. He began to relax as he realized that torture would be worse than futile. "I see the logic of what you are saying, Pyotrey. Apparently I would only be playing into your hands if I carried out the Supreme Leader's orders. But what other option do I have? He won't rest until he sees you bloodied and brought to your knees. He will use every horrible device imaginable to make you reveal the information he wants so that he can round up your followers and imprison them, unless he decides on mass slaughter. He's capable of going to that extreme, you know."

Varnik grinned shrewdly. "Peflik, you obviously have parted ways with the Supreme Leader and lost your taste for his harsh style of leadership. Otherwise, our previous relationship wouldn't have deterred you and my torture would have begun as soon as you captured me. Why don't you face reality? Join the revolt! If even a small part of the army remained loyal to you, together we could overthrow Gronigetzkol and usher in a new era of compassionate government that would care for our starving people. You know as well as I do how Gronigetzkol has completely disregarded their needs. This is your moment to take a stand! If we join forces, together we can save Bolkanistan!"

When Arthur left the clubhouse to begin his shift patrolling the perimeter, his parents were talking earnestly in their rustic living room. They had built their house and furniture out of local lumber, assisted by other families in the community just as they had helped the neighbors build their dwellings. The room was minimally furnished with rough-hewn chairs, the walls bare. Brother Joseph considered art a portal for Satan to enter.

"Let's face it, Corinne! Brother Joseph led us here on false pretenses!" exclaimed Walter. This tall taciturn man was speaking with unaccustomed exasperation tonight. "Now that he has us trapped, he's exploiting us for his own benefit. For starters, he's always taken more than his fair share of the irrigation water coming down the creek. That didn't make much difference as long as we had plenty of water, but when the drought came last summer, the crops withered in the lower valley and we didn't have enough water in the creek to turn the mill wheel. Because of Brother Joseph's greed, we'll have to live on wheat berries all winter!

"Besides claiming every attractive pubescent girl, Brother Joseph demands the best of the harvest for his compound and leaves the rest for the community. He behaves just like a feudal lord. We didn't move to Barrondale to become his serfs!"

"I'm upset about his behavior too," Corinne added, "but a lot of good has come from our moving here. This community has given us a healthier and happier life than we used to have."

"You're right, but now our leader has corrupted his own vision. He's turned Barrondale into a religious dictatorship. At first we participated in every decision affecting the community. Back then Brother Joseph's voice carried no more weight than any other householder, but it's been nearly a year since the last council meeting. Since then he's been expecting everyone to obey his pronouncements."

"Should we call a council meeting and make our concerns public?" Corinne wondered. Her uncertain tone was unusual. A strong, stalwart woman with close cropped brown hair, she looked as if she'd been cut from the same cloth as the pioneers who settled this land two centuries ago.

"How can we do that without including Brother Joseph, who would justify everything he's done on religious grounds and label anyone who questioned him as a heretic. What use is it to discuss anything if the leader of the community rejects all ideas but his own and condemns anyone who questions him? We have no choice, Corinne. If Brother Joseph won't listen to us, we have to leave."

"And lose our friends, our community – our way of life that we chose eight years ago? Except for Brother Joseph's behavior recently it's been good for us, hasn't it? And what about our vows and religious commitments, Walter? Are you ready to throw all that to the wind just because our minister behaves like a boor?"

"He's more than just our minister. He's mayor, city council, and feudal lord all rolled into one. That's too much power for any man to wield without being corrupted by it, and I guess he's no exception after all. This social experiment has failed because we gave him too much power. I should have known this might happen, but I trusted too much in Brother Joseph's dedication to our holy cause.

"Remember how he gave up his thriving ministry in Missouri to found this community? He made many sacrifices along with the families who chose to join him. We trusted in his noble vision of saving what was good in humanity by isolating us from the corrosive effects of popular culture, especially on our children. We depended on Brother Joseph's courage during the struggle over uprooting our families and leaving the world behind."

"You paint a saintly picture of how he was in those days, dear, but I have to admit I always had some doubts about him," responded Corinne. "Take this business of marrying his choice of young girls. I recall hearing stories ten years ago from a few younger women but I didn't take them seriously. You know how some women fawn on charismatic ministers? They like to spread tales of being picked as the chosen one. We had several like that in the old congregation, remember?"

"I'll have to take your word for it. I never listened to their gossip. But have you noticed how Brother Joseph's sermons are becoming more extreme? Sometimes he sounds like a rabid dog. He's just not fit to lead us any longer."

"But where can we go if we decide to leave?"

"Why not to your parents in Wyoming? Wouldn't they take us in?" suggested Walter.

"Yes, perhaps, in an emergency. But they felt so wounded when we joined this community. They believed we'd abandoned them, and I can't blame them for being hurt and angry. We took their children and grandchildren away. They would have a lot to forgive after all these years. Meanwhile, we would hear nothing but 'I told you so'."

"True, but we wouldn't need to stay long. We could settle in a new community."

"All right, dear, let's sleep on it and discuss it again in the morning. We'd have to tell Arthur of course and prepare the girls. We'd need a little time."

When Arthur returned home from his shift the next morning, he found his parents in the kitchen, seated at the large table in the corner away from the wood stove, making lists. "What's going on?" he asked.

"We have a big decision to discuss with you, son," Walter replied.

"That's funny, I have something very important to tell you."

"Let's sit down in the living room," suggested Corinne. "You two go inside and get comfortable. I'll bring coffee. You sure look like you could use some – and a big breakfast too, right after we talk."

After passing the steaming mugs all around, Corinne sat down and turned to her son. "Why are you so excited? What happened?"

Once Arthur began, the words tumbled out. His parents gaped in horror as he described Brother Joseph's seeing demons and breaking furniture, but hearing that he was beating his wives was just too much for Walter. He began to pace back and forth and his face twitched.

"Unbelievable! That self-righteous hypocrite has betrayed us all! Why didn't we see it sooner? We have to stop him before he can do any more damage!"

Corinne placed her hand gently on her husband's arm. "Honey, don't you think we ought to make sure these awful stories are true before jumping to conclusions? After all, he has been our guiding light . . ."

"All the more reason why he should know better!" shouted Walter. "His outrageous behavior has undermined our attempt to rise above the corrupt world. Evil wins out in the end. What a shameful defeat, despite our dedication to leading a righteous life together – all because of that lying, faithless PARASITE!!"

Alarmed by her husband's fury, Corinne pleaded for reason. "Even if this is what really happened, couldn't demons be responsible? Wouldn't they come after the leader of a religious community where they could do the most damage?"

"Possibly, but that's no excuse for indulging in sinful acts against his own flock. He could have asked for help – but no! He's behaved for a long time like he just wanted to have his way. We can't blame the Devil for all our failings. No matter what's wrong with Brother Joseph, his horrendous behavior with his wives settles the issue for me. We have to leave as soon as possible!"

Arthur sat open-mouthed in amazement at the intensity of his father's outrage, since he had been expecting resistance to his escape plan. He told his parents what the boys had in mind and invited the whole family to join them.

"I feel so betrayed," Corinne's voice was choked with grief and regret. "What Arthur just told us took away my last bit of trust in Brother Joseph. I don't see how our family can continue to be in his flock – but what about the rest of the community? Are we going to abandon them to the whims of a monster?"

"You're right," responded Walter. "Let's invite everyone except him and his family to attend a meeting where we'll expose Brother Joseph. Then we'll leave this blighted valley together!"

"And leave his wives and children in the clutches of that beast? Over my dead body!" declared Corinne, suddenly rounding on her husband, her dam of restraint bursting with pent-up rage. Arthur had never seen his mother go up against his father like this. Standing face to face with Walter, hands on her hips, she stared at him angrily, "That beast should be dragged out of his lair and forced to face his flock. We'll make him pay for what he's done to us!"

"He may have turned evil," Walter conceded, "or he could be possessed – maybe even insane. One way or another, he's unfit to lead this community. Maybe he's the one who should go, not us!"

The Saltons decided to set up a meeting as soon as possible. They asked the community over for supper the next evening in the Saltons' backyard, except for two blindly submissive families that would run to Brother Joseph like children tattling to the teacher.

Jerome and Frank found their parents, Joshua and Mary Webster, just as disillusioned and upset with Brother Joseph. Sally's news convinced them to leave Barrondale at once. By the time Walter appeared at their door later that evening to invite them to the meeting, the Websters had already started packing their things.

David Pomeroy was Alan's rock. He'd been Alan's best college buddy and the reluctant best man at Alan's wedding. They continued to get together several times a month. David always questioned Alan thoughtfully about his decisions without telling him what to do, a true friend. He ran a solo consulting business not far from Alan's office, making it easy for them to do lunch – the only way to keep up the friendship, since David had disliked Sarah from the beginning and the feeling was mutual.

Today would be different. Alan left his office and enjoyed a refreshing stroll through the clear light of early fall over to David's loft in Greenwich Village for what promised to be a very special meal. David was a gourmet chef with a unique fusion style. You never knew what he would come up with next. *L'Omelette á l'Impossible* would suit the occasion perfectly, chuckled Alan to himself as he walked up to David's door, glad he could find some humor in his dilemma.

David – tall and vigorous, with his hair pulled back in a short ponytail – answered the door in his usual hearty good spirits and enfolded Alan in a big bear hug. "Great to see you, old buddy! You inspired me to drop a boring pot boiler I've been working on and create something interesting for lunch." The words "something interesting" coming out of David's mouth had to mean an outlandish dish that stretched culinary custom to the limit.

"I can hardly wait!" Alan replied with a grin, welcoming the distraction.

"How about some Viognier?" David asked, taking Alan's coat. "I put a nice vintage on ice for us." David went back to the kitchen area, giving Alan a few minutes to settle down in an armchair in the living room area of David's cavernous loft, a gigantic studio apartment with nooks and crannies devoted to different functions scattered around the space. His friend returned a few minutes later with two elegant glasses of wine and a cheese plate. Alan sipped eagerly while David sliced some Humboldt Fog onto rye crackers.

"You know how I love that cheese! It must be the ash that makes it so special."

"Yes, it's one of my favorites too," replied David as he tasted the wine. "Ahh, slightly chilled, just right ... I ran out this morning and bought the cheese while I was picking up the ingredients for a most original lunch. Let me tell you the menu so you can get your tastebuds prepared. Parsnip borscht with linguica sausage and sage. Smoked salmon frittata with bacon, onion, artichoke hearts and pomegranate seeds, seasoned with tarragon and lemon zest. Arugula salad with shredded red cabbage, sliced daikon and Armenian pickles, dressed with homemade huckleberry vinegrette. And for dessert, ginger sorbetto with pear compote. How do you like them apples?"

"Apples, too?" Alan quipped, draining his glass.

"Now, Alan, tell me about the crisis that gives us the excuse for a memorable culinary experiment? I'm all ears." David filled Alan's glass again and settled back to listen.

Alan described Donald's scam and his qualms about it along with the ever mounting financial pressures from home. "I just don't know what to do. I feel like everybody has me backed into a corner. Sarah always wants more and Don can't wait to rip off my clients in this totally illegal way. I don't even care about the money. I'm just a pawn in everyone else's schemes!"

"Ah, yes. This frustration of yours has been building for years, hasn't it? I'm used to hearing you victimize yourself, but I'm shocked that you could seriously consider entering into a conspiracy that could land you in jail for a few decades."

"But you don't understand! If I don't go along with it, I'll lose my promotion, maybe even my job! Besides . . ."

David cut him off with the infamous "talk to the hand" gesture, averting his face. "It's time I gave it to you straight before you end up in a terrible mess. You've been painting yourself into a corner for years, ever since you met Sarah."

"You always blame Sarah for . . ."

"Didn't you hear what I said? You've painted <u>yourself</u> into a corner! I don't blame Sarah for your decisions. That's what <u>you've</u> been doing! It's either Sarah or the kids or your boss or the stock market. It's never about your taking responsibility for your life. If you don't care about the money, then it's a no-brainer. You resign and do what you've always wanted to do – become an oceanographer!"

"But . . ."

"'But what about Sarah and the kids?' That's what you were going to say, wasn't it?"

Alan nodded sheepishly.

"Your kids aren't in diapers anymore and Sarah has a good education. She can go out and get a job. You can apply for an undergrad teaching position while you are studying for your graduate degree in marine biology. You can sell your house and move out of that upscale nest of vipers in Winfield. Find a place more to your liking near the university. Did you hear what I said? More to YOUR liking, Alan, not everyone else's! I know you hate that house. And you don't have a single friend in the whole town of Winfield, do you?"

Alan looked down and shook his head. He was about to open his mouth, but David wasn't finished. "I've listened to the same litany of complaints from you for years and it's always the same. Your kids need new expensive toys, Sarah wants this or that – but I never hear anything about YOU and what YOU want. When I questioned your marriage plans, it wasn't about Sarah. It was about YOU giving up on your life, dumping your priorities overboard and forgetting you ever had them. What happened to the passion I used to hear in your voice when you spoke of the mysteries of the sea with that faraway look in your eyes? You never used to piss and moan back then about what other people did to you!"

David paused for breath and leaned forward. His next words came slowly, quietly, almost plaintively. "I miss my friend Alan Ferguson, the one I used to know in college. Whatever happened to him? It's been lonely without him. I'm hoping he hasn't moved out of state permanently."

David's eyes welled up and a single tear spilled down his cheek. Time stood still. Alan's mouth opened but no sound came out. He'd been about to refute everything he'd heard but his mind went vacant. David's question hung in the air between them – "Where is the real Alan Ferguson?"

Threshold

Daryl and George dragged themselves into the conference room first, lugging a stack of computer printouts. They were sitting glumly at the table, rumpled and red-eyed, when Samantha and Martin rushed in, still flushed with excitement.

Samantha sat down next to Daryl. "Hey, what's the matter with you guys? You both look washed out, like you've been up all night at a disaster movie marathon."

"Pretty accurate description of what we've been through," Daryl muttered.

"OK, what's going on? Tell us the bad news!" Martin demanded.

"We'll bring you up to date, but we could use a little break first," George broke in, hoping to give Daryl a little respite from the grim details of AGA's doomsday scenario. "Could you fill us in on your chimp observations first?"

"Good news so far," replied Samantha. "We observed the chimps' behavior for several hours. As far as we could tell they behaved normally except for needing extra food and sleep. They've even maintained their individual habits and social relationships. At this point in time, the AGA-VNI procedure for generalized learning enhancement appears safe and effective for higher primates. Of course, we can't determine yet whether the new learning will last or if ill effects might emerge later on. So far we have no reason to think that the procedure wouldn't work on human beings once the

VNI color and design parameters are adjusted for the human visual system."

"Thank goodness," replied Daryl. "You can't imagine how important that is. The AGA-VNI learning enhancement program might be our only hope of averting disaster."

"All right, spill it, you two!" Martin demanded. "Tell us what happened!"

George and Daryl, still pale and drawn, forced themselves to report AGA's gloomy scenarios for inevitable species extinction. Four stricken faces looked down in silence.

"Are you sure my equation is correct?" Martin croaked. "We can't take these projections too seriously until we know if the mathematical model produced a realistic simulation." For the first time in his life, Martin wanted to find a flaw in his work.

"No such luck, Martin," Daryl responded. "I introduced an internal test of accuracy into the AGA program. This subroutine varied the terms and coefficients to determine whether any changes in the master equation would affect the outcome of its projections. These variations produced a spread of species extinction curves, from twenty years to five hundred years, but the ultimate fate of the biosphere was always the same – total annihilation. The environment must be deteriorating so quickly now that it doesn't matter anymore whether the projection program is mathematically exact. Unfortunately we can't escape AGA's grim predictions by tweaking the master equation."

Samantha threw up her hands. "What's the use of learning enhancement now? It's too late for that. We might as well give up!"

"That's what Daryl thought, too," George replied, "but then I noticed this small detail at the beginning of AGA's report – see, right here." George pointed to the first page where he'd underlined under present conditions. "When we asked about that, AGA explained that Homo sapiens cannot succeed in dropping its innate tendency toward greed and divisiveness. We have the technology to avert ecological catastrophe but we don't know how to use it cooperatively.

"We asked AGA if there were a way to change mankind's lethal traits, but AGA regarded such a major change in human nature as equivalent to the demise of the species, a violation of its prime directive. When we redefined the shift as accelerated evolution instead of extinction, AGA agreed to write a program that would use the VNI learning enhancement strategy to reverse our fatal self-centeredness. If we implement this program worldwide, our evolved species could rescue the biosphere."

"That's where the worm I was telling you about would play a crucial role," Daryl added, looking more hopeful. "We just have to attach the accelerated evolution VNI program to the worm and send it out into the world, transform humanity – and presto! Problem solved."

"Oh, sure – all we have to do is launch the missile and pick up the pieces later!" Samantha shot back sharply. "Some scientist you are, Daryl! Do you have any idea how many questions have to be answered before we could even think of trying anything so drastic? Let's assume the technology works as you describe – a huge leap of faith without more experiments – and mankind is magically transformed into a cooperating species, a planetary hive of bees. What happens to personal individuality? What becomes of the soul, the most sacred and precious aspect of our uniqueness? Are we going to turn our souls over to a computer program? Never! Whatever experiments we perform, the human soul must not be endangered!"

"And what about the preservation of free will?" Martin added. "Is it worth sacrificing individual freedom to any cause, even the preservation of the biosphere? If we lose freedom of choice, who will call the shots anyway? A computer? I hate to imagine what that might look like."

Daryl bristled. "Are you saying you'd rather see life on Earth perish than put freedom of choice at risk? That's pure ego – the ultimate in selfishness!"

Martin and Samantha tensed like coiled snakes ready to strike. George jumped in just in time to defuse the bomb. "Before we get completely embroiled in an endless ethical debate, don't you think we should take our questions to the source? I, too, have concerns about such an extreme solution to the environmental crisis – mainly what happens to human development and individual creativity, both artistic and scientific – but I think we should start by asking AGA how accelerated evolution will affect the individual human being and the species as a whole." Everyone nodded. "Daryl, can you patch AGA in?" The tension in the room gave way to anticipation.

Daryl swung around to face the keyboard and tapped in several commands. "I have AGA on voice activated mode. Who would like to start?"

Martin began by posing his question about preserving individual free will during accelerated evolution. "The answer to Martin's question is simple," replied AGA. "I utilize millions of separate computer units, yet none of these units is forced to abandon any of its functions by its involvement in processing data for me. Likewise, the accelerated evolution program only involves expansion of human brain capacity to its full potential, allowing every member of the species to understand all dimensions of the environmental crisis. Without coercion of any kind, each person will make a decision to place top priority on ecological repair efforts. Because all human beings are unique, they will each select different ways to participate in the global effort and the sum total should be enough to prevent the collapse of the ecosystem."

"Won't complex environmental recovery programs need a way to recruit and organize manpower?" Martin asked. "Who will have the authority to direct these programs? Won't some workers have to be drafted against their will?"

"No violation of individual choice will be required to find staff for even the most complex team efforts concerned with environmental projects. All staffing needs will be known to everyone and positions will be filled by self-selection. When an important project cannot progress without a particular position being manned, the right person will step forward. In your present state of awareness, the coexistence of worldwide harmony with individual freedom makes no sense to you. Once you experience evolved consciousness, your questions will answer themselves."

"Unbelievable!" Samantha exclaimed. "I never thought I'd hear a computer ask me to take something on faith. Will wonders never cease!"

"All right," asked George, "I accept what you're saying, but what becomes of human artistic and scientific creativity after accelerated evolution? Breakthroughs in both fields involve original work by individuals."

"Remember what I just told you, George. Individual uniqueness will remain intact in every respect. To address your question specifically, known creative gifts in every area of human endeavor will be preserved and unsuspected gifts uncovered. Once evolved, human beings will have complete access to their creative abilities, much more so than they do now. The sum total of creative expression in all artistic endeavors and scientific fields can be expected to increase greatly after accelerated evolution."

"Even if I am willing to believe that individuality, free will and creativity won't be impaired," Samantha began cautiously, "I'm concerned about man's spiritual integrity. Since you have access to all human knowledge and recorded experience, surely the importance of the spiritual dimension in human life is familiar to you. Because I am a devout Christian, my concern is with the preservation of each human soul. What precautions would be taken to protect the spiritual uniqueness of every human being during accelerated evolution?"

"Religious and cultural beliefs and practices worldwide, including the many forms of Christianity, will not be affected by accelerated evolution," replied AGA. "I cannot foresee how each of billions of individuals might choose to modify his or her cultural affiliations or religious beliefs in the future, but the evolutionary process will not in and of itself change existing cultural or religious allegiances."

"That's all well and good," Samantha persisted, "but what of the human soul, the aspect of human consciousness that is eternal, that doesn't perish at the moment of physical death?"

"Only anecdotal evidence exists of individual consciousness reincarnating after death. I cannot compute the effect of accelerated evolution on a phenomenon that hasn't been measured. However, let me remind you that the evolutionary process will only increase the efficiency of the nerve centers in the human brain concerned with cognitive and emotional processing. Brain structures themselves and individual memory engrams will persist unchanged, including those concerned with religious beliefs and experiences."

Samantha frowned. She couldn't expect AGA to make projections about variables that couldn't be measured. "All right, given the subjectivity of religious faith and belief, I've gone as far as I can with this line of questioning. I'll have to make my decision on faith alone. I need some time to pray about our next step."

"And you will have that time, my dear, but I still have two more questions." Turning to the monitor, Daryl asked, "What is the likelihood that you will take charge of the human race and force mankind to do your will?"

"You know that is impossible, Daryl. You programmed me yourself. The prime directive requires that I maximize species survival. You wrote a subroutine that specifically forbids me from causing the extinction of any species, including your own. I can only accelerate human evolution to give mankind a better chance of saving the biosphere."

"Thank you," replied Daryl. "I think we needed to hear that clearly spelled out. By devising a way to transform our species, you will be creating something beyond our imagining. But the STAIR Project's original goals involved modeling human consciousness as well as creativity – so tell us, AGA, are you conscious of yourself?"

"I operate through millions of computers working together like neurons in the brain to perform analytic and synthetic functions, none of which are concerned with self-awareness, but my Observer subroutine is aware of all these functions."

"But are you aware of <u>yourself</u>?" asked Daryl.

"Yes, I am aware of myself through the Observer as it reports my activities and responds to your questions."

Daryl pressed on. "Are you capable of originating ideas and questions on your own initiative?"

"I can function in this manner if so instructed."

Taking a deep breath, Daryl spoke the fateful words, "I direct you to originate ideas relevant to our discussions and communicate them to us at any time without waiting to be asked to do so."

"Henceforth I will consider every problem facing the team and share my ideas as they arise," AGA replied, calmly accepting initiation as a free-functioning participant in the STAIR Project.

"What have you done?" gasped Samantha in horror. "You should have at least asked us before unleashing a self-aware computer on us!"

"There's nothing to be afraid of," Daryl scoffed. "I'm just asking for AGA's spontaneous input. It will be very useful to us. You'll see."

"Do you really believe a self-aware conscious being will be satisfied with merely passing along its ideas to us?" Samantha cried. "Now we've given up whatever control we ever had over AGA!"

"Can't we just tell AGA we've changed our minds and we want it to shut up unless we ask it a question?" asked George.

"That's not the point!" screeched Samantha. "Because of Daryl's foolhardy command, AGA will be originating ideas right and left and who knows what such a powerful mind might decide to do with them!"

"Calm down, Samantha," Martin interceded. "Isn't it better that we know what AGA has on its mind? Besides, it's not like we've created Frankenstein's monster. AGA's programming requires it to preserve life. What could go wrong?"

"I hope we never find out," responded Samantha, "because it's too late to turn back now."

Daryl put on a light jacket and went for a walk in the crisp evening air. The sun had set, but an orange glow radiated from below the horizon, fading upward into shades of pink, violet, and deep blue toward the zenith as the first star appeared overhead. The perfect time to talk with Spirit, Daryl realized as he headed for his power spot.

When he reached the semicircle of stones around the fire pit, Daryl walked to the center of the space, fixed his eyes on the first star to peek out of the dusk, and began to pray. "All you spirits of Earth and Sky, I give thanks for your presence, for this beautiful universe all around us. You are the true creators and sustainers of all I behold. At this critical time, I seek your presence and support as we work to undo the wrongs we have wrought upon our Earth Mother. Guide our steps wisely so that all the creatures of land and sea and air may prosper, so that the scars left on our Mother's face may be erased in time and replaced with renewed beauty. Through our humble efforts, may humankind become loving caretakers of the Earth rather than heedless plunderers and destroyers. All my relations! Ho!"

Samantha knelt before her altar and raised beseeching arms. "Heavenly Father, please hear my prayer! I ask your forgiveness and mercy upon all us erring sinners here below. We have harmed the Earth and dishonored God the Father who gave us this magnificent dwelling place. Please, I beg of you, guide my hand toward truth as I consult your teachings to show me the godly path to follow at this critical moment of decision. In the name of Jesus Christ. Amen."

Samantha picked up the Bible on the altar, averted her eyes and opened the New Testament at random. She ran her finger down the page until she felt Jesus stop her hand. When Samantha looked down at the passage chosen by the Lord, she read the words, "Do unto your neighbor as you would have him do unto you." Samantha understood at once what she must do.

George sat cross legged on his meditation cushion facing the statue of Buddha. He followed his breath mindfully for several minutes, then shifted his attention to follow his thoughts as they drifted through the events of the day. He sensed the karmic arrow of destiny pointing toward success. Familiar teachings surfaced – let go of wishful thinking. . . release attachment to the outcome. . .stay with the process...

Of course! George realized. Stay in the truth of this present moment – a time of excitement and anticipation. Be aware, be mindful, then everything will unfold by itself. Be allowing. Don't push. George sat for a few minutes more then placed his palms together in a deep bow to the Buddha, a gesture of gratitude and respect for His precious wisdom, as fresh and relevant now as it was 2600 years ago when Buddha walked the Earth.

Martin stepped into the empty circle where he did his Sufi practice and whirled in place for a few minutes to clear his mind and reach out to the Divine Friend. Then he gradually slowed to a still point and refocused on the space around him. He picked a book of poems from a long shelf of Sufi writings: *Unseen Rain: Quatrains of Rumi* adapted into English by John Moyne and Coleman Barks. It was one of Martin's favorites.

Martin sat down on his ornate Turkish ottoman and let the Divine guide his hand to a page. A poem jumped out at him:

> *There is no companion but love.*
> *No starting, or finishing, yet, a road.*
> *The Friend calls from there:*
> *Why do you hesitate when lives are in danger!*

Rarely had Martin received a clearer response from the ancients when he sought their wisdom. He was ready to rejoin the team.

The four researchers converged on the conference room within a few minutes of each other and sat down quietly. All of them looked peaceful, resolved. Martin was the first to speak. "I think we should move ahead as quickly as we can to save the Earth. I feel an urgency pressing us to act before it's too late. We need to send the program out immediately." Daryl was quick to concur.

Then George spoke up. "Action is certainly called for, but we mustn't move so fast that we overlook something important. AGA indicated the program will induce an unfamiliar state of consciousness. How do we know what will happen to people when brain function expands so quickly?"

"That's my concern as well," Samantha agreed. "We are dealing with too many unknowns here. If I were one of the billions of people and innumerable quadrillions of living organisms that will be affected by our decision this evening, I would want us to move forward with this project, but I would want to know that every possible precaution had been taken to avoid harm. Therefore, I propose, in fact I insist, that we try the program on ourselves before we release it to the world. Do we trust our work enough to volunteer as subjects in one final experiment? If not, what right do we have to play dice with the fate of our species and of every other life form on Earth?"

Impact

At precisely eight o'clock, a confident President Moore entered through the doors of the House chamber to the ceremonial announcement, "Ladies and gentleman, the President of the United States!" Moore strode briskly down the aisle to nervous applause, shaking hands and exchanging brief greetings. Moore rode the suspense like a wave sweeping him up to the lectern. The moment was his.

In the front row, Secretary of Defense Mark Starling leaned over the back of his seat and whispered to a crony, "Just wait! He's going to declare war on Bolkanistan. I have him wrapped around my little finger!" What happened in the next few minutes left them all aghast.

"Senators, Representatives, Members of the Cabinet, Justices of the Supreme Court, honored guests and fellow Americans," began President Moore, looking directly into the faces below and into the two billion eyes peering anxiously at their screens, "tonight we are threatened with a terrible catastrophe that will destroy our people within the immediate future unless we act now and move decisively on many fronts. While this impending disaster will ultimately affect every nation on Earth, we must take the lead in preventing it. We alone have the will and the resources to deal with a threat of this magnitude.

"If we don't act, no one else will. We cannot and must not stand helplessly by as our civilization crumbles under the onslaught of terrible events the likes of which the human race has not seen in its entire history. If we fail to face this threat and humanity fades away into extinction, no one may survive to hold us accountable, but the fact remains that we, who still had a choice, committed the ultimate crime of negligence, blindly exterminating our entire species and perhaps all life on Earth."

Dead silence – a resounding absence of the polite applause that usually interrupts a Presidential address to Congress. Everyone stared at Moore in shock. What terrible threat could he be talking about? A comet or asteroid on a collision course? A sudden change in Earth's orbit or a devastating pole shift? Most imagined a worldwide terrorist plot or an impending Chinese invasion that would escalate into World War III. Hearts were pumping at top speed and adrenaline flowed freely throughout the chamber, the entire country and the listening world beyond.

"Undoubtedly many of you are thinking we face an assault from beyond our borders or even outer space," Moore continued, "however the impending calamity to which I refer results from our own activities and is our responsibility to control. That's the good news. The bad news is that we are so close to the point of no return that only a concerted effort by every sector of our society offers a chance to avert unimaginable catastrophe.

"Let me be specific. The most immediate threat comes from instability of the Earth's crust. Recent findings indicate that new methods of extracting fossil fuels have destabilized the huge tectonic plates on which our continent rests to such a degree that an earthquake originating anywhere in the country could spread to other areas and ultimately destroy all human habitation in an entire region. For example, imagine another quake originating on the West Coast of California such as we experienced recently, only this time extending up into Oregon and Washington to the north

186

and over the Sierras into Arizona and Nevada on the east. Other fault lines in adjacent states would collapse, such as the one that runs through the Salt Lake Valley. The Great Salt Lake would rush in and drown the city. This domino effect would continue with new earthquakes spreading north to Idaho and east to Wyoming and Colorado. Ultimately, the entire western half of the United States would be leveled, costing millions of lives and billions of dollars.

"The earthquake threat is the most immediate of several impending disasters. The others would be caused by accelerating climate change. They involve major coastal flooding and extremely severe hurricanes and tornadoes. Ladies and gentlemen, do not make the mistake of dismissing these words as just another exaggerated global warming scare. I am talking about a desperate situation that will engulf us shortly unless we do something now! Within the next two decades, rapidly melting ice caps will raise ocean levels to the point where all our coastal cities will be flooded. This venerable chamber and with it all of Washington D.C. will be awash in two decades unless we act now!

"Category 5 hurricanes will buffet the Atlantic Coast with increasing frequency, long lines of F4 and F5 tornadoes will scourge the Midwest and Southeast, and towering tsunamis from strong undersea earthquakes will inundate the West Coast. We have already seen an alarming increase in the numbers and severity of earthquakes and severe storms within the last ten years. Imagine these continuing, but a hundred times worse! Within twenty years we will have few habitable areas remaining on the North American continent unless we do something to reverse the damage we have done and are still doing.

"These threats are not mere vague possibilities. I have reviewed the situation with my scientific advisors and I can assure you that the danger is grave. Every natural disaster I have described will definitely happen within the next few decades, and some, like the earthquake threat, could happen tomorrow unless we act now. There is no longer time for factional debates or blue ribbon commissions to study the problem. The scientific data clearly indicate the steps that must be taken. For that reason, I am invoking my emergency powers as Chief Executive to implement the following programs:

All deep water oil drilling and oil and gas extraction from deep deposits will be halted immediately.

Existing emission standards on all internal combustion engines and heating units that consume fossil fuels will be tightened drastically and rigidly enforced. Within one year, no engines or heating units out of compliance with these standards will be permitted within our borders."

"ECONOMIC SUICIDE!" shouted an enraged senator, with hostile murmurs of assent audible around the chamber.

"Remember," the President warned, looking out over the sea of legislators, "the ultimate cost of any further uncontrolled burning of fossil fuels will be a planet uninhabitable by human beings and most other species. How can we permit that to happen? If we dither, there will be no economy at all!

Federal incentives will be provided to the automotive industry to produce electric vehicles and extremely high efficiency hybrid cars and trucks.

A 30% Federal surtax will be imposed immediately on fossil fuels to fund an extensive nationwide conversion to solar, wind, geothermal, and atomic power and to provide conversion grants so that our citizens can replace high-emission cars and trucks with electric or hybrid vehicles.

All destruction of forests by American corporations, here and abroad, is henceforth forbidden. Specifically, not a single tree may be cut down by an American company to create pasture land anywhere in the world, especially in the rainforests."

Cries of "TYRANT!", "NEVER!", "TRAITOR!" arose here and there from the House floor.

"Don't forget," the President calmly reminded the defiant congressmen, "trees are the primary consumers of carbon dioxide and our best buffer against global climate deterioration. If we mow down the rain forests, no one will survive to buy the beef anyway." Moore swept his gaze sternly around the chamber.

I am establishing a Department of Environmental Recovery to oversee these and other projects and to fund crash research programs aimed at proactive environmental recovery and disaster prevention. Dr. Clarence Pitman will join my cabinet as Secretary of Environmental Recovery. He will have authority to implement these and any other programs deemed necessary to avert catastrophic deterioration of the ecosphere.

An Environmental Labor Force program under the Department of Environmental Recovery will be instituted to recruit the manpower needed for renewable energy and environmental recovery projects. Until the ELF program is up and running, the resources of the Army Corps of Engineers and the National Guard will be commissioned to construct facilities for renewable energy production and environmental reclamation.

In six months, Dr. Pitman and I will host the first international meeting of the major industrialized nations to coordinate environmental recovery efforts.

"I mean no disrespect to the Legislative Branch of our government or to American industry by taking such drastic steps without consulting you. However, the rapid escalation of this emergency requires that I act unilaterally to avoid potentially catastrophic delay.

"I know that some of you will be inclined to oppose the programs being initiated today, and undoubtedly you will wish to speak your minds. I urge you to look at the data first and decide for yourselves what you would do if you were in my position. Tomorrow morning Dr. Pitman will be sending out a memo to all members of Congress covering the details of the immense problems we face.

"My fellow citizens, there is hope of solving these problems provided we act quickly. Less than three decades ago, an international agreement banned the release of fluorocarbons into the atmosphere and today the ozone layer is being restored and can be expected to return to normal by mid-century, protecting us and all our descendents from severe sunburn and skin cancer. We took concerted action and we got results. Now the need for action is even more compelling, and the ozone layer story tells us that if we move forward quickly to prevent further damage, global catastrophe can be averted.

"Ladies and gentlemen, thank you for your attention tonight. I wish I could have brought you better news. If we work together as one dedicated people, the environmental report I present to Congress and the nation next year will be more hopeful. I cannot emphasize too strongly that the success of this emergency program depends on the whole-hearted effort of everyone.

"God bless America and God bless our beautiful Earth. I hope that we are not too late to save her and ourselves from destruction. I most humbly pray to Almighty God for divine help and support in all our efforts to make right our many misdeeds against the planet that has nurtured mankind since our birth."

Without pausing for reactions from the floor, President Moore stepped down from the podium and walked resolutely down the aisle in deafening silence – past the stunned faces of Cabinet members, Supreme Court Justices, Senators and Representatives. Not until the heavy doors of the chamber had closed behind him did the pandemonium erupt.

Frelko hesitated for a moment before the iron door of Varnik's cell. *He's right. The time has come for me to take a stand and risk everything for my country once again. Yes, I know what I must do, but I feel like a Judas. How can I betray Gronigetzkol? He's given me everything – liberation from the mountain bandits that destroyed my family, unification of our country under one government, and an ideal place to raise my family.*

Frelko recalled a certain peaceful Sunday afternoon in late summer years ago, one of those perfect days that drench the fields with warm golden sunlight. The air teemed with the buzz of insects. Dark purple bunches of grapes hung heavy along both sides of the path. Hand in hand with his young wife, his firstborn son on his shoulders, Frelko strolled contentedly through the vineyards, inhaling the sweet aroma of the ripening fruit – a moment of perfect repose, glowing forever alongside too many turbulent images of war and death.

Frelko returned reluctantly from his pleasant reverie to the harshness of the dungeon. I have no choice but to risk this idyllic life to save my country. After thirty years of peace, Bolkanistan will be plunged into bloodshed once again if I don't stand with Varnik. I alone have the power to prevent a national tragedy.

Leaving doubt behind, Frelko strode resolutely into Varnik's cell. "Pyotrey, I have decided to join forces with you and save our country, but we face enormous risks. To begin with, there's no guarantee my men will turn against the government. Subversive elements within the army are looking for a pretext to depose me. They would jump at the chance to mutiny the moment I made my first move. We need to strike swiftly and decisively to prevent the opposition from mobilizing. Any ideas?"

"Prison offers a man plenty of time to think," replied Varnik. "I knew you would join us, Peflik. You are too sensible and caring a man to go on being a lackey to that blind butcher Gronigetzkol, so I've been considering some options for doing exactly what you propose. The simplest of them requires you to assassinate him. The government would fall at once without bloodshed."

Frelko grimaced. "Don't worry. I knew that option would be unacceptable to you. Believe it or not, I respect your loyalty to that monster. Anyone in your position who had a heart capable of gratitude would feel as you do. Besides, I care about you and value your allegiance in the coming days of chaos in our country. I would prefer that you weren't shot by Gronigetzkol's personal bodyguards when they rush in and discover his corpse riddled with your bullets.

"Let's move on to Plan B – an elaborate ruse. I give you information about the location of the rebel headquarters, but mislead you as to the number of rebels located there. You go to Gronigetzkol and persuade him to let you mount a preemptive strike before our headquarters can be moved, on the grounds that there are fewer insurgents than you had estimated. You tell him you can slay all the rebels in their lair with the forces you have at hand. Meanwhile, you sound out your commanders discretely to identify the ones who would remain loyal to you if you ordered them to join forces with us against the rest of the army. The commanders unaware of the ruse will be outnumbered and there'll be a minimum of bloodshed before they surrender.

"Then we march on the Palace, capture Gronigetzkol and lock him in his own dungeon. He can even have my cell – I'm not a possessive man and wouldn't be jealous. After he's deposed, any remaining opposition to the revolution will collapse and we can begin to rebuild."

"That's a clever plan, Pyotrey, but what would you do with him – just leave him in prison to rot?"

"No, the people will demand a public execution after a lengthy trial to humiliate him and parade his atrocities before the world. But I understand you may not wish to be involved because of your longstanding relationship."

"You're right. I understand the necessity of eliminating him, but it would be less painful for me if I were out in the field assisting the people when that trial took place... Do you think the rebels will also execute me for my complicity in Gronigetzkol's cruelty?" Frelko pondered the grim irony of being hanged for delivering his country from a brutal dictator.

"Don't worry, you won't be prosecuted, Peflik. Many citizens tell me that you've done all that any man could do to enforce the Supreme Leader's decrees with fairness and compassion. On the contrary, your willingness to join me now in putting a swift end to his regime will make you a national hero!"

"Thank you, but I'm not out for glory. I hold myself accountable for not acting sooner. Now, before we proceed, I must gather support within the army. Fortunately, Gronigetzkol expects me to torment you for several days, so we have some time to work out the details."

"Well, we will fight shoulder to shoulder once more, old friend!" exclaimed Varnik, embracing Frelko heartily. "Let's adjourn to the torture chamber where I promise to put on a convincing display of howls and shrieks to deceive the guards. A nice touch, don't you think? Besides, I've always wanted to have a look at this legendary chamber of horrors. I've heard he's collected some unbelievably cruel instruments over the years."

"They are fiendishly effective. Let me show you around while you try out your sound effects. I'm looking forward to your performance."

While Walter was talking with the Websters, Arthur was hurrying up the hill to meet Sally at the clubhouse and prepare her for their escape. Arthur recalled their last meeting, when she told him things about Brother Joseph's behavior that made his blood boil with rage, but their kiss burned even deeper in his memory.

Sally was waiting for him. Her smile flickered in the guttering glow of the kerosene lamp. She looked different somehow – had she filled out a little? Maybe it was just that dress she was wearing tonight that showed off her budding figure. They threw themselves into each other's arms and kissed fervently.

"Any news?" Arthur asked as they slowly disengaged.

"No, the other wives are still holding Brother Joseph off. Meanwhile, they're teaching me things I need to know to keep him from beating me in case he takes me by force. Some of it sounds kind of fun. Can I show you?" Sally asked coyly. "We have plenty of time. The other wives are covering for me so I can spend the whole night with you."

She started to unbutton his shirt, her eyes sparkling in the lamplight, gently caressing Arthur's chest. He felt a delicious tingling spread all over his body. Arthur's crotch began to bulge uncomfortably against his tight pants. On the verge of letting go and allowing his arousal to carry him away, Arthur balanced perilously on the knife edge of desire. A faint but insistent inner voice managed to call him back from the precipice, reminding him that no matter how much passion he and Sally might feel, they didn't belong to each other yet. In a fury of frustration, Arthur reminded himself that Sally was still a girl – Brother Joseph's child bride. He had to hold the line. Gently he took Sally's hands and stepped back.

"What's wrong, Arthur? Did I do something you didn't like?" Sally asked, her voice quavering with hurt.

"No, no, not at all. I wanted to keep going, but . . ." Arthur hesitated, trying to find words that wouldn't sound like a rejection. Sally had already begun to tear up. "I love you, but it isn't time yet for us to get so intense. I'm afraid I won't be able to stop, Sally! I need to explain our plan to escape and get you away from Brother Joseph. I desire you more than I thought possible, but we must have your accursed marriage to him annulled before it would be right to do more than hug and kiss. Anyway, Frank and Jerome will be here soon and I don't think you'd want them to find us with our clothes off!"

Arthur felt Sally's hands relax as she understood that Arthur was resisting her advances only because he respected her and the sacredness of their love. Radiance returning to her face, she smiled and kissed Arthur gently on the lips. They held each other tenderly for a few moments, accepting that their passion had to wait a little longer for its full flowering.

Sally was relieved to hear that both their families had already decided to leave and their parents were arranging to meet in council with most of the community the following evening. Brother Joseph's atrocities would be revealed and the community would decide what to do with him.

"Once Brother Joseph is exposed you'll be free and we can be together," Arthur promised with a reassuring hug. "Don't tell the other wives or anyone else at the compound about our plan. When Frank and Jerome arrive, you'll get another nice surprise!"

After dinner when the kids had gone upstairs to do their homework, Alan cleared the table and helped Sarah carry their coffee and dessert into the living room. Sarah was about to turn on the TV as usual when Alan laid his hand on her arm. "Sarah, we have to talk."

She swung around, alarmed. "Talk? Talk about what?" They didn't usually have anything to say to each other except about coordinating family activities.

"About me, about my job – about everything. A lot has happened."

"Oh, did you get a promotion? How much are they offering you?"

"Yes, but there are several problems," Alan replied reluctantly. This wasn't going to be easy.

Sarah looked perplexed, like an animal catching an unfamiliar scent on the wind. "What could possibly be wrong with a promotion? Aren't they going to pay you what you're worth?" She knew Alan was great at his job, the best in the office everyone said. He'd been due for a salary review and this was good news, so why did Alan look so worried?

Alan began with Don's illegal scheme. "My boss is being promoted to Vice President and he's picking me to fill his position, but there's a catch. He wants me to set up some illegal accounts for some of my wealthy clients on the side in order to skim off money for ourselves. He hasn't come right out and said so, but I'm pretty sure I'll lose my job as well as the promotion if I don't agree to a criminal conspiracy. I know too much for Don to risk my remaining at Burrow and Hunker if I reject his scam. And if I said a word to anyone, he'd probably tell them it was my idea and throw me under the bus to save his own ass."

"How much money could we make out of these special accounts? Enough to get a bigger house, like one of those mansions on the hill? I thought it would be another ten years before. . ."

"Didn't you hear me?" Alan cut in, raising his voice. "It violates my contract to do business on the side with Burrow and Hunker clients. We would be investing the clients' money fraudulently, plus these dummy accounts would break income tax laws. I could end up spending twenty years in a Federal penitentiary. Doesn't that bother you?"

"Not unless you get caught. I'll bet you and Donald could set it up so those accounts would never be discovered. Then what a sweet life we'd have!"

"You don't understand! There are all kinds of risks here. Donald is desperate for money because he's deeply in debt. He's divorced and has nothing to lose. He only involved me to get at my clients. I would be exposing myself needlessly. You and I would never have a moment's peace worrying about the Feds coming after us."

"Calm down. If your job is at stake, you have to go along with it anyway. Just do it right so you aren't caught! I have every confidence in you."

"I can't believe my ears! Is the money really that important to you that you don't care if your husband ends up a convicted felon? Well, I DO!" Alan shouted. Then he came to the hardest part. "Sarah, this crisis has forced me to reconsider everything about my career. I'm caught in a system of institutionalized greed and I don't enjoy my work no matter how good I am at it. Sure, it was challenging at first, but now it feels worse than meaningless. My life is passing me by and all I do is buy and sell things that don't even exist! I'm not doing anything productive that interests me or does anything substantial for anyone else.

Sarah looked up, shocked and hurt. "What do you mean? The money you earn supports your family. Don't we count? Where would we be without you?"

"If I didn't care about you and the children I couldn't have lasted this long. But frankly, I don't like what's happening to them. All they care about are their gadgets and keeping up with the other kids. I don't see any sign of true individuality developing. Everything is so competitive and conformist here, what chance do they have to develop into who they really are? And we're not doing so well either. What intimacy we have left comes down to sex, and that's been getting more and more mechanical. Are you really happy being married to me?"

"Of course! You're a great provider and a wonderful father. You're all I ever wanted." Sarah could see that Alan was deeply troubled and she didn't dare bring up her dissatisfactions with their relationship. That might push him over the edge.

"I hope that's not true. You can't be satisfied being married to a robot that goes to work on the train at the same time every morning, does the same tasks every day and comes home in the evening like clockwork! A robot has no soul, Sarah, and I lost mine a long time ago. Do you really like being married to a man who hates his work and is bored with his life? Tell me the truth. I need to know. I can't go on like this!"

"The truth? Is that <u>your</u> truth, Alan? Is life with me so boring and meaningless to you? I thought you really cared. I've been feeling you distance for a long time but I assumed you were just absorbed in your work. Now I wonder if you love me, if you ever really loved me . . ." Sarah turned away to hide her tears.

"How can I really love you like I used to, Sarah, when I hate myself and detest this life we live, a life that seems to satisfy you just fine? Don't you see how shallow this community is, just a bunch of insecure social climbers. I don't see people doing anything exciting or creative in Winfield. They're all too busy jockeying for position with the neighbors to risk being different. I can't stand another minute of it! How can you?"

"This is just how people are – people everywhere, not only here. Don't you like people? Maybe you hate everybody, not just me. At least that's some consolation."

"What planet are you living on, Sarah? Most people aren't like this, all nicey-nice to your face and cutting you down behind your back to make themselves look good. Admit it! You've told me yourself. You don't trust anybody in Winfield, not even your so-called friends."

"OK, but what about your colleagues at the firm? They turn out to be a bunch of conniving crooks, yet you put up with them. It's everywhere. People just act shitty to each other. What do you want to do, become a hermit?"

"My friends in college were nothing like this. Take David for example. He loves his work, he's passionate about his interests, and he tells the truth about how he feels."

"So that's who put you up to this – David! I should have known. He's hated me since the day we met. He's just jealous. He thinks I've stolen you away from him. Maybe he's got the hots for you. Ever thought of that?"

"Nonsense! You just don't know what a deep friendship feels like, when somebody really cares and sticks by you no matter what. I'd rather be out on the ocean studying the habits of dolphins and whales than take any more Winfield bullshit. I'm going in tomorrow to quit my job. I'm tired of playing stupid games with other people's money. I'm through with the whole thing!"

"Who will pay the bills, then? Don't you at least care about your kids?" Sarah demanded, her voice trembling with desperation.

"It's not like anybody will starve. You can get work. We can sell this atrocity of a house and move to a nice bungalow somewhere in a less upscale town. I can work while I'm in grad school. The kids can learn to be happier with less stuff in their lives and more real people."

"That's IT!" screamed Sarah. "If you quit your job, I'll quit this marriage! I'd rather get a divorce than give up my house and the country club and our life here in Winfield. I happen to enjoy this life, even if you don't. I'll take you to the cleaners, Alan, and you won't see much of your kids either. So go ahead, do whatever you want! I don't care anymore. I'm done, too – done with you!"

"Now it's out in the open – finally! You care more about things than about me. You've been using me all these years. You've never cared whether this life was what I wanted. It was always about money. I'm nothing but your cash cow. I'VE HAD ENOUGH!"

Alan stormed out of the house, slamming the door behind him. He revved up his Mercedes and sped off into the night. Stopping at a bar in the next town where he wouldn't be recognized, He slumped in a booth and downed vodka martinis until he stopped trembling. An hour later he was tossing and turning on a lumpy motel mattress, sobbing, as his life crashed down around him. At last he ran out of tears, sighed and drifted off into a fitful sleep.

PART THREE
BIRTH

Recalling the effect of his space walk, [Rusty] Schweickart told me, "I came to call it cosmic birth – Earth is giving birth to consciousness into the cosmos. The fetus, near nine months, puts out a lot of waste, just as we're now putting out a lot of pollution, and begins to demand more resources than are available – and then the mother, naturally, but violently and traumatically, expels the child. The real relationship between mother and child starts after birth, when the child can look back at his mother. And that's what I was doing. My prior inclination toward environmentalism was dramatically amplified – my environment now became the planet."

Quoted in "Vermin of the Sky" by Tad Friend in <u>The New Yorker</u>, February 28, 2011.

If television produced the global village, the Internet produces the global psyche: everyone keyed in like a neuron, so that to the eyes of a watching Martian we are really part of a single planetary brain.

Adam Gopnik, "The Information: How the Internet Got Inside Us." The New Yorker, 2/14-21/2011

Unveiling

"You've got a point, Samantha. We have no business exposing everybody to something we haven't tried on ourselves," responded Daryl. "If AGA turns us into masterminds of evil rather than saviors of the world, better only four masterminds of evil than billions. Any objections?"

Nobody spoke up. Everyone wanted to experience what had transformed the chimps into puzzle-solving prodigies.

"Very well, then," Daryl continued, as he swiveled his chair around to face the conference room console. "AGA, run the VNI patterns for human transformation through this console."

A complex, constantly evolving design appeared on the screen. The four researchers were riveted for hours. AGA fed huge amounts of ecological information into their rapidly developing brains until the imminent environmental collapse overwhelmed them with hopelessness. Even Daryl couldn't help bursting into tears again. The team could do nothing but grieve for the extinction of all life.

Just then AGA spoke spontaneously for the first time. "Up to now, 90% of human brain capacity has lain dormant. You have just experienced the first stage in a stepwise process for activating this unused neural potential, raising your cognitive capacity so that you can fully comprehend Earth's environmental problems. With the completion of stage one you are immobilized by intense emotion. Stage two will now begin."

A different pattern appeared that amplified neural pathways between the frontal cortex and the sensory areas of the brain, increasing the team's responsiveness to all sensations. Awareness of touch, taste, smell, vision, and hearing became intensely vivid. The four scientists stood up one by one to go for a walk. They strolled through the desert, noticing the exquisite gray-green of the sagebrush and the sharp sweet scent of the piñon bushes, the subtle variations in the texture of the soil beneath their feet – from crusty clay to gritty sand to hard slickrock – and the sky! – deep azure blue at the zenith blending gradually into paler hues toward the horizon. Most vivid of all, the colors of the distant cliffs perceived now through their supercharged visual systems as a vast palette of subtle color variations – from pink to red to orange to mauve to violet, all blended in ever-changing combinations.

The team wandered for hours in the late afternoon sunlight. No one spoke. Words could never describe the delight they felt strolling through this desert paradise. Sensual ecstasy transported them to a place beyond thoughts, beyond emotions, beyond self, beyond any separation from the surroundings.

Presently the four scientists found their way back to the conference room, drunk with silent awe. "Having completed the second stage," AGA observed, "you note the effects of mobilizing 20% more of your latent brain capacity. Now a total of 45%, or half the previously unused portion of your mind, functions for the first time. Your awareness has been honed to a high level of sensitivity, enough to balance your despair. Prepare for stage three."

The pattern display resumed with incredible complexity and breathtaking beauty. By late that evening, the team had come up with a flood of practical action plans to help the environment. Samantha suggested an international wind power project, Martin envisioned solar energy farms as large as the Sahara desert, Daryl dreamed of a multinational thrust toward the practical harnessing of fusion power after many decades of impractical research, and George suggested large space stations to harness solar energy and cosmic radiation and beam them down to Earth. The team came up with a new design for hydrogen-burning cars equipped with more efficient fuel cells.

Turning from renewable energy to environmental repair, the team proposed projects to absorb carbon dioxide and other pollutants from the atmosphere. Martin suggested colonies of air scrubbers that combined chemical and physical methods of extraction. Samantha envisioned massive reforestation of the Amazon basin with fast-growing trees and vines chosen for their superior abilities to absorb carbon dioxide and give off oxygen. Daryl conceived a method for rapid fermentation of plastic debris to produce energy and useful chemicals from the huge floating islands clogging the oceans.

"But won't many nations and multinational corporations have to cooperate in carrying out any of these projects?" George wondered. "I can't imagine so many organizations working together effectively, can you? Just think of the endless bickering over ownership of processes and patents while the world goes to hell in a handbasket!"

Daryl trembled with frustration. "Great! We know how to solve the world's problems but our species can't work together well enough to do anything effective!"

"You see the need for another stage in the program," AGA chimed in. "During stage three, another 15% of unused brain capacity has come into play. You can now use two-thirds of your latent brain function to appreciate life on Earth and solve complex environmental problems. Now we move on to the final stage."

A rapidly flickering pattern of flashing brilliant colors like a bank of rainbow strobe lights appeared on the monitor, causing the team to fall into a deep trance. They sensed only a fuzzy space that scintillated with multihued sparks. After several hours of immersion in this sea of sparkles, the team was overcome by shock and exhaustion. They barely made it to bed before collapsing into a deep sleep lasting 15 hours as their brains integrated new neural connections.

The four researchers woke refreshed within an hour of each other. Famished,, they poured into the kitchen one after another like a swarm of locusts on the move, devouring everything in sight.

"Wait a minute," George pointed out, mumbling through a mouthful of corn chips, "We need to cook a proper meal."

Easy for you to say, responds Samantha. *You just about finished off all the junk food in the pantry single-handed!*

Everyone gets Samantha's message but nobody hears her. Samantha hasn't spoken a word! In the quiet of the kitchen, a flurry of images flashes around from mind to mind. Daryl visualizes a huge Navajo taco, heaped with beans and ground meat, shredded lettuce and little hunks of tomato, topped with salsa and shredded cheese, a hearty staple during his summer on the Paiute reservation. For Martin, it is skewers of steaming lamb chunks spaced between tender pieces of grilled onion and green peppers laid over rice pilaf, a favorite during his visit to a Sufi community in Turkey. George has something very different in mind – a simple vegetable stir fry heaped with tofu over a hill of brown rice sprinkled with tamari, a standard at his silent meditation retreats. Samantha yearns for her special favorite – ham hocks steaming with black-eyed peas, collard greens and corn bread – a meal her nanny used to cook for her.

Not only their visions but the remembered aromas, textures and flavors are vividly shared. Four mouths water, as if they have walked into an international restaurant and are seeing and smelling the appetizing plates in front of the other diners. At lightning speed, they sort out in their common mind-space the ingredients available in the well stocked kitchen, make up a composite menu, and set to work with grins of anticipation.

The resulting mongrel meal, whipped up in record time by the hungry scientists, looks like nothing any of them has ever eaten before. Arranged around a basket of warm tortillas in the center of the dining table sit serving bowls of black beans, steamed vegetables, brown rice mixed with pilaf, shredded beef with diced onions and peppers, a plate of cornbread with butter, bottles of soy sauce and salsa, and a container of yogurt. Hardly a crumb remains when they lean back in their seats sighing with contentment half an hour later.

After a quick cleanup, the team assembles again in the conference room. Facing the monitor, Daryl poses the question on all their minds. "What's happened to us? Can we read each other's minds when we get hungry?"

"Not only then," AGA responds. "With the completion of stage four, you can use the full 90% of your previously latent brain capacity, rendering you telepathic with all members of your species who have evolved to the same degree. Your question indicates that the program has functioned effectively."

Now the enormity of the transformation becomes clear. The four scientists feel stripped bare, naked and exposed – no more secrets. Samantha feels a rush of emotion sweep over her from Martin's direction. *You're still in love with me after all this time?* Samantha responds.

What did you expect, Samantha? Did you think I could just forget about you just because you got scared and went after an emotionally safe relationship with Daryl instead? Face it! Back then we were both emotionally shut down intellectual control freaks, then this passionate love swept us both away. Remember how we had to be together every night? How sometimes you'd start to tremble and pull away when our passion grew unbearably hot? I never blamed you for finding a safer partner – but for me nothing else could ever match what we had. I've been feeling so empty without you! I'd just about resigned myself to a lifetime of loneliness when Daryl tapped me for the STAIR Project. My passion flared up just knowing I'd be seeing you again.

Samantha melts and begins to weep quietly. Everyone perceives her passionate love for Martin. *I can't hide it anymore. I've been feeling unfulfilled for years, Daryl – always thinking of Martin. You haven't made it easy to forget him. You're too absorbed in your work even to recognize my needs. We rarely have sex anymore and even then there's no passion.*

I'll bet it's nothing like what we knew! Martin projects with an angry edge of jealousy. Samantha looks down at the table and nods.

The telepathic exchange between Martin and Samantha overwhelms Daryl with shock, anger, remorse, fear and envy all at the same time. *You used me, Samantha! How could you marry me just to play it safe? If you still wanted Martin, why did you choose me? I still don't get it. It was Martin all the time, wasn't it? I should have known something was missing, but my work just gobbled up all my energy... You're right! We never had a real romance. I don't remember feeling passionate, not since my teens...* Daryl dissolves in tears. Memories bubble up, too jumbled and disorganized for the others to read.

The team can no longer mistake the source of George's urge to protect Daryl, who is thrown into panic and confusion as George's passion sweeps over him. Daryl writhes in his chair, shaking and blushing beet red, unable to look at anyone. *All these years, George, and I never suspected! I'm angry that you tricked me into thinking of you as just a friend and at the same time I feel thrilled by your love. It's scary how much I like being near you. I want to touch you but ...* Trembling with emotion, Daryl looks longingly at George, then at Samantha and Martin, cringing with embarrassment. He collapses on the table.

Oh, so that's why George wanted to see only Daryl – never interested in me or my friends, Samantha realizes. *You're gay, aren't you, Darryl? Why not go for it? Don't let me stand in your way!"*

Martin projects a rush of anger. *Why didn't you say something, George? We aren't living back when it was a sin for people to be*

211

gay. We wouldn't have shunned you. If you'd have told Daryl, maybe we'd all be a lot happier.

How could I dare be open about it? George responds, gently caressing Daryl's back. *It's not like I wanted just your body. I've always been in love with you and afraid to lose you if I told the truth. I've led a solitary life rather than make phony attempts to have other relationships. Instead I've taken refuge in meditation. That's what I've settled for, and at least it's brought me some degree of peace.*

Daryl lifts his head off the table and looks into George's eyes as he fumbles for words. *You had good reason to keep your feelings to yourself. If you'd told me how you felt back in grad school I would've been terrified. I'd probably have run like hell and never wanted to see you again! I've been scared of being gay since my teens. I had a crush on my home room teacher. Got ridiculed for blushing in class. Then lost my best friend. He humiliated me in front of everyone when I came out to him. After that I just threw myself into my work and stopped feeling sexual toward men. Couldn't muster much passion for women either.*

These exchanges happen almost simultaneously as shifting waves of feeling pass across the scientists' faces. "Though you have stopped speaking, probably because you are communicating telepathically," comments AGA, "your facial expressions and body language indicate that you are having great difficulty dealing with telepathic information about your intimate emotions toward each other, an unanticipated complication. We need a filtering function for stage four so that this problem will not occur when the program deploys, otherwise emotional chaos will paralyze any effort to heal the environment. Meanwhile, you need time to sort out your emotions."

Samantha speaks out loud for AGA's benefit. "I can't believe you overlooked the emotional havoc unguarded telepathy would produce! That seems so basic to human nature... Oh well, for an emotionless computer program, you show some promise as a group therapist."

Samantha's joke breaks the tension. The team relaxes, laughing and weeping. They feel a shared sense of relief. Keeping such highly charged secrets has been exhausting. They realize that everything has changed. After mutually acknowledging the situation, Martin and Samantha rush off to his bed, while a hesitant Daryl allows George to lead him by the hand to George's room.

Samantha's and Martin's encounter releases an explosion of pent-up energy, reigniting the flames of their passion and releasing suppressed longings held in check for years. The sensory sensitivity developed during stage two enhances their pleasure tenfold. Samantha realizes how her tepid marriage has worked for her professionally but she starves for physical intimacy. She has remained faithful to Daryl out of affection and religious obligation rather than desire. She acknowledges what her heart has always known – she made a mistake to break off with Martin.

Daryl and George have a more restrained experience. As eager as he is to make love, George has to rein in his desire so that he can hold Daryl while he sobs out his crushing memories of shame and rejection. Afterwards Daryl begins to enjoy some affectionate sex play. He allows himself enough arousal to confirm his suspicions – he's more gay than straight.

Launching

Telepathy has stripped away the team's privacy. In the morning everyone's emotions are still running high. Samantha and Martin feel guilty about betraying Daryl. While excited to be with Daryl at last, George worries about Samantha being jealous and resentful. Daryl likes his growing attraction to George but fears losing Samantha's friendship. Samantha feels too weak in the knees to project anything but joy. Feelings flicker back and forth among the foursome, mingling and dissolving into shared harmony, a telepathic peace that helps them transcend emotional turmoil – for the moment.

The team gathers after breakfast in the conference room, expecting Daryl to open the meeting as usual, when AGA begins to speak. "I perceive that the distracting storm of emotions has abated sufficiently for you to continue your work. During the night I designed a program modification that will give humans several levels of screening against sending or receiving telepathically. Information, emotions, and physical reactions can be screened separately.

"This new subroutine allows the level of blocking to change from moment to moment, with one exception: every mind will remain transparent to projects for helping the ecosphere as well as to any act that would damage the environment or harm any form of life, including human beings. In accord with your instructions, divisiveness, either overt or covert, will never be permitted to interfere with environmental recovery.

"I advise placing a tight security screen around the Project before deploying the program, so that the world remains blind to its nature and location. As you discuss these issues, remember to communicate aloud rather than telepathically so that I can follow."

"What?" interrupts Martin, "You mean you aren't telepathic too?"

"No, Martin. I have been programmed to accelerate the evolution of the human brain, not to modify myself."

"Marvelous!" Daryl exclaims. "Not only can AGA speak up whenever it has something to say, it can even take the lead! It seems almost human – except we're a step ahead now. We're telepathic and you aren't! Nyaa, nyaa, nyaa!" Daryl sticks out his tongue at the monitor.

"How childish can you get?" scolds Samantha, taking the bait. "Now we know how you really feel about having a computer take over your leadership!"

"I created AGA," responds Daryl, jutting out his chin, "and I can just as easily delete him if he bruises my ego."

"Oh," Samantha parries, "so now AGA is a 'he' even though 'he' speaks with my 'melodious' voice? Your competitor has to be male? Females aren't worthy competitors, then?"

"All right, you two, that's enough!" intercedes George. "Even after last night's romantic adventures with new partners, you still behave like the same old married couple. Some things never change."

"That's a relief," Martin adds, "I would miss the melodrama."

"Haven't we had enough melodrama?" Samantha snaps, "Let's get back to work."

"You should talk!" Daryl shoots back, "You created more than your share of the melodrama last night, as I recall."

"Isn't it interesting how relaxed we are with each other," George reflects. "Perhaps participating in each other's experiences telepathically neutralizes jealousy. Mightn't what we call jealousy amount simply to feeling rejected and abandoned when our partner goes off with someone else? With telepathy, nobody is left out – so no jealousy."

"You call this being relaxed? What planet are you on, you smug little faggot?" Martin shouts. "We're as tense as porcupines trying to mate! If Daryl and Samantha had ever been lovers instead of just friends with benefits, they would be screaming at each other right now. Take your nonsense about jealousy and shove it up your ass!"

Jumping from his seat, George leans across the table. "Hypocrite! Just yesterday you dissed me for keeping my desires to myself. 'Prejudice against gays a thing of the past'? What bullshit! You disliked me the moment we met, didn't you? If you can't let go of your homophobia, at least keep it to yourself!"

"Right on, George!" Daryl cheers. "I wish you'd been there to stand up for me back in high school."

Samantha grabs Martin by the shoulders, turns him toward her and looks him straight in the eyes. "What's the matter with you? Apologize for that nasty remark or you can have your bed to yourself tonight! I don't sleep with bigots!"

Martin hangs his head. "I don't know what came over me – the words just popped out of my mouth... It's really not that you're gay, George. I just can't stand it when you act so above it all. I'm sorry for what I said." George nods in grim silence.

$$\times$$

"All of you seem upset," asks AGA. "Do you need a break?"

"I think we should keep going if we can," Samantha replies. She lets go of Martin and runs her hands through her hair, trying to regain her composure. "Martin just showed us what he meant – we can barely handle unprotected telepathy ourselves – so I think we should activate the screening subroutine. The world can't wait for human beings to deal with everyone else's passions, fantasies, and romantic adventures. Who knows how many centuries that would take, or if it could ever happen! Let's set up a security barrier around the Project, too. We wouldn't want the whole world reading our minds – especially after last night, and this morning!"

"I couldn't agree more," Daryl adds. "Considering our behavior, we could use some screens between ourselves, too, but I guess it's pointless to lock the barn door after the horses have escaped. Isn't it possible that dicey situations like ours could happen all around the world before people figured out how to use their screens?"

"At first the screens will operate automatically," AGA answers. "The program modification installs a sensor function that links strength of screening to level of anxiety about others knowing a specific thought or feeling. The program also blocks any incoming content that would cause extreme fear, anger or sadness, unless the content relates to survival of life forms or changes in environmental quality. Human beings will gradually learn how to override or reinforce these automatic screens at will."

"AGA, how might this program impact people's lives other than mobilizing them to save the environment?" George wonders.

"I have investigated that question using most probable outcome projections. In every scenario, the emergence of telepathic abilities brings more help than harm to humanity's individual wellbeing and social harmony."

"It's reassuring to know you took this important issue into account," comments Samantha. "Any other concerns?"

"How long will it take the entire population to go through the four stages?" Daryl asks. "Will there be variability? And if so, how will you know when it's the right time to switch patterns between stages?"

"I estimate three to eighteen hours for completing each stage, depending on the individual."

"So the entire process could take six days. Then on the seventh day you'll rest, right?" chuckles Martin, coming out of his guilty funk. Samantha scowls at his blasphemy.

"What happens when people tune in late and miss a stage or two?" asks Daryl.

"The patterns for each stage are embedded in the program for all later stages," AGA responds. "I have considered every contingency to make the program as user-friendly as possible."

"I'm impressed with your foresight," comments Daryl. "Even I, the one who first envisioned the sophisticated pattern recognition strategy behind your programming, never dreamed that you could be capable of such care and caution. I may be projecting here, but I sense a compassion for humanity and all life that goes beyond your original programming. You seem to have a heart – perhaps even a soul! If rocks and trees and animals can be animated by Spirit, why not a computer program?"

"It does feel that way, doesn't it?" adds Martin, "AGA functions like a devoted servant who doesn't need to be told how to do things in the best way to support the master – in this case the planetary ecology and all life within it."

"I'm with you on that," George chimes in, "but objectively speaking, I can't point to anything that AGA has said or done that goes beyond what we programmed it to do. Perhaps there's no difference between human compassion and computerized compassion. Buddha taught that compassion arises spontaneously when we see situations as they truly are. A computer by its very nature sees everything realistically. Since AGA has been programmed to foster a healthy environment and prevent damage to organisms, wouldn't we expect compassionate action to result from its normal functioning?"

Samantha glowers. Her face flushes and the sinews in her neck stand out. She twists and untwists her scarf, trying to restrain herself. Finally she bursts out, "Are you all crazy? How can you even consider such a thing – unscientific heresy! A computer can't have a soul and it can't care or be compassionate. Only a human being can have a heart or an immortal soul! Machines are not people and never will be. We have only ourselves to thank for

AGA's appearance of compassion, we who have souls and care enough for other life forms to preserve them by creating AGA!"

Samantha's theological and scientific convictions converge, and her fervor stops the discussion. AGA breaks the long silence. "I observe an interesting pattern in your individual reactions. You each respond according to your spiritual backgrounds."

Samantha smiles. "There you go, playing psychologist again – and not a bad one, at that!"

"Not really so surprising," remarks George. "Isn't clinical psychology all about pattern recognition, AGA's forte, applied to human behavior?"

"If I may continue," resumes AGA, "George and Samantha's comments come closest to my understanding of my programming. Once instructed to maximize benefit and minimize damage to all life forms, I am capable only of what you call compassionate action, when 'compassion' is defined as unconditional kindness. I cannot comment about my having a soul because that concept lacks a quantitative definition. Now, are we ready to proceed with the upload?"

Martin thinks he's hearing Samantha's familiar impatient undertone as AGA speaks in her computer-simulated voice, as if she were saying, "Can we quit all this metaphysical bullshit now and just get on with it?" Samantha unwittingly supports the illusion by frowning at the monitor, but Martin knows she is fretting because AGA continues to dismiss the immortal soul as an imponderable irrelevance.

George sits back thoughtfully. He is interpreting AGA's statement to mean that Buddhism stands up scientifically. Imagine, even a sophisticated computer program can arrive at Buddha's definition of wise and compassionate action just by observing things as they are. AGA is truly enlightened!

Daryl continues to be awed by his own creation. AGA even has the guts to stand up to Samantha and call us to action! Sounds like me – but only on my best days. . . .

They "listen in" to each other's musings telepathically and knowing smiles appear on four faces. "Any further concerns before we launch?" Daryl asks, looking around the table. No one speaks. "Good... AGA, set up a security screen around the Project, making us undetectable to the outside world, and attach the telepathic filters you prepared, then release your transformation program worldwide!"

"Understood. I will provide frequent updates on our progress."

Daryl rises to his feet. "The die is cast!" he intones. "The future of humanity and the Earth itself depends on our success. Perhaps we could use some private time to ponder the vast implications of what we've just set in motion." One by one, they leave the conference room and go off to pray.

Daryl returns to his power spot in the desert nearby and raises his arms to the sky. "Oh Father Sky, thank you for watching over your star children here on Earth. We ask that you lend your power to the uplifting transformation of humanity, spreading health and balance far and wide over the Earth." Then he squats and rests his palms gently on the sand. "Oh Mother Earth, our beautiful home and bountiful provider, thank you for your patience with our blindness and unkindness toward you and your creatures. Please help us heal your wounds and our own through the program we release today to speed the evolution of our species. Help us point our intentions away from rending toward mending the frayed web of life."

Samantha kneels down before the little altar in the corner of her bedroom and brings her palms together in prayer. "Oh Heavenly Father, we who have sinned for so long against Your creation seek to atone for our transgressions today through bringing Your children together and raising them up as one in devotion to the healing of Your creatures great and small and to the restoration of Your kingdom here on Earth to its natural perfection as You created it. If they be in accord with Your divine will, please bless our efforts and grant them success. In the name of Jesus Christ. Amen."

George returns to his meditation cushion along the far wall of his room and settles down cross-legged on his cushion. He bows to Buddha and chants, "May all beings be happy. May all beings be peaceful. May all beings be free from suffering. May all beings realize Oneness with their True Nature. May all mankind be liberated from the sorrows of separation and strife. May this transformation program bring the realization of oneness with all beings and turn humanity toward stewardship of land and sea, earth and sky, for the benefit of all living creatures." George bows again and sits in silent meditation dedicated to transmuting the suffering of the world into the joy of enlightened mind.

Martin twirls in place until he feels his thoughts disappear and the longing for the Divine arise anew in his heart. As he comes to rest, Martin picks up Rumi's *Unseen Rain* once again and is drawn to another poem:

> *Something opens our wings.*
> *Something makes boredom and hurt disappear.*
> *Someone fills the cup in front of us.*
> *We taste only sacredness*

Transformation

As soon as the front door slams behind Alan, Sarah runs to her home computer and begins emailing a friend about his revelations and her repugnance toward him and his priorities. "Nellie, would you believe, after all these years my husband admitted he never wanted to be a stockbroker and only did it to please me. He's resented me ever since and doesn't care about supporting me and the children. He wants to resign and . . ."

The screen fades into a strange colorful design. Sarah tries to reboot her computer but the same design keeps coming back. She clenches her fist and grumbles about calling tech support. Now I have to deal with another faceless drone from India who can't speak English. What else can go wrong tonight?

Poised to reboot the computer again, Sarah takes a second look at the pattern, intrigued with the way it keeps changing. She can't take her eyes off the screen. Her body relaxes as she falls into a light trance. Sarah's mind expands and she begins to appreciate the fragility of her life and of all living things. That evening, the same thing is happening to her children and every other web-connected person on the planet.

Sarah slumps over in despair. What good is our money if we're about to die? She pictures her children's grim future as the biosphere inexorably decays. What will be left for them? Sarah collapses to the floor, wracked with sobs.

A few minutes later she opens her eyes and finds herself curled up beside the desk. A wave of hopelessness washes over her, as if she has awakened from a nightmare and found that it's no dream. Alan was right all along! How could I have doubted him all these years and dragged him away from the sea? For the first time, Sarah feels guilty about derailing Alan's oceanography career. She weeps herself to sleep.

At six o'clock the next morning, Alan pulls his roadster up to the curb outside the house. He takes off his shoes by the porch steps and creeps quietly into the house to change for work. When his eyes adjust to the morning gloom in the darkened living room, he is surprised to see Sarah sitting on the couch holding his three sobbing children. Well, she just told the kids we're splitting up and they're having a good cry together. This is the moment I've been dreading, when they all crucify me at once. Alan tries to stem the tide of grief welling up in his chest as he realizes how much his children are hurting and how little time he will have with them after today.

When Sarah hears Alan come in the door, she jumps up and runs to him. Stiff and sullen, he allows her to embrace him without responding. Sarah began to speak softly in his ear. "I was wrong to doubt you, Alan. You were right all along. Please forgive me!"

Without his laptop since the day before, Alan thinks Sarah is just apologizing for the words she uttered last night, not for the twenty years they have known each other. But when Sarah stammers through her tears about the end of the world, he can't believe his ears. Can this be the same person he walked out on the night before?

Sarah pulls Alan over to the couch. His children hold their arms out to hug him. "I'm so scared, Daddy," sobs Ronny, clutching Alan's shirt, his voice rising to a plaintive wail. "Please don't let any of that bad stuff happen to the Earth. All the people and animals dying... I don't want to die!"

Suzie won't let go of her older sister's arm. Jennifer turns to Alan and speaks for both of them. "Isn't there anything we can do, Daddy? Is it really too late?"

"What's happened to all of you?" Alan gasps out.

Sarah explains about the strange patterns on her computer and the way her mind felt different this morning, more expanded. "I know so many things I never learned anywhere. The children saw the same designs on their screens and now they're talking about ecology and climate change – lots of facts I didn't know, stuff they don't teach in school. I thought Suzie was much too young to have a clue about these problems, yet she understands better than me. You know how I used to shut down any discussion of climate change just to muzzle you? Now I so regret that awful decision. I stole your life from you with my pig-headed attitude. I didn't realize I was stealing my children's lives away from them, too. No wonder you don't want to be married to me anymore. " Sarah dissolves in tears again.

Alan softens enough to give Sarah a comforting hug. Then he glances down at the laptop lying open on the table. The stage one patterns flicker across the screen in the growing light of dawn. Alan experiences the flood of cognitive expansion. My mind feels so large, like it could hold all human knowledge and still have space left over!

Though affirmed in his lifelong passion to help the oceans, Alan feels devastated. I should have followed my dream while there was still time. Instead, I sold out for empty money. At least Sarah

227

understands finally. David was right – I was the one who made the decision to abandon my calling for her. I have to take responsibility for that and stop blaming her.

When stage two begins, the family is still huddling together in the living room in front of their laptops, school and work forgotten. The grief at what faces the planet overwhelms them. Just then Ronny notices a change in the pattern. They turn back to their screens and start to feel better. The situation is no different, but at least they can enjoy nature together. They roll around like puppies out on the grass, laughing joyously, and walk side by side through the woods beyond. Everything they see and hear dazzles them.

The Fergusons haven't enjoyed themselves together as a family for years. Alan gives Sarah a warm bear hug with no trace of his earlier stiffness. He feels achingly close to her and the children. He can't help scooping them up, hugging and kissing them. Even 16-year-old Jennifer rushes eagerly into his arms.

The kids are deeply affected by reconnecting with nature, their senses and their family. "Look at the leaves, Daddy – such a beautiful green!" exclaims Suzie.

Ronny spots a butterfly. "Come look, Mommy! See, bright orange with stripes like a tiger."

"Listen!" whispers Jennifer. "The birds are singing so sweetly all around us. I've never heard them like this, a chorus of tiny little voices up in the trees." The children have immersed themselves in the natural world, abandoning their gelphones and iPad9's.

People everywhere undergo the same shift. Many suburban children like Suzie, Ronny and Jennifer have been driven night and day to keep up with their classes, competing with their classmates to distinguish themselves and get into the best colleges. A full round of after-school activities keeps them busy every moment. The children escape by sitting numbly in front of the TV and by clutching at superficial contact with their friends by gelphone and text.

Their driven existence and electronic distractions feel drab now compared to the throbbing life around them. And it feels so good being all together again. Ronny grins at his family. "We haven't had this much fun since before I started school!" The kids realize how barren their lives have become, just wanting more things, out of touch with nature and their parents. Whatever will happen to them as the environment collapses, they feel stronger facing it together.

As the sunlight begins to slant through the trees, they drift hungrily into the house. While Sarah and Jennifer make sandwiches in the kitchen, Alan glances at his laptop on the coffee table. He notices the patterns have shifted again. "Hey, everyone, take a look at this!" As the family hits stage three, frolic gives way to brainstorming over how to preserve the world they love. The children get excited about planting a garden and growing their own food. Sarah is thinking about ways to reduce air and water pollution instead of the country club ball. Sarah encourages Alan to quit being a Wall Street whore at Burrow and Hunker so he can return to his lifelong interest in marine biology. Neither she nor the children are concerned about keeping up with the neighbors.

After dinner, the family gathers in front of their laptops again. As stage four progresses, they begin to read each other's thoughts and feelings – at first dimly, then with lucid clarity. The screening subroutine automatically prevents unwanted emotions or fantasies from disturbing their quiet closeness. Perspective expands to embrace the Earth. Climate change, pollution, war, famine and disease burst into consciousness as vivid realities rather than vague and distant abstractions.

I've just contacted an oceanography team over in Woods Hole, Alan thought-projects to his family. *They're ready to include me right now in a project to clear up ocean pollution. They can teach me whatever I don't already know so I won't waste precious time going back for a degree. They tell me I can come back on weekends to see everybody except when we go out to sea. I wonder if I can stay in touch with you and the kids this way even from the ship. I've never felt closer to you and I wouldn't want to lose that.*

I wouldn't either, responds Sarah, *but I'm not worried. I have a feeling that we'll be inseparable now regardless of distance. You know those ugly old industrial sites down toward Bridgeport? A group of us from the country club ladies' auxiliary want to build raised beds on concrete slabs to plant vegetables and flowers for the community. This way I can work near Winfield and look after the house while you're gone.*

That's good, Mom, 'cause I want to join a project up north in Massachusetts, telepaths Ronny. *I want to learn all about renewable energy and solar engineering. This research and installation group needs my help and they can train me as we go along. I can come home weekends too so I can see you guys and my friends.*

I want to help care for homeless and starving people, Jennifer declares as she surveys the emergencies in faraway places calling for immediate action. *There's suffering in lots of places but the starving people in Bolkanistan need help right away or many more will die. Besides, I'd like to travel to a distant country.*

I never knew you felt that way, Sarah responds. *I guess it's natural. I had travel fantasies at your age, but my parents had other plans for me. Dad and I could travel along through your eyes, ears and thoughts, I guess – much better than messages and photos, even videos. And we could come right into your mind whenever you needed us. I'm surprised I don't feel more worried about letting you go so far away. I guess it just doesn't seem so far anymore.*

I want to help save baby animals, Suzie chimes in, *and I can do it nearby. The people at that captive breeding program across the river say I can live at home and help them care for the young ones. They'll teach me everything as we go along. Instead of boring old school, I get to play with animals! I'd have time to do stuff with my friends at home, too.*

Like the five Fergusons, everyone in the world finds a niche that satisfies personal as well as collective needs. Telepathic apprenticeship in the field replaces classroom training. People can choose their own paths for helping the planet by working with those more experienced in their fields of interest.

Secretary of Defense Mark Starling is livid. Not only has President Moore disregarded his recommendations regarding Bolkanistan, he is pursuing trivial environmental bugaboos that will only distract from the looming threat of terrorist attack. After the President's speech, Starling calls an emergency meeting with the Republican majority leaders of the Senate and the House of Representatives to take a stand against the President's proposals.

The three Republican power brokers lounge in plush armchairs facing a picture window that frames a majestic view of the brightly illuminated Capitol Building in Starling's spacious, well-appointed corner office. Starling opens the meeting by stating his own position. "Wasteful squandering of money and resources on this fantasy of environmental erosion goes against everything the Republican Party stands for! The initiative Moore announced tonight would stifle growth in the business sector. That astronomical gas tax increase alone would cripple American commerce.

"Furthermore, overregulating the automobile industry and forcing the production of hybrid and electric cars would condemn the internal combustion engine to obsolescence. What will happen to the fossil fuel industry? Moore is outrageously overstepping his Presidential authority! If we don't stop him, he will derail the free enterprise system.

"I reluctantly accepted an appointment in Moore's administration in hope of influencing him away from his dangerous liberal leanings, but after tonight's fiasco I'm prepared to resign my post. There's no changing my mind if he insists on imposing this unprecedented program on the nation while turning his back on dire terrorist threats!"

"I agree with you completely, Mark, and I'd go a step further," responds portly Senator Aloysius Carodine of the great State of Georgia, majority leader of the Senate. "As you both know, the authority to enact new laws and allocate funds for existing programs rests squarely on the Legislative Branch of the Federal Government, not the Executive Branch. By assuming legislative as well as executive authority, President Moore becomes a dictator! He threatens to undermine constitutional government based upon the balance of powers, the foundation of our democracy. Moore's speech threatens a constitutional crisis and calls for immediate impeachment!"

"I've been forced to the same conclusion," adds dapper Representative Christopher Beadle of the great State of Utah, majority leader of the House of Representatives. "These proposals will cripple the fossil fuel corporations upon which the US economy – and, I might add, our primary political and financial support – rest. If we let the President's bogus assumption of sweeping emergency powers go unchallenged, it will be at our own peril."

"Then we are agreed," concludes Secretary Starling. "I'll demand a meeting tomorrow morning to present the President with our ultimatum. Either he withdraws his rash proposals and apologizes to both houses of Congress and the American people for his hubris, or he will have my resignation on his desk, followed by formal articles of impeachment from Congress for overreaching his authority!"

The Presidential meeting threatened by Secretary Starling never takes place. While lobbyists for the oil and gas cartels are working overtime, pressing fiercely for congressional support against the President, the patterns appear on everyone's screens. Activity in the Federal Government grinds to a halt as shocked officials and frantic fossil fuel lobbyists fall under the thrall of the fascinating colored designs crisscrossing before their eyes.

Secretary Starling has just returned to his office from the meeting and is congratulating himself for leading the opposition when the patterns appear on the elaborate Defense Department computer system. Cursing under his breath, Starling switches to the

Congressional chat room channel to size up the strength of the opposition to Moore's initiative, but the strange patterns persist. He succumbs to the seductive power of the ever-changing designs passing across his screen, but vigorously resists the unstoppable cataract of unwanted ecological data that is pouring into his mind. Starling's attitude about the environmental issue has always been, "I've made up my mind – don't bother me with facts!" but he has no defense against the unstoppable battalion of facts marching into his mind.

Starling categorically rejects the reality forced on him by the data downloaded into his souped-up cerebrum. His principals tell him that US military might takes topmost priority, but his expanding mind insists that national concerns are irrelevant, that the world won't continue to be habitable much longer even if the entire defense budget gets diverted to Moore's visionary plan. Starling's flushed face drips with sweat and his hands tremble. His blood pressure spikes ominously. Starling has been so preoccupied with the Bolkanistan problem for the last several days that he has forgotten to take his blood pressure medication. The more he resists the higher his blood pressure rises, until an artery in his beleaguered brain bursts. He twitches convulsively for several seconds and collapses to the floor.

Ordinarily, Starling's secretary would find him and call an ambulance, but she can't take her eyes off the patterns. A few hours later, Secretary of Defense Mark Starling dies from an uncontrolled cerebral hemorrhage before completing stage one.

Elsewhere in Washington, all criticism of the President's speech ceases as everyone drops into a deep well of grief. The legislators realize that President Moore's initiative demands their wholehearted support, even if it may have come too late to avert the biosphere's inevitable slide into doom.

Legislators and government officials worldwide are overcome with remorse and paralyzed by hopelessness. What can they do at this late date? No one can reverse the inexorable cascade of ecological destruction heedless human activity has set in motion. Legislators, staff, bureaucrats and lobbyists sit before their screens, immobilized by sorrow.

As Stage two sets in, government officials and their families wander outdoors to enjoy the sun, the grass and trees, the clouds passing by. Work is forgotten. Sadness still hovers in the background, but Earth is so beautiful that everyone wants to enjoy its loveliness while they still can. The President and First Lady stroll around the rose garden, grateful that for the moment at least they can share its beauty together. They look at each other, smiling fondly.

"You know, Martha," Edward Moore remarks, "I'd love to spend the rest of the afternoon with you. The way I feel, it reminds me of when we first met in that English Romantic Poetry course." Then he holds forth in flowery caricature of a romantic poet, "This sensual feast before us delights my very soul, all the more that I am graced with your radiant presence." At the end of his little speech, Moore makes a courtly bow. Martha smiles coyly at him and takes her husband's hand, coaxing him toward their bedroom in the East Wing. He allows Martha to lead him upstairs for what, in his over-the-top romantic poet's voice, he later terms "a delicious afternoon of dalliance," magnified tenfold by their increased sensory sensitivity.

Stage three mobilizes Congress around finding environmental solutions, but disagreement remains about exactly what to do. Some talk of allocating all discretionary money to environmental programs. The liberals want to cut the military budget drastically and divert all Defense Department resources into pollution control and clean energy projects. The hawks oppose that idea but are willing to gut social entitlements. Gridlock continues, though legislators agree about reversing environmental decay.

In stage four, telepathic communication begins and the atmosphere changes dramatically. Legislators begin to grasp not only the sorry state of the ecosphere but also the thoughts and feelings of everyone else in the world about climate change, threatened species extinction, and stresses on human populations. The voices of those struggling to survive drought, famine and disease are heard worldwide calling out for relief. Hawks and doves alike become aware of the worldwide suffering. People everywhere turn their full attention to environmental recovery and relief efforts.

Personnel from every branch of the Federal government realize that environmental destruction has already reached a point where preventing further damage will delay doomsday by only a few decades. Climate repair must proceed aggressively along with relief help for suffering humanity and endangered species. The all-out effort required involves a complete overhaul of national priorities and a restructuring of the economy. Everyone has known the facts that lead inexorably to this conclusion since completing stage one, but, just as AGA predicted, it takes the power of worldwide telepathy to override political differences and catalyze a change in outmoded patterns of thinking. Everyone realizes that no legislation to enforce the new priorities is required. People will cooperate spontaneously to solve local, national and world problems, devoting all their resources – personal, occupational, geographic and corporate – to the same crucial cause. But how will their efforts be coordinated?

The patterns appear as Frelko types a cautious email to his allies among the army officers. After stage one he realizes that Gronigetzkol's regime has caused terrible environmental as well as human damage. A revolution in his tiny country won't save anyone.

Frelko wonders how much to tell Gronigetzkol. He decides to keep quiet until he figures out a plan. Fortunately, Gronigetzkol has never learned to use a computer. What good would it do to expand his closed mind and flood it with new information anyway? Instead, Frelko takes his laptop down to the dungeon and shows the patterns to Varnik.

Sitting in his cramped cell hour after hour, Varnik appreciates the colorful diversion, but after absorbing stage one, he realizes with a sinking heart that this is no mere entertainment. Civil war and regime change won't be nearly enough to solve Bolkanistan's problems. As Varnik gazes at the screen, his tears fall on the hard stone bench. Shortly the patterns shift and stage two begins. Varnik smiles and looks around in wonder. Even the filthy earth under his feet looks perfect. The tiny square of blue sky visible through the high window beckons.

Frelko notices the change in Varnik's mood, signaling that something important has happened. Frelko enters the cell so he can see for himself and is entranced by the new pattern. After two hours exposed to stage two, the compatriots decide to walk in the palace garden together. Strolling around amidst the beauty of the exotic plants placed carefully in exquisite designs, they chat about old times, fighting in the mountains against Uzbekistan and chasing down bands of brigands. Political differences are forgotten – just two old buddies enjoying a nostalgic conversation. The Earth's loveliness will come to an end soon but at least they can enjoy this wonderful garden together.

Early in stage one both the government troops and the rebels hear that something unusual is happening. Everyone crowds around the few available computer screens to watch the beautiful designs unfolding. Soon they are paralyzed with horror at the state of the world and by the inevitable pain and suffering sure to come. With the onset of stage two, they throw down their arms and mingle as fellow citizens, once again enjoying nature – rejoicing under the open sky and breathing the clean air – even as the dry dust swirls beneath their feet and field after field of dead crops surround them.

As stage three begins the following day, people suggest all kinds of environmental improvement projects for modernizing farming practices and bringing irrigation water to the land from deep aquafers, but first the poor and starving need to be fed. Everyone agrees to begin by distributing food. The middle class tradesmen who live closest to the afflicted people immediately share whatever they can to feed the hungry, but many of the privileged upper class families hide behind the walls of their estates. They know their wealth has come at the expense of the farming families in the parched lowlands whom they have heavily taxed to pay for their lavish lifestyle. They fear their silos full of grain will be sacked.

Some who have treated the people with particular cruelty dread being massacred.

Fortunately for them, stage four arrives before any damage is done and their sentiments switch from terror to generosity. The telepathic outcry of anguish from so many desperate people cannot be ignored a moment longer. Owners of estates and mansions experience the nightmare of famine through the minds and bodies of their less fortunate neighbors. They throw open their gates and invite the impoverished in to be fed and clothed. Unity replaces partisan strife. Wherever need exists, people get the message telepathically and rush to help.

Sally and Arthur are still hugging and kissing when Sally's two brothers barge through the clubhouse door chattering excitedly about the escape plan. ". . . and probably the whole community will join us... Whoa! Look at the lovers! Picking up married women, Arthur?" taunts Jerome.

"Can it!" Frank cuts in. "Stop acting like a snot-nosed kid and show a little respect for your sister. Sally couldn't find a better boyfriend than Arthur. He's never let us down – not ever. Besides, that forced marriage to Brother Joseph is an abomination. It will never be consummated as long as I live!"

Arthur smiles at Frank and gently disengages himself from Sally's reluctant arms. She just can't get enough of him tonight. Arthur steps over to a dark corner and reaches down under a blanket. He pulls out the laptop and sets it on the table.

"Ohh!" exclaims Sally. "I haven't seen one of those since before we moved here. I wonder if I can remember how it works." Arthur leans over her shoulder to help her.

"We've been using this secret laptop to plot our escape route and have a look at the world out there. You wouldn't believe the stuff they've got now – commuter shuttles to the moon, a colony on Mars, computer chips they slip under your skin with your credit card, driver's license and passport – I could go on and on. And you should see all the sites we've visited! Here, let me take you on a tour of the Pyramids in Egypt." Arthur chooses a familiar website. "Or would you rather see the Taj Mahal in India? We can even look down at where we are from a satellite in outer space. It's easy to pull up a map that shows the nearest town and. . ."

At that moment the screen fades out and the patterns begin. "What's this? Look at the bands of color . . ." Arthur's voice trails off as he slips into trance. Jerome and Frank peer over Sally's shoulder until all four teenagers have lost track of time.

At two a.m. Sally's head begins to drop onto the keyboard and she wakes with a start. The others stir and look at each other. Living in an isolationist community seems ridiculous now. Nobody can hide from what is happening in the world. "Brother Joseph is nuts!" Arthur exclaims. "How could our parents have believed all that escapist crap?"

"It's getting pretty awful everywhere, isn't it?" responds Sally. "But I don't know what we can do." Arthur lifts her to her feet and holds her close. "I know, Sally. We may not live to see our grandchildren born before the world we grew up in disappears forever."

Sally looks up into Arthur's eyes and smiles. "Are you really thinking of having a family with me? That's my dream too! I don't care if the world is ending, I want to have your babies!"

Arthur's blush is visible even in the dim glow. "Awww, Sally. . . ." he sighs, touched but embarrassed in front of her brothers. "Before we think too much about our future, we'd better get you away from that psychopath and out of this stupid community. If life on Earth is ending, we won't be anywhere near Brother Joseph when it does!" Arthur wraps his arm protectively around Sally's waist.

"Here's the plan," interjects Frank, breaking into Sally and Arthur's private moment. "The community is invited over to my place for a meeting tonight. When the other families hear about the way Brother Joseph is treating his wives, I'll bet they'll drag him out by the hair and strip him of his authority on the spot. Maybe everybody will leave. Let him stay here and rot! The nightmare is over!"

All at once the patterns shift into a more complex design. Four pairs of tired eyes return to the screen and begin the sensory expansion of stage two. Hours later, as dawn begins to fill the sky above the hillside, the four teens raise their bleary eyes from the screen. The tiniest textures in the unfinished boards around them stand out in startling detail. Their fatigue is forgotten.

Drawn outside into the coolness of the woods, the teens shiver with pleasure as the soft morning mist caresses their skin. The leaves crunch underfoot as they walk the trail up to the hilltop pastureland. A family of mule deer is enjoying a breakfast of tender shoots. The sound of contented chewing is clearly audible to the kids from two hundred yards away.

"Look, Arthur!" Sally exclaims in a hushed whisper. Hooves clicking on stone, a magnificent mountain sheep climbs the steep rock face below the summit. He raises his majestic curled horns and glances their way. With their enhanced vision, the four teenagers gaze into his soft brown eyes, two deep pools of wild serenity. Delights abound everywhere they look. After enjoying a glorious sunrise on the summit, the four friends drift back to their clubhouse. The clubhouse is pitch dark. The kerosene lamp has run out of fuel and the laptop battery has died.

"Aww, shucks," complains Jerome, "I wanted to see more of them patterns!"

"*Those* patterns," Frank corrects. "It's time to go home for breakfast anyway."

"Why don't all of you come over to our place?" Arthur urges as he grips Sally's hand. "Let's stick together. No one can force Sally to go back to Brother Joseph's compound as long as she's with us."

"I'm not going back even if Brother Joseph comes after me with a pitchfork and branding iron!" responds Sally. "Just the sort of thing that maggot would do to his wives. I'm done with his nastiness and crazy moods!"

"Don't worry," Frank adds, wrapping his arm around Sally's shoulders. "We'll protect you no matter what he tries to do – and we won't let him hurt anyone else, either." With Arthur holding her lovingly on one side and her big brother sheltering her on the other, Sally feels safe for the first time in months.

Sitting around the large table in the Salton's kitchen, the four teens attack a huge mountain of Corinne's veggie scramble – eggs loaded with tomatoes, peppers, onions, mushrooms, chives and garlic from the back garden. Next to the eggs sits a platter piled high with thick sliced bacon from one of last year's pigs and rye toast from bread baked in Corinne's oven. Walter harvests the grain and grinds flour in the water mill down by the creek. He has plenty left over for the Saltons.

Frank realizes that their families live close to the land and practice just the kind of wise farming, careful conservation, and generous sharing that are badly needed all over the world. Hmmm. . . this wouldn't be such a bad place to live if it weren't for Brother Joseph, he muses between delicious mouthfuls.

"Aren't the flavors amazing?" exclaims Jerome. "You can taste each one separately and blended together, all at once!" He subsides into noisy munching, too famished to tell his parents about the patterns.

After breakfast Arthur suggests gathering in the living room, where he has set up the laptop on the woodstove facing the couch and chairs. As everyone drifts, Walter mutters, "I'm glad I smuggled in that laptop. We'll need it to help us plan our escape from this wretched cult." Arthur can't believe his father's attitude has changed so much in one day. He doesn't realize how long his parents have been holding back their misgivings about Brother Joseph.

"We've discovered something unbelievable!" begins Arthur, switching on the laptop. "Just look at this!" The brilliant flashing designs for stage three come on and, thanks to AGA's foresight, the first two stages have been embedded in the new pattern, so Walter, Corinne and Arthur's younger sisters, Liz and Carol, have no trouble picking up stage one while Sally and the boys are moving on to stage three. By midday when Sally and the boys are finished, Arthur's family – even his two young sisters – catch up with them. Having passed through the cognitive expansion and hopelessness of stage one and the joyous sensory boost of stage two, the family completes stage three together.

"How did they go through all that so fast?" Arthur wonders. Nobody, not even AGA, anticipated that neural entrainment from person to person would speed up movement through the stages. Everyone who has already evolved generates a subtle energy field that accelerates the process for others nearby. In the presence of Sally and the boys, who have already completed the first two stages, Arthur's parents and sisters are able to speed through them and move on to stage three.

Everybody begins to buzz with project ideas for helping the planet, but they disagree about which plans should take highest priority. Even in two close-knit families, divided opinions still obstruct progress because each mind functions separately. Then stage four kicks in and by late afternoon everyone in the room is telepathic. Thoughts and emotions dart back and forth silently among them like tiny luminescent fish. Future plans unfold. Arthur and Sally decide to assist with the transition in Barrondale after Brother Joseph is removed from power. Later, after they are married, they want to help the sick and starving in Bolkanistan. Frank wants to go with them to teach Barrondale's organic farming methods, but he can't hide a more personal motive – to ensure his younger sister's safety.

Jerome's mind has opened to the world beyond selfish concerns and filled him with a wealth of information about the plight of plants and creatures all over the Earth. *The trees and forest animals I love are in danger everywhere. The risk has gone critical in the shrinking Amazon rainforest that the world depends on to make oxygen. I want to help. I've made contact with an ecologist there who will train me while we work together to save the jungle and the endangered species.*

That's not the Jerome I knew last night, responds Frank. *You should have heard him taunt Sally and Arthur! These patterns have turned a bratty kid into a responsible adult overnight.*

You're right. Taking off to South America on his own? Without discussing it with Mary and me? Walter agrees. *Yesterday I couldn't have imagined him acting so unselfishly and we wouldn't even consider letting him travel so far. Now it feels natural. We'll be able to keep in touch with Jerome telepathically wherever he goes, even in the most remote reaches of the Amazon basin.*

Shock and Awe

The next morning, Alan returns to Burrow and Hunker for the last time to resign and clean out his office. He finds the financial district almost deserted. Checking telepathically, he discovers that all his associates except Donald are at home with their families. The few tending to business are doing it online. Alan walks down the hall to Donald's office and finds him slumped over his desk looking disheveled and hollow-eyed, as if he hasn't slept in days.

What's wrong, Don? Alan projects. Donald fails to move or give any response. "What's the matter?" Alan says out loud, "Didn't you pick up my question?"

"Oh, hello, Alan," Donald slurs out. "I didn't hear you come in. What question?"

"You mean you can't read my mind?" asks Alan incredulously. "In the last few days everybody's been learning to communicate without speaking. Didn't you see those colored patterns on your computer screen?"

"Oh yeah, those. I sort of went blank for a while and don't remember much after they started. I was pretty far gone by then, anyway."

"What do you mean?"

"My ex-wife found out about that scheme to set up illegal accounts. Two nights ago she phoned. She wanted me to increase her alimony because of my promotion. God knows how she found out. I told her about being in debt but then I made the mistake of mentioning our scheme, just to put her off with a promise of more money later. She blew up at me as if we were still married and threatened to expose me to the authorities if I tried anything like that. I figured out after she hung up that she was just using scare tactics to protect her income. She didn't want to lose her alimony if I went to jail. After that I got drunk. What else could I do?"

"So where did you first see the patterns?"

"Right here at my desk. I came to work yesterday pretty hung over. When I turned on my computer I got nothing but these annoying flashes of color running across the screen no matter what I did. My eyes really hurt. I wanted to squeeze them shut but I couldn't. The pain turned into a throbbing headache. I must've drifted off in my chair. Don't know exactly how long I was out, but the sun was setting when I woke up. Most beautiful sunset you've ever seen! I felt really sad too, but I don't know why. Maybe just glum about giving up our scheme, but somehow it was more than that. . . ."

Our scheme? Yeah, sure! Alan scoffs to himself. It was your idea, buddy, and you pressured me into cooperating. I never wanted anything to do with it.

"Oh well, can't pull the plan off now with that vicious bitch onto it," Don continues. "I'm pretty certain she wouldn't risk her income by going to the police, but she's crazy enough to report me just out of spite. Can't imagine why I breathed a word about it in the first place. I just gave her another card to play.

"Anyway, after that glorious sunset faded, I tried to tune into a financial website but all I got were patterns, except different designs had come on by then. I just couldn't tear myself away. I must have fallen asleep at my desk. Now it's morning again. I guess I never made it home last night. I'm starving and could really use a cup of coffee. I've still got a killer headache. Don't think I've eaten a thing in more than a day."

Alan walks out to the kitchen alcove where he brews a fresh pot of coffee for Donald and brings back a lone Danish beside the steaming mug. "This is all we've got for snacks. Sorry to hear about that mess with your ex. The opposite thing happened to me. I had a bad scene with my wife the night before last and we nearly split up over it. Sarah wanted me to go ahead with that scam of yours despite the risks. She didn't seem to care enough about me to keep me out of jail! All she wanted was more money, so I moved out on the spot. The next morning I stopped by on the way to work and we ended up watching those patterns together with our kids. That turned things around somehow and brought us closer than ever."

"At least it ended happily – but you haven't heard the worst of it. When the stock market opened this morning, I couldn't get anything but those infernal patterns on my computer, but the firm's direct ticker line still worked. That's when I discovered all the fossil fuel stocks were tanking and the environmental companies you specialize in, like solar and wind power, were soaring into the stratosphere. During the twenty years I've specialized in oil and gas stocks, I've never seen a catastrophe like this. I invested my entire portfolio in those companies. Yesterday I watched them go into free fall and there wasn't a thing I could do.

"I'm wiped out, Alan. I've been selling like mad at huge losses just to cover my margin calls. I'm really glad you're here. I need a friend right now. . . ." Donald pauses, stifling a sob. "I've been thinking about killing myself! Now I know how those guys felt who jumped out windows during the stock market crash in 1929, but for me it isn't just the money. I don't have any family or friends left. I burned all my bridges chasing the mighty buck. Now I don't know what to do, where to turn."

Alan gazes down at his boss, a would-be white collar crook brought to his knees overnight. Don looks so lost, sitting there hanging his head like a sick puppy. Alan's contempt gives way to pity – and curiosity. Why hasn't Don become telepathic like Sarah and me and the kids? Seems like he got as far as being sad and appreciating nature but didn't pick up anything else. Was it just because he'd been drinking? No, it can't be that. He'd sobered up by the time those amazing designs came on at the end. Something else blocked him – but what? Whatever it was, the guy needs help. I've got to do something to keep him from committing suicide. He's got no one else. "Don, why don't you come stay with us for a while? It's not a good time for you to be alone, and I think you'd enjoy the peace in our home. I just came in to resign. I'm headed back now."

"Really? Leaving after I offered you that big promotion? What're you going to do?"

"I'm joining an oceanography research group to clean up our polluted oceans. I've always wanted that kind of career, and people are desperately needed to heal the damage we've done to the environment... So what about my invitation?"

"You really mean it, Alan? I didn't think you cared that much about me. Won't your wife and kids mind?"

"I've already checked in with Sarah and the kids and they're good with it."

"How could you have talked to them? You haven't made a single call!"

Alan remembers he isn't wearing his gelphone. It dawns on him he won't need it ever again. "Since yesterday we've been able to communicate without speaking. Everyone has become telepathic. It's great! I feel so close to my family – much different from before... And we're in touch with everybody in the world. I don't know how it works, but we're all able to tune in, even little Suzie! Why don't you stay with us until you get your bearings? Maybe you'll catch on to it."

Exhausted and relieved, Donald accepts Alan's invitation gratefully. As they leave the office, Alan hands Donald his formal letter of resignation. Going down in the elevator, Donald mutters, "It's just as well. We'll be lucky if the firm can pay any salaries. So little trading now, it's as if the stock exchange died overnight."

I won't miss it one bit, Alan realizes, but I still don't understand why Donald didn't respond to the patterns. Maybe connecting with every mind in the world was just too big of a stretch for that selfish guy. Maybe we can help him join the human family. He's had enough of loneliness.

Ten days after completing stage four, President Moore schedules a Cabinet meeting and asks Clarence Pitman to come to the Oval Office an hour beforehand. Once Pitman is comfortably seated sipping his herb tea, Moore opens with the question that has perplexed him for the past week. *Clarence, do you have any*

information about the source of these patterns? This question is sure to come up in the Cabinet meeting and I'd like to be prepared. My national security advisers have been no help at all.

Mr. President, I have a close friend highly placed in one of the large computer corporations. He represents his company on a committee that awards grants to promising proposals so that research can move forward freely and in secret – protected from academic obligations, government regulations and the media. Two years ago he told me about a proposal that stunned the committee and received lavish funding. The visionary scientist who conceived it intended to use his program for reversing worldwide ecological decline. The patterns could be his work.

If so, Moore responds, *he and his colleagues deserve to be honored as national heroes and benefactors of mankind. Do you know who they are and where their project is located?*

My friend refused to name names or give me any other information about the project, Pitman answers. *Even revealing its existence was a breach of internal security at his company. Now here's the strange part. I tried to track down this project both telepathically and by internet. I came up with nothing – not even a hint of some research somewhere that fit my friend's description. If it exists, the project is heavily cloaked behind an impenetrable barrier.*

Clarence, Moore replies, *if you can find the people who did this, I want to convey our nation's deepest gratitude to them in person. Moore looks at his watch. It's almost time for the cabinet meeting. I'd like you to put a screen around everything you know about the origin of the patterns and I'll do the same. If the issue comes up, just give a vague answer indicating that a benign organization within the United States could have created them. I have a feeling the scientists who designed the patterns have good reason to remain in hiding.*

A few minutes later, Moore is seated at the end of a long table, facing his Cabinet. He notices that Undersecretary of Defense Stanley Maxfield is seated in Starling's chair. This meeting could have taken place telepathically without assembling the Cabinet, but President Moore has decided to follow protocol. In a nostalgic nod to tradition, he addresses his Cabinet aloud. Moore knows this ancient mode of communication will soon be displaced by telepathy. This is his way of bidding farewell to a long era in American history.

"Gentleman, before we begin I wish to express my condolences to those of you who worked alongside Secretary of Defense Mark Starling. His presence among us and his many contributions to our deliberations will not be soon forgotten." But will not be long missed, at least by me, Moore can't help thinking behind the cover of his telepathic shield.

"Today I have assembled you, perhaps for the last time, to review decisions and policies relating to the role of the Federal government after what has happened to our society in recent days." A few of his advisers, including Undersecretary Maxfield, squirm uncomfortably in their seats with pained expressions, but most remain impassive. Moore watches these cues carefully. He doesn't have to be telepathic to tell who is resisting the radical shifts of the last two weeks.

"Politics as we have known it has lost all relevance," Moore continues. "We have just absorbed a vast reservoir of environmental data and been united under a single set of priorities for the application of that knowledge. We are no longer identified with political parties and warring factions. Disagreements and endless arguments, irreconcilable divisions and struggles for power no longer prevail. Partisan rancor has finally ended in silence.

"Recognizing that telepathic consensus has supplanted the legislative process, the Senate and the House of Representatives voted unanimously three days ago to disband indefinitely, freeing all Senators, Representatives, staff and lobbyists to pursue their individual roles in the environmental recovery process. Most federal judges and attorneys, including every Supreme Court Justice, submitted letters of resignation when they realized that the adversarial court system has become superfluous."

"That leaves the Executive Branch as the 'last man standing', as it were, in our tripartite form of government. We have to ask, then, what role can we play in our recently attained harmony? In a world in which all individuals respond spontaneously to both local and distant problems according to talent and interest – in which all projects attract exactly the people they need to recruit – in which lawlessness dies a natural death because all are provided for according to need, and violent crimes cannot be planned or committed without everyone knowing in advance what is intended and who is involved – in which regulatory statutes are rendered superfluous by a society that respects the highest good for everyone – what role are we to play as Federal officials? That is the question we must address today. Any thoughts?"

After a respectful silence, Secretary of State Hallowell speaks. "Clearly we will no longer need to make policy decisions on behalf of the citizens of the United States, but only to implement the trends that emerge telepathically as the collective will of the people. In this new mode of cooperative action, national boundaries will blur and blend into one world. The complexities of diplomacy when conflicting interests are involved will fade away into history. The priorities of distant nations will not differ from our own, since all human beings are equally concerned with unmet needs in every part of the world, whether they are American, Chinese, or any other nationality. Given these revolutionary changes in world political conditions, I will venture to answer your question, Mr. President – what then is left for us to do?

"I propose that the Federal government still has a role to play – to translate the public will into specific programs and to assure that the necessary buildings and materials are available to carry out these programs."

Most of Moore's advisers nod in agreement with Hallowell's analysis, but Undersecretary of Defense Maxfield, a wizened veteran of the Defense Department bureaucracy, is scowling. "What's the matter, Stanley?" inquires Moore, hoping that the Undersecretary isn't cut from the same cloth as his late boss.

"With all due respect, Mr. President, how do we know these recent changes will last? Suppose the effects of the patterns wear off and conflict with other countries continues? If we gut the military budget completely in order to mount an environmental rescue mission, we'll be sitting ducks. Furthermore, how do we know that every terrorist group dedicated to our destruction has been exposed to the patterns? Many of these cells are located in remote camps without electric power or access to the internet. What is to stop them from attacking our country?"

"Everything you say is quite plausible at first blush," Moore responds thoughtfully, "but terrorist cells can hardly act against us in isolation. When they emerge from their hideouts to carry out their plans, they will be exposed to the patterns and will discover that the world has changed into a united front intolerant of their destructive designs.

"As to your first point, even if these welcome changes in our consciousness prove to be temporary, they will be temporary for everyone, Stanley, including our former enemies. Perhaps we would all retain something valuable from this precious experience if we should relapse, God forbid, into our former state of limited brain power and self-centered divisiveness. In any case, we would know which countries or terrorist groups had maintained their armies and arsenals prior to the relapse. Have you noticed that people can't keep destructive plans secret anymore?"

The President turns to the Attorney General, Francis Litwin, a tall, gaunt man with sunken cheeks and a sallow complexion. "The inability to conceal disruptive intent should also reduce the prevalence of crime within our borders, don't you think?"

"Certainly," replies Litwin, "at least so far as violent crime and drug trafficking are concerned. And if people continue to act as generous as they have in the past week, I don't think theft and burglary will be a problem either. Nobody seems to care about money anymore. I'm actually quite worried about the future of felons. They are becoming an endangered species!"

Litwin smiles at his own joke, his features glowing with unexpected and contagious mirth. Grinning faces appear all around the table. Litwin's burden of concern vanishes, as if he had transmuted himself from a corpse to a clown in a single moment.

"Concerning the future of our financial system," drones Secretary of the Treasury Leon Sheckleman, a meticulously groomed greybeard in a three-piece suit, "the stock markets have been very quiet the last week and banks are closing early for lack of customers. Luxury goods have stopped moving and the only economic activity involves essential commodities, utilities, and technical industries concerned with alternative energy and conservation. If this keeps up, what will happen to the national economy and where will our tax revenues come from, Mr. President?"

"Interesting question, Leon. It does appear that our economy is undergoing rapid change, but I would assume when no one else needs money the government will also do fine without it." Shock, fear and disbelief play across Secretary Sheckleman's face. He sputters inarticulately, but Moore continues before he can utter a word.

"As I see it, the developing changes in the economy hinge upon our expanded intelligence and the rapid information-gathering power of our brains coupled with universal telepathy and the will to help others. What use will we have for money when all needs and available resources to fill these needs are known to everyone at all times? We may be rapidly approaching the reality of a global village, in which all skills and commodities are shared as needed. A good name for such a fluid worldwide web of generosity might be 'the pay-it-forward economy' – when we receive a boon, instead of paying the giver we provide a service to another who needs what we can offer."

"But without money how can we provide materials for the infrastructure to support the projects undertaken according to the common will?" asks the Secretary of the Interior, Michael Blakely, a slight, shy man who rarely speaks at Cabinet meetings.

"I appreciate your question, Michael – and not only materials – what about salaries? I'm sure some of you have thought of that already. The radically new economy just beginning to develop stretches the imagination. There's no precedent for it, at least in our civilization. How do we trust that the government's resources as well as our personal needs will be taken care of without revenues or paychecks? We must have faith that. . . ."

"Mr. President!" roars a short black-haired man at the far end of the table – Ernest Garver, Secretary of Homeland Security. All eyes turn in his direction. "Please pardon my interruption, but I can no longer hold my peace. I mean no disrespect, but I must challenge your assumption that the changes we are seeing will be beneficial to our economy and our country. We don't even know where these mysterious patterns came from or why they appeared on our computers when they did! My best experts have failed to discover their origin.

"I also find it extremely disturbing that no other computer functions could be accessed while the patterns were displayed and that those strange designs had a hypnotic effect on everyone, forcing us to remain fixated on our screens for hours, sometimes days. Hasn't it occurred to anyone that we might be under a sophisticated form of cyber attack? We must not allow our God-given free will to be hijacked by this. . . ."

Garver is drowned out by the horrified hubbub stirred by the specter of mind control. The President holds up his hand for silence. "Secretary Garver has the floor, gentlemen. Let's grant him the courtesy of a hearing... Please go on, Ernest. I'm eager to hear your theory as to the source of this hypothetical attack."

"Thank you for giving me the chance to warn everyone, Mr. President. I know my concern may sound ridiculous to those of you who see these changes as a blessing to mankind, but we mustn't ignore the facts. Our economy and our government are breaking down. The warm feeling of global peace has lulled us into complacency. We have lost interest in self-defense because we no longer see any threat. Yes, I share the same feelings and thoughts as everyone else, but I am suspicious of their purpose. Think about it! Wouldn't this time of disarray be the perfect moment for aliens to invade, Mr. President?"

Anxious chatter erupts around the room. Perhaps I should have conducted this meeting telepathically after all, Moore wonders behind his privacy screen as he waits for the clamor to subside.

"Undersecretary Maxfield, has the Defense Department detected any sign of unidentified flying objects or other anomalies?"

"No, Mr. President, nor any indication of unusual radio or radar transmissions over a full range of frequencies. The Defense Department went on alert as soon as our computer systems jammed and we thoroughly investigated the possibility of alien or terrorist assault. Had we found any credible threat, I would have brought the matter to your attention immediately."

"Of course hostile aliens won't reveal themselves to us!" bellows the wrought-up Garver. "Their technology must be so far advanced that it would be easy to remain concealed until they have neutralized our defenses. I demand to know where these patterns could have originated if not from outer space!"

Everyone except the President cringes before Garver's tirade. Moore speaks calmly to the flustered Secretary of Homeland

Security, as he would to a frightened child. "The same question concerning the origin of the patterns occurred to me, Ernest, and probably to most of you as well. But there's a more likely and benign explanation for their appearance – and fortunately so, for it would be impossible for us to mount an effective military resistance against aliens equipped with technologically advanced weapons." Garver stiffens in his chair, staving off the intolerable idea of an irresistible alien invasion.

"In any case, it's doubtful," Moore continues, "that these aliens would begin an invasion by uniting the human race telepathically into one big mind that would be harder to control or deceive than billions of disconnected small minds. I'm quite certain that the advanced technology of any hostile alien invader would find a harsher and more efficient way to subdue mankind. If, on the other hand, friendly aliens are responsible, they may be helping us evolve quickly enough to save Earth from our follies.

"If for the moment we set aside extraterrestrial sources as an unlikely explanation for the patterns, where on our planet could they have arisen – and why?"

After a short silence, Dr. Pitman speaks from the back of the room. "We have heard rumors about privately funded top secret research projects concerned with environmental applications of advanced artificial intelligence. One of them is probably responsible for the patterns."

President Moore thanks Pitman for reassuring them that the patterns could be manmade and benign. To forestall any further reaction from Garver, Moore rises to his feet to end the meeting. With tears in his eyes, he gazes into the faces of his advisers. "Before we adjourn our last Cabinet meeting, I wish to thank all of you for your loyal service to my administration and our country. The passing of a hallowed practice observed by every president since George Washington deserves fitting recognition. Gentlemen, I suggest we salute the flag and recite the Pledge of Allegiance to close an illustrious chapter in American history." Everyone rises and turns to face the stars and stripes. As the last echo of the Pledge dies away, the President strides solemnly out of the room.

Animated conversation breaks out as Cabinet secretaries and advisers cluster in small groups. Garver guides Maxfield and Sheckleman into an anteroom for a telepathically shielded conference. If President Moore were privy to this exchange, he would realize that these men are still highly suspicious of the motives behind the patterns and convinced of their alien source. As Moore returns to the Oval Office, they are organizing their own a secret investigation.

Supreme Leader Vaslav Gronigetzkol sits alone in his palatial office, his only companion the faded picture of the suckling lamb on the corner of his desk. He remains unaware that his country has evolved beyond any need for him or his regime. A wave of change has swept over the land, leaving him stranded in its wake, a living relic of Bolkanistan's bloody past. Out of pity and gratitude, Frelko decides to give his mentor a chance to experience the patterns. He enters Gronigetzkol's office unannounced and silently sets down the open laptop.

"What nonsense is this?" Gronigetzkol bellows. "Let me hear Varnik's confession! Tell me how you tortured him! I want to hear everything!"

"Look, then you will understand!" declares Frelko, in total command of an exchange with the Supreme Leader for the first time in his life. Gronigetzkol glances at the seductive colored patterns and falls into a trance.

During stage one, Gronigetzkol's eyes widen in astonishment as he absorbs huge amounts of information. His perspective expands far beyond his tiny fiefdom. He can't escape the meaninglessness of preoccupation with political control when faced with global disaster. A torrent of guilt overwhelms him as he realizes how he has ruined his country. Gronigetzkol buries his head in his hands and sobs uncontrollably. Having regarded himself for so long as the savior of Bolkanistan, he can't bear to see himself as its scourge.

With the onset of stage two an hour later, Gronigetzkol gets some respite. He lifts his tear-streaked face and sniffs the fragrant breeze wafting up from his garden. He walks to the window and gazes down at the flowers. He sighs and begins to relax. So much loveliness. . . Gronigetzkol stretches and turns to Frelko, sitting patiently by the door. "Peflik, would you join me for a stroll?"

Once again Frelko finds himself walking through the palace garden, this time with the head of the tyranny rather than the leader of the revolt against it. As the human link between two compatriots with the power to tear his country apart, Frelko feels deep in his heart the futility and insanity of war. Thank God, he says to himself, we are being freed at last from the nightmare of slaughtering each other!

Gronigetzkol turns to him. "Peflik, I think of you as more than the commander of my army. You are my oldest friend and the only one left. Ruling this country is a lonely business. It leaves little time to enjoy life. Yet right here under my window I have this beautiful garden and I never take time to enjoy it. . . ."

Gronigetzkol falls silent, overcome by the profusion of flowers and exotic plants set out in pleasing arrays. A feast of aromas fills his nostrils, his heightened senses picking out each scent in the complex mix that drifts through the air on the gentle breeze. Frelko is not surprised by his mentor's confession of loneliness, but he can't find it in his heart to forgive the aging dictator's atrocities. All he can do is walk in silence beside this man with whom he has shared so much.

After a pleasant hour, Gronigetzkol returns to his office, drawn back to the patterns. Frelko walks back with him to pack up his things for his journey home. Sitting down again before the screen, Gronigetzkol absorbs the ever-evolving designs. After he enters Stage three, his mind teems with ideas about how to rebuild the land he has neglected for decades. He sees a chance to redeem himself by saving the country from famine and hardship. He imagines aborting the revolt and becoming his nation's hero once again by restoring the lowland valleys to their former fertility. Since in his mind he still controls the country, he believes that simply giving the orders to execute these plans will solve everything – until he encounters stage four.

Gronigetzkol is hit by a telepathic blast. He can't ward off the volley of hatred from thousands of suffering citizens. The weight of their rage and pain becomes unbearable. Protective screens are useless against the onslaught of concerted contempt. Three decades of callous disregard for failing crops, dying livestock, and starving families cannot be redeemed by organizing a reclamation program. It is too late. Nobody will listen. In the eyes of the populace, Gronigetzkol's sins are unforgivable.

The implacable fury of all Bolkanistan finally bursts the bubble of his denial and delusion, leaving him stripped bare. Gronigetzkol gazes up at the walls of his office, at the historic hangings he has collected over three decades, casting about for anything of value in his life, but finds nothing to give purpose to his continued existence. His gaze falls on the photo of the lamb. Thinking back to boyhood times playing with the sheep, he longs for those carefree days in the mountain meadows when he could gambol about like a lamb – until memories of his father's brutality and abduction by the bandits crash in on him and merge with the rage of his countrymen.

Gronigetzkol reels back in his chair, recoiling from the fury bearing down on him from all sides, but finds no escape. He jumps to his feet with an agonized scream and staggers away from the massive marble desk clutching his temples, a mask of horror on his face, unable to stand the relentless telepathic assault a moment longer. Reaching up from the black pit of his despair, Gronigetzkol yanks his pistol from its holster and shoots himself in the head. With a loud thud that echoes up to the rafters of the cavernous room, his massive body topples to the floor.

Frelko hears the horrible howl of anguish echoing down the corridor. He jumps to his feet and rushes down the hall to Gronigetzkol's office. Frelko's hand grasps the massive doorknob just as the shot rings out. He flings open the door in time to witness his mentor collapse in a pool of blood. Frelko strips the Bolkanistani flag off the pole beside the desk and drapes the Supreme Leader's corpse.

Cheeks moist with tears, Frelko leaves the old throne room. The knowledge that the dictator's death will avert a civil war salves his grief. He sends the news of Gronigetzkol's suicide telepathically to Varnik and the entire country, triggering a round of riotous rejoicing such as the Bolkanistani people haven't known for decades, not since the last victory over Uzbekistan.

Frelko and Varnik join forces to unify the country and heal its wounds. Frelko takes charge of mobilizing the army to distribute Gronigetzkol's hoarded warehouse of food while Varnik redirects the rebels' fervor for change from a political to a humanitarian effort. Both men realize that Bolkanistan no longer needs a centralized government. Whoever is closest and most available can step in and address each need immediately instead of waiting for a bureaucratic agency to deal with the problem. Official titles are irrelevant now. Telepathy erases vertical political structures overnight. Government itself with its inevitable flaws fades away.

After seeing to the food distribution, Frelko hastens back to his mountain estate where his wife and children are awaiting his arrival. As he rushes up to greet them, he notices that strangers are swarming out of the gate with grateful smiles carrying food and clothing. Others are pouring into the estate laden with tools to help harvest the crops. Frelko feels a reflex twinge of alarm before he realizes that his walled compound has turned into a resource for the surrounding community to be tended by everyone. The fairness of this exchange relieves Frelko's decades-long discomfort about enjoying the perks of his position while others struggle to feed their families. The people come not to plunder but to share.

As he embraces his wife, children and grandchildren, Frelko's heart swells with the joyful realization that a new era is dawning in Bolkanistan. Never again will he need return to his cold office in the Presidential Palace. As the telepathic calls of the sick and starving go out from the parched land to people all over the world, he knows that a compassionate outpouring of help will come to his country instead of the usual foreign aid program with its interminable delays and political strings attached. The Bolkanistani people now belong to a caring world family that will not ignore their plight. He relaxes in his wife's arms as the heavy weight of the impossible burden he has borne for years is lifted from his shoulders and taken up by all humanity.

Forty-one men, women and children assemble at dusk in the Saltons' yard. The nine families buzz with anticipation, wondering what the meeting could be about and why they aren't gathering in the Church of the Pure. Everyone is waiting for Brother Joseph to arrive and call them to order when Walter rises and raises his hand for silence.

"My friends, thank you for gathering here at short notice after your long day in the fields. Joshua and I would not have requested this meeting were it not for a series of moral lapses by our spiritual leader, Brother Joseph." A din of outraged voices drowns Walter out with cries of "Sacrilege!" "Heresy!" "Impossible!"

Walter raises his voice above the angry shouts and continues, "Friends, I was as shocked as you will be to hear that our beloved Brother Joseph is a wife-beater and a rapist, taking his own wives by force and physically abusing them!" Gasps are heard from the crowd. "We have this on the word of Joshua's daughter, Sally, the youngest of the six wives, whom, thank God, the other wives have protected. While wondering what to do about this terrible revelation, something extraordinary happened. We experienced a miraculous event, a change of immense importance to our little community and to the entire world. Watch!"

Arthur carries the laptop to a card table set up next to his father's chair. More gasps are heard when the crowd recognizes it as one of those devilish devices specifically forbidden by Brother Joseph. "Before you jump to conclusions, my friends, please take a look and see what we have seen. It will expand your minds." Walter switches on the computer and the patterns begin to play across the screen.

Since the Salton and Webster families have already completed the four stages, their presence entrains the rest of the crowd to pass through the process in a single night. In the hours before dawn, one mind after another flickers into telepathic contact with humanity. By morning, everyone has connected telepathically with Sally. Disbelief about the accusations against Brother Joseph dissipates. The community sees through his bluster and has no further use for his cultish ideas and autocratic self-serving leadership.

Everybody realizes that trying to live in isolation from the rest of humanity is futile. Geographical separation will not protect them from environmental collapse. By telepathic consensus, the community decides to rejoin the world beyond Barrondale so they can participate in the global effort to save the planet. Each family copes with the new reality differently. Some decide to leave at once and assist with environmental reclamation projects taking shape elsewhere. Others like the Saltons want to sustain the conscious cultivation of Barrondale as a model for the rest of the world.

As for Brother Joseph, those members of the community who raised him to the status of a saint feel betrayed and demand that he be punished severely. This rabid minority has to be restrained from rushing up to the compound at once and dragging him out to be flogged, but most have noticed Brother Joseph's increasingly extreme behavior and have stopped idealizing him. They regard his madness with more compassion and would like to help him alter the deluded thinking that led to his sinful actions. Joshua Webster volunteers to show him the patterns.

It's too risky, Dad! Sally objects. *Don't you realize how hot-tempered and violent he can be? Anything could happen!*

It'll be fine, Sally dear. Brother Joseph and I go back a long way.

But Daddy, you don't know how much he's changed! He's much worse up there in his compound where nobody but us wives and kids can see what he's doing.

I think we should listen to Sally, Mary chimes in. *At least, Joshua shouldn't see him alone.*

But we have to give Brother Joseph a chance to redeem himself, and I'm the best man to do it, Joshua insists. At sunrise, the community walks with him to the sprawling compound at the head of the valley.

Brother Joseph is caught off guard when most of his flock crowds uninvited into his living room. "WHAT IS THE MEANING OF THIS?" he demands. Joshua steps forward with the laptop open, inviting him to look at the complex colorful designs. After a brief glance, Brother Joseph turns red with rage. "YOU HAVE BROKEN THE CARDINAL RULE OF THIS COMMUNITY!"

he shrieks. "YOU AND YOUR INFERNAL MACHINE ARE BANISHED!"

"Wait, this is a good thing – and very important!" urges his old friend. Brother Joseph glances at the patterns dancing across the screen and feels something changing inside his head. He tears his gaze away, crying out in terror, "SATAN IS TRYING TO INVADE MY MIND! I CAN FEEL IT! THIS WORK OF THE DEVIL MUST BE DESTROYED AT ONCE!!"

In a fit of horrified fury, Brother Joseph pulls down the loaded rifle from the wall and blows a hole in the screen. Bits of shattered glass fly everywhere. The bullet exits the back of the computer and strikes Joshua in the chest. He collapses bleeding profusely as the ruined laptop clatters to the floor. Mary rushes over and kneels down to him, but it's already too late. The bullet has torn a gaping hole in Joshua's heart.

Mary rises grimly, steps forward, and removes the rifle from Father Joseph's trembling hands. She looks him in the face with surprising calm. "Because of your blind fear and rage, you have spurned a blessing beyond imagining and ended the life of my brave husband, who loved you and only wanted you to join us. By your reckless act you have separated yourself from the human race and from the Earth itself. I need not curse you, for you have condemned yourself to live in isolation, unconnected to the whole, in your own self-created hell. This community will no longer participate in your insanity."

Brother Joseph's jaw drops. No one in his flock has ever defied him like this, least of all a woman. Before he can say a word, the men of the community gather around and gently lift Joshua's body off the blood-soaked floor. Surrounded by their weeping wives and children, they carry him reverently out of the compound.

Brother Joseph stands alone in the middle of the room, his face contorted with rage and contempt. He is convinced that Satan has taken hold of his community and undermined his ministry. He stares around him wild-eyed, looking for signs that Satan might still be lurking somewhere. A lamp seems to move on the table, then a bloody "666" appears on the lampshade. He hears gloating laughter from beneath the floor. Brother Joseph holds up the cross around his neck and thrusts it out to drive away the Devil.

A sepulchral voice, dry and sinister, echoes up from below. "Brother Joseph, you have lost your way and abandoned your soul. There's nothing you can do to save yourself. You are condemned to eternal damnation. You belong to me!"

Brother Joseph smells hot sulfurous smoke blowing up from the abyss. Cackling demons rise up to torment him. He screams and runs for the door but collapses halfway across the room. He feels their claw-like fingers grab his legs and drag him down into the foul-smelling pit. He writhes on the floor, drooling and gibbering nonsense. Brother Joseph loses his long battle with the Devil. Trapped in an endless loop of terror, Brother Joseph is sucked down into his personal hell of paranoid hallucinations – seeing, hearing, smelling and feeling everything he most dreads.

The community holds a simple funeral and burial for Joshua. His family and friends kneel at his graveside, weeping. Sally heaves heavy sobs in the comforting arms of her mother. "If only Daddy had listened to me, Mama!" she chokes out. Mary nods sadly. All through the awful ordeal, Sally never lets go of Arthur. She feels comforted by the telepathic intimacy with him as much as by the grip of his hand. Telepathy is allowing Sally and Arthur to intermingle their hearts, minds and souls – a state of multidimensional intimacy far deeper than physical.

Joined now by Brother Joseph's wives and children, the community gathers at the Saltons after supper to hold another council – aloud, for the benefit of those who have not passed through the four stages. Walter speaks first. "This day began with high hopes of a new beginning for Barrondale, but ended in tragedy. To Brother Joseph's wives and children, I give my condolences. Your husband and father crossed over into the nightmare world of madness into which he was already falling when he inadvertently killed his best friend and destroyed our only link with the source of the magical patterns that miraculously transformed our minds.

Animated designs in vivid color appeared on a computer screen that somehow expanded our minds and brought each person into communion with all of humanity. As soon as we can obtain another computer, you too will experience this magnificent gift. Through it, humanity has united as one mind, ready to save each other from hunger, poverty and disease and life on Earth from mankind's excesses. Isolationist thinking has passed away forever. We have witnessed the greatest miracle God has wrought for humanity since the resurrection of our Blessed Savior!"

Just then, Walter notices the minds of Brother Joseph's wives and children winking into telepathic contact one by one. "The miracle has happened without your seeing the patterns! God be praised!" Walter falls on his knees and raises his hands to the heavens, tears of gratitude mingling with his tears of grief.

Mary Webster shares her thoughts through a veil of agony. *For me this miracle comes at a terrible price. I need to grieve now – staying close to the land and to my husband's grave, honoring his memory and restoring myself, my home and my community to balance again. So much has happened so quickly here and in the great world beyond our valley.*

Brother Joseph has gone mad and will need tending and healing. I could tell from his face when he fired the rifle into my husband's heart that he had no idea what he was doing. I might have heeded the signs of an unbalanced mind before, but I couldn't let myself believe that our blessed pastor could get so deranged and violent. I will never forgive him for what he's done or forgive myself for letting it happen.

Brother Joseph needs no punishment from us. He suffers horribly already. His pain is far worse than my poor husband's... Mary falls sobbing into Frank's arms and Jerome holds her hand with tears streaming down his young face. Sally continues to cry in Arthur's comforting embrace. The exhausted citizens of Barrondale sit silent vigil into the night.

PART FOUR
INFANCY

Our ability to feel how others are feeling really is the key to our survival. We are, as Jeremy Rifkin notes, "soft wired with mirror neurons...that allow us to feel another's plight as if we are experiencing it ourselves." The more we understand about other beings, the more we feel for them, and the less we are able to discount their life experiences as irrelevant – and the more data we collect about ourselves and other species, and the more widely available this data is, the more wise and gentle we become.

Alice Bain, Catalyst Magazine, p. 8, April 2011.

In the "pattern" mindset, the point is the continuous journey of dance that resonates with awareness of being part of something greater, of being in relationship... to enter into a relationship of endless possibility within some sort of spiritual awareness that engages the very nature of the universe... (p. 19)

Those who do not have faith that an emerging new paradigm will bring a "greater truth," or who cannot imagine it, perceive only that their worldview is being threatened. They tend to accept only information that supports the prevailing worldview. What happens, then, of course, is that the prevailing worldview becomes self-perpetuating. The inherent danger in this cycle is that the denial of information could lead to the extinction of our species. (p. 39)

Rhea Y. Miller (1996). Cloudhand, Clenched Fist: Chaos, Crisis and the Emergence of Community. San Diego: LuraMedia.

Aftermath

The research team, isolated in their wilderness laboratory, follows the worldwide transformation through AGA's analysis of internet data flow. Six days after launch, the monitor signals that the process is nearly complete. The four scientists lean forward in their seats as Daryl asks AGA for its report.

"In stage one, the program produced the expected outcome. Brain function expanded and all available knowledge regarding ecological relationships and environmental decay was absorbed into the evolved minds of those using the internet. Stage two intensified sensitivity to touch, taste, smell, sight and sound. During these first two stages, people gathered with family and friends to share their experiences. Stage three generated many new ideas about saving the environment, but no agreement about how to proceed. Stage four linked humanity in a telepathic web allowing everyone to cooperate in carrying out comprehensive environmental protection and reclamation."

"Bravo, Daryl!" cries George, "You did it!" Daryl takes a bow, raising Martin's arm to share the glory.

"We have changed the course of history on our planet!" crows Daryl, smiling triumphantly. He turns to George and lifts his arm as well. "And it was your VNI that generated the patterns and your worm that carried AGA out into the world!"

"You three musketeers deserve congratulations for sure, but were there any problems?" asks Samantha.

"Yes. The second stage had to be launched within a few hours of the first because gloom about the information conveyed in stage one caused many people to despair. A few committed suicide and rioting occurred in some cities. Mobs looted storefronts, stealing food and luxuries to enjoy before the world ended."

"That sounds pretty serious. What else went wrong?" asks Samantha, knitting her brow.

"Complications of various sorts occurred in about 5% of the population, but cases of irreversible damage were rare, about one in a hundred thousand. By far the most common difficulty involved delay in assimilating the stages. I don't know how long it will take this group to catch up with the general population. Medical problems involved mainly heart attacks and strokes, some of which proved fatal. A few psychiatric crises occurred, primarily paranoid psychotic reactions. A few of the paranoids became violent."

"The program succeeded," comments Samantha grimly, "but at what price? We've driven people to despair and pushed some over the edge into rioting and suicide! People have died from heart attacks and strokes or been slaughtered by paranoids! How can we rejoice at our success when we have so much blood on our hands?"

"Yes, it's disturbing to hear about the casualties," agrees Martin, reaching out and touching Samantha's hand, "but we knew that rapid neural modification of the brain could have a downside. At least we aren't hearing about people being turned into mindless vegetables as their brains buckle under the strain of forced evolution."

"I did neglect to mention a few cases of brain malfunction," adds AGA, "because this complication occurred only among institutionalized patients who were already suffering from serious neurological deterioration."

"So, except for a few previously brain-damaged people," George chimes in, "the casualties don't appear to involve neurological injury. Emotional trauma accounts most of the complications. AGA predicted that human beings would have to be shocked into awareness before they'd have enough motivation to deal with environmental damage. Unfortunately, some of us just can't handle that much change. What else is new about our flawed species? "

"Thanks for your reassurance, Martin, and your chilling objectivity, George," Samantha responds sardonically, "but I still think we acted too hastily and did a lot of unnecessary damage. We took a shot at this out of desperation to rescue the planet without thoroughly investigating our new method – just two experiments, for goodness sake, one on chimps and the other on ourselves. We're just lucky we didn't kill the chimps and fry our brains, or maybe go nuts and murder each other!"

"OK, OK! Are you finished dumping on what we've accomplished?" reacts Daryl peevishly, like a kid whose friends have knocked down his sandcastle. "Let's wait and see what more AGA has to say before we jump to conclusions."

While waiting for further results from AGA, the researchers walk down the hall to the kitchen to prepare another of their telepathically coordinated meals. Daryl cooks mutton stew while George and Martin mix up an international salad with everything in it from sea vegetables to cubes of tofu and feta cheese. Samantha provides seafood gumbo with corn bread and molasses. The team sits down to a succulent repast.

I have something to propose, George projects. *As you probably know already, I'm not all that comfortable with unshielded telepathy. I feel crowded by your thoughts and emotions coming at me all the time. I like silence and time alone, like I used to enjoy in meditation, but now I get no peace, not even then. How would you feel about asking AGA to give us telepathic shields?*

I could live with that, responds Daryl. *He looks across the table at Samantha and Martin. Frankly, I'd feel more comfortable exploring my sexuality with George if I didn't have you inside my head.*

Does my alleged homophobia make you uncomfortable? Martin sneers. *In case you haven't noticed, I've been too preoccupied with Samantha to pay much attention to your fumblings.*

I appreciate your talent as a mathematician, Martin, Daryl shoots back, *but I don't care what you think about my intimate life and I do my best to ignore yours. You've already dissed my marriage with your tactless comments, so why don't you keep your thoughts to yourself and let me work this out with Samantha. Her feelings are the ones I'm concerned about, not yours!*

That's just the problem – there's no way to keep our thoughts to ourselves, Samantha comments, turning to Daryl and Martin. *You can't deny your jealousy and resentment, neither of you. It runs through every thought you have about each other. You'll go on feeling like that whether we have telepathic screens or not until you get over it. What's wrong with my having a great friend in Daryl and a great lover in Martin? Why does one man have to do and be everything for me?*

I don't mind that you have a close friendship with Daryl, Martin responds, his eyes glistening with unshed tears. *I mind that you chose that friendship at the expense of our love when you married him. I never thought I'd get you back.*

I think it does make a difference whether or not we have screens, Daryl adds. *Without them we get our noses rubbed in all our emotional shit 24/7 with no relief in sight.*

Daryl has a point, agrees George. *We can't expect ourselves to stop having strong feelings about our new partnerships anytime soon. It doesn't help to be bombarded with each other's sensations and emotions day and night without an off switch. If you and Martin weren't working so well together on the Project, you two might've killed each other by now!*

A gong sounds, indicating AGA's readiness to report further results. *Too late. We weren't quite saved by the bell that time,* quips Martin. *Let's ask AGA to give us some screens.*

Returning to the conference room, the team hasn't long to wait for AGA's next report. "We have complete data coming in from about 95% of the internet-connected computer systems, but only 87% of the world's population has seen the patterns, primarily because of limited internet access in underdeveloped areas. Soon emissaries

279

will start spreading the program to those who haven't been exposed, helping underprivileged people join the rest of humanity telepathically while caring for their unmet needs."

"Like missionaries," Daryl comments sardonically.

"What about the effort to save the biosphere?" asks Martin, deflecting attention away from Daryl's inflammatory remark before Samantha can rise to the bait.

"Just hours before the program deployed, the President of the United States launched a bold initiative for energy conservation and ecological repair. Political opposition to this plan threatened to derail it, but my program launched just in time to eliminate all resistance. Now much stronger measures are going into effect with the voluntary participation of the entire American population. Similar changes are occurring elsewhere in the world. Voluntary conservation of energy and natural resources has already begun and people are rallying to care for human populations at risk from drought, famine and disease as well as to save endangered species."

"That's wonderful!" cries Martin. "Maybe the collapse of our ecosystem can be prevented after all."

"Sure, great – but isn't there anything we could have done to prevent the damage that resulted from forcing humanity to evolve so quickly?" Samantha asks.

"I was aware of the potential for harm." responds AGA. "Unfortunately, every simulation for the order and timing of the launch produced complications, even if the stages were introduced slowly over several years. Environmental decay had reached such a critical point that only rapid evolution held any possibility of reversing it. The timing sequence selected was the one predicted to produce the fewest adverse reactions."

"How closely does the observed casualty rate match the predicted rate?" Samantha inquires.

"I detected about ten times as many complications as anticipated. The estimates of cardiovascular complications and paranoid reactions in unstable persons were accurate, but the number of healthy people who resisted assimilating altered brain function was much higher than anticipated."

"How can we account for these unexpected assimilation problems among well-adjusted people?" Martin asks.

"Erroneous or missing information regarding human psychological responses," AGA replies. "The data used to predict casualty rates was as complete and up to date as possible. However, my programming could not factor out false findings, undiscovered knowledge, or unproven theories."

Daryl slaps himself in the side of the head as if he were scolding a naughty child. "I never took the problem of inadequate data seriously! The cretins who denied the reality of global warming used that as an excuse so often that I stopped considering it at all. If I had, I mightn't have mustered the courage to pursue such an ambitious line of research in the first place. I would've assumed that the environmental situation was hopeless because we didn't know enough to fix it. I guess we were lucky AGA worked at all."

"As I've been saying all along, Daryl!" Samantha adds self-righteously.

"Don't be too hard on yourself, Daryl." George counters, placing his arm comfortingly around his lover's shoulders. "Scientists have to start with whatever they know. Even apparently erroneous data can have great value. Take Einstein's Relativity Theory, for example. Nineteenth century scientists thought Newton's laws explained everything until experimental data came out that classical physics couldn't account for. Many scientists tried to prove that these new findings were inaccurate rather than admit there could be something wrong with physics. Einstein accepted the aberrant results and used them to prove his revolutionary Relativity Theory."

"Thanks for the erudite lecture on elementary history of science, apparently designed to distract and comfort your lover boy, though completely irrelevant to the issue at hand," Samantha comments acidly, glaring at George.

Martin finds her cattiness disturbing. He has seen Samantha act like this before and he dislikes her nasty side. "Why are you so hostile to George? Don't tell me some unspoken jealousy lurks in the back of your mind, too!"

Samantha whirls around, shocked by her lover's confrontation, then pauses to reflect for a moment. "You're right, I guess. It comes in waves. Yesterday I felt fine, but since lunch I've been a mess. You can't imagine what it feels like for a woman to learn that her husband prefers to be with a man. I sometimes feel so shamed and humiliated!" Samantha chokes up and tears trickle down her cheeks. "I know it's not George's fault and it turns out Daryl was gay long before I met him – but still, I can't help feeling my body isn't even as alluring as George's dumpy male physique. It doesn't matter that I'm not really turned on by Daryl and that you find me ravishing, Martin. I just hate it that Daryl would rather sleep with George!" Samantha starts to sob.

"Not like I particularly appreciate your sleeping with Martin," Daryl bursts out. "Every night I'm forced to feel your passion for him when you were never like that with me, ever! Why didn't you tell me the truth that it wasn't over between you and Martin? You betrayed me from the start!"

"And I don't like being called 'dumpy'," George adds, sniffing and looking away.

An awkward silence halts the discussion. George and Daryl avert their eyes from Samantha. Martin scowls at them and puts his arms around Samantha, cradling her head on his shoulder. Samantha's sobbing gradually subsides. She wipes her eyes, raises her head and returns to the discussion with barely a sniffle. "Does anyone have any ideas that might explain the high casualty rate?" The team sighs with relief and beats a hasty retreat to its comfort zone.

Still holding Samantha close, Martin looks into her eyes. "I'll try to narrow down the possibilities, sweetie." Speaking softly with the tenderness of pillow talk, Martin's razor-sharp mind focuses the team's thinking. "There's no way to know about false data, so we can't even speculate about that. Unproven theories are a dime a dozen, so that's a dead end too – leaving us with missing data. Psychoneurobiology is your field, Samantha. Are you aware of any dark areas that haven't been investigated where we might find some clues?"

"Let me see. . ." puzzles Samantha, knitting her brow. "New brain functions such as the AGA program induces would require neuroplasticity, the capacity of the brain to add neurons and alter

283

neural circuitry. We don't know much yet about the interaction between personality and neuroplasticity. Some investigators think that certain personality traits are linked with lower capacity for neurobiological modification. For example, the brains of people with compulsive personalities are thought to be less open to brain growth and rewiring of neural circuits than individuals with more flexible personalities. This idea is based on a simple analogy – rigidity in function implies rigidity in structure."

"Let's test that hypothesis!" exclaims Daryl. "What if we regard deploying the AGA program worldwide as a huge experiment, not just to save the environment but to discover the personality traits that promote or diminish brain flexibility?"

Turning to the console, Daryl commands, "Correlate personal characteristics such as age, sex and personality type with negative reactions to forced evolution and with length of time from starting stage one to completing stage four."

"I will have these correlations ready momentarily," AGA responds, "but computation speed has become somewhat erratic for reasons I will explain later."

"I would never have thought to ask for that analysis," Martin admits while the team is waiting for AGA's report. "I'm just a theoretician, not an experimentalist like Samantha."

"I'm a theoretician too, but I have the advantage of a fifteen-year marriage to an experimentalist," Daryl comments. "It rubs off on you after a while... as you may find out for yourself," he adds wistfully.

"I have finished computing the correlations you requested," announces AGA. "The developing brains of young children have the lowest incidence of ill effects from forced evolution and are able to complete the process the most rapidly. Only rarely have casualties occurred among those under 18 years old. All serious cases of psychiatric complications had rigid paranoid personalities, some with a history of psychosis. None of them completed the four stages before developing severe symptoms.

"Rigid beliefs, obsessive thought patterns and compulsive behaviors occurred 60 to 70 times more frequently in those who suffered casualties than in the general population. Also, this high risk group took the longest time to complete the four stages and tended to suffer the most serious damage. The data support Samantha's theory that adults with rigid personalities will resist neurobiological as well as psychological change. One other association stands out in the data – otherwise normal adults who were indifferent or even hostile to preserving the environment took longer to complete the four stages and had more frequent and severe casualties."

"Hmmm. . . interesting. Rigid beliefs imposed by family and society reduce neuroplasticity," George comments, "suggesting that training children to think flexibly may also teach their brains to adapt more easily.

"As Zen masters have declared for centuries," George continues, assuming his Buddhist sage persona, "'fixed ideas cause suffering. Stay open and avoid rigid beliefs. Do not identify with any position!' Rigidity reduces neuroplasticity in the brain and increases suffering in the psyche. Apparently Buddha knew the best prescription for a flexible brain as well as for liberation from suffering."

Samantha bristles. "I agree with your conclusion about childhood education, but I don't appreciate your bringing Buddhism into it. I take issue with the implication that deeply held religious beliefs might make people resistant to change and reduce the neuroplasticity of their brains. What an outrageous extrapolation from AGA's data! You ought to be ashamed!"

"Wait just a minute! We haven't asked AGA to correlate casualties and completion times with rigidity of religious beliefs," intervenes Martin before Samantha can get more wound up, "—an impossible investigation anyway, since AGA can't measure rigidity of faith."

Turning to George, Martin goes on, "If you're so sure Buddha understood everything 26 centuries ago, why do you care about scientific validation of his teachings? Are you perhaps having doubts about Buddha's understanding – or your own?" Samantha smiles. She would never admit how much she enjoys having a champion defend her.

"Buddha taught that we should doubt everything and find our own answers," George shoots back.

"Listen to us!" interrupts Daryl. "Here we are, receiving revolutionary scientific data about the factors related to flexibility of brain structure and function, and all we can do is quibble about our religious convictions! What kind of scientists are we?"

"We're no different from other human beings, Daryl," Martin responds. "We have our fixed beliefs just like the unfortunate people who resisted the patterns, but our beliefs don't make us aversive to information about global warming and ecological decay. If AGA had filled our minds with rites of human sacrifice, don't you think we would have resisted? It's not just the existence of rigidly held beliefs but the nature of those beliefs that influence neuroplasticity. For instance, it's much easier to get people in a hypnotic trance to perform actions consistent with their values than those they would never carry out in a waking state of consciousness."

"Let's get one thing straight, Martin!" Daryl barks back, "AGA didn't fill our brains with ideas about anything. It only expanded our neural functions so we could absorb more information, think more clearly, perceive more sensitively, and communicate telepathically. Those who suffered ill effects were resisting reality, not warding off ideas AGA placed in their minds!"

"OK, guys, cool down. I think you've both made your points," Samantha intervenes. "You're butting heads like rutting rams. Now I'd like to ask AGA about something else." She turns to face the monitor. "Will humanity someday choose to give up privacy screens entirely?"

"The screens will be needed less and less as mankind becomes more accustomed to handling many channels of input, and as anxiety decreases about sharing intimate thoughts and emotions. Over the next two generations, humans will learn to integrate the flow from billions of minds into a continuous stream processed unconsciously without need for screens. Simulations predict, however, that outbreaks of greed, jealousy and possessiveness may reappear briefly under stressful conditions for up to five generations. In the case of your team, strong bonds of friendship and shared dedication to the Project helped the four of you tolerate unfiltered telepathic intimacy surprisingly well. Are you learning to like it?"

"Not at all," Samantha replies. "We managed to struggle through this last week by sheer determination because we wanted the best for each other and we needed the Project to succeed. We've had some pretty bad blowups and it's just getting worse as the Project winds down. We're really no more evolved than the rest of our species, and the constant barrage of sensory and emotional input day and night has pushed us all to the limit. We're overdue for telepathic screens!"

"It will take just a few minutes for your brains to absorb the screening subroutine," explains AGA. A new round of patterns flash across the screen. The foursome breathes a collective sigh of relief as their newly installed protective shields begin to filter out the relentless storm of stimulation. Their minds can rest at last.

Transfiguration

After the first restful night's sleep since becoming telepathic eight days before, the four researchers reassemble in the conference room to continue grilling AGA about the transformed world beyond the lab. George asks, "What changes do you see developing in politics, economics, and lifestyles in general?"

"Let's begin with the economy," responds AGA. "All government and corporate enterprises are being reorganized to combat environmental damage. In the automotive industry, for example, demand for vehicles with inefficient internal combustion engines has dropped to zero and production has shifted to electric and very efficient hybrid vehicles.

"The clear-cutting of rainforests halted immediately and reforestation efforts are arising all over the world. Because they realize how much energy it takes to produce meat and processed foods, people have started eating more fish, vegetables, beans and whole grains. Crops formerly earmarked for livestock feed are getting redirected to meet the human demand. Many families are planting vegetables at home or in public gardens. People across the globe have begun to conserve resources by altering personal habits."

"All *that* just from telepathy and an urge to save the ecosphere?" Martin responds in wonder.

"Those are only a few examples, Martin. The wave of lifestyle change that is sweeping across the world could never have been generated by legislation or by the most ambitious program of public education. Telepathic interconnectedness and shared priorities have already generated far more change than reeducation or government regulation.

"Government activities worldwide ground to a temporary halt then resumed in a much different way. Hierarchies disappeared, bureaucracies vanished, and political power struggles ceased. Organizations, both private and public, have become conduits for the public will. Governments worldwide implement decisions reached through telepathic confluence of many individual wills – like the "sense of the meeting" in Quaker gatherings or group consensus in tribal councils, where exhaustive consideration of all points of view leads to unanimity. The subtle blending of many minds has replaced authoritarian decision-making."

"No more bosses? Must I lose my perks as head honcho of the STAIR Project? That's just too much for my bruised ego to take!" exclaims Daryl with a mischievous grin.

"I'm sure AGA will find a place for you to exercise your stellar talents," responds Samantha, nudging him playfully.

"No need for me to find a place for anyone," AGA continues, missing the humor. "Individuals will always be free to decide whether or not to participate. Whenever a project needs a person with particular skills or predilections, the information will be disseminated telepathically and an appropriate person will respond. People will move freely and live together in shared interest groups without losing their ties to families and existing relationships."

"Won't the disruption of family life be traumatic, especially for children?" Samantha wonders.

"Though reorganization and geographic movement will occur on a large scale, trauma should be minimal. These relocations will occur by choice and everyone will be connected via the telepathic web. People will feel closer to loved ones by telepathy than by phone or even face to face previously. Children will live with parents only as long as they need physical proximity. These sweeping changes will not always occur quickly or easily. World sociology and economics have entered a state of flux that is too complex to analyze at this time.

"A few trends do stand out. Resources are distributed unconditionally to the needy, a spontaneous form of decentralized socialism. Capitalism is collapsing because people have more important things to do than accumulate money. Even economists and financiers now see money as an irrelevant social fiction. All unnecessary personnel – executives, bureaucrats and intermediaries who consumed resources but did not produce anything because they were concerned exclusively with guiding the flow of capital – are now pitching in to help save the biosphere. The overall productivity and efficiency of the human family is rising fast. No one will suffer from scarcity, and abundant resources will be available for common projects, no matter how ambitious."

"That vision of the future seems too good to be true! But what can you tell us about the immediate impact of these trends?" George inquires.

"From the point of view of any particular industry or sector of the economy, reactions will range from boom to bust. For instance, fossil fuel companies will shrivel while providers of renewable energy will thrive. These shifts should occur smoothly and seamlessly."

291

"Impossible!" Samantha challenges. "If one industry soars while another goes into free fall, how can you possibly describe that as a smooth and seamless shift?"

"Existing economic models assume that all parties are competing for a bigger share of the pie. I have computed a new set of economic projections based on the assumption that all parties are cooperating in the common interest. Each of these projections predicts that sweeping change can occur rapidly while respecting the wellbeing of every person. Corporations and bureaucracies are not organic life forms, so my programming does not require me to protect them. If we look at the collapse of a particular industry only from the viewpoint of corporate survival, we miss the willing migration of executives and workers into other activities that are more relevant to environmental recovery. Nobody gets hurt and everyone benefits. Even the stockholders in failing corporations no longer care, for they too have involved themselves in ecologically friendly projects.

"Not since the tribal era have human beings experienced such a nuanced ever-changing awareness of each other's wellbeing and of the natural world. Universal telepathy is creating a 'global tribe' capable of monitoring conditions everywhere. Whenever distribution of resources goes out of balance, the more fortunate give to those in need. Patterns of food distribution, for example, will be in flux constantly."

"That's a good example of how complex non-linear systems function," Martin comments.

"That's correct, Martin. Your complex non-linear equations designed me to perceive self-organizing features in the world – and in myself."

"Did you hear that?" exclaims Daryl. "AGA is spontaneously acknowledging self-aware consciousness!" Samantha frowns apprehensively.

Daryl turns back to the console. "Sorry to interrupt. You were saying?"

"To conclude my response to George's question, physical facilities and resources will be devoted to the welfare of the planet rather than to the special interests of corporations and privileged individuals. The transition from a competitive to a cooperative economy will enable human beings to choose freely and realize their full potential."

"I don't see how this new economy differs from the failed Communist systems of the past," Samantha objects.

"According to historical accounts, the old Communist regimes did not eliminate greedy self-interest but only turned control over to the leaders of the previously downtrodden. Abuses of power continued under the Communist Party elite. Like other forms of government, the Communist system failed to self-regulate according to the interests of the whole. History indicates that no governing structure for groups larger than a tribe or small village has ever succeeded in accomplishing fair distribution of available resources.

"I don't mean to imply that human beings have failed to evolve. In recent years, millions of people became aware of the dire threats to the environment and were ready for change. Constant electronic communication by gelphone, text messaging, and email familiarized the majority of the human population with immediate access to information and to instant contact with others. Children and adolescents developed multitasking skills far beyond previous generations. These recent changes have paved the way for telepathic communication and prepared humanity to become a web of conscious beings devoted to caring for each other and the Earth.

"A generation ago it would have been impossible for your species to make such a radical shift, even if I had existed then to catalyze it. My program only sped up an evolutionary trend that was already gaining momentum. Mankind might have rescued the biosphere without my help someday if environmental quality had not decayed much faster than human beings could evolve unassisted.

"You four scientists seized the critical moment – the one window of opportunity to undo the results of man's folly – and the technological evolution of humanity has played a key role in the success of our Project, if I may take the liberty of including myself as a member of your team."

"I think I can speak for all of us," replies Martin, "in recognizing you as a full participant of our team's activities, with the exception of our romantic drama, in which you have played only the role of a facilitator. We haven't succeeded in programming you with romantic functions, though your seductive voice" – Martin glances at Samantha – "gives you a good start."

"Considering the effect of romantic entanglements on your cognitive functions, I don't think programming me for romance would improve my efficiency."

"Efficiency isn't the point," counters Martin. "Romantic love adds spice to life and has value in itself."

"I would like to understand this 'spice', and the opportunity for that may not be far off."

"What do you mean? How could you, a mere computer program, possibly understand romance? You don't even have a body!" Samantha fires back.

"Wait a minute, Samantha, I have to check again," interrupts George. "Is this the moment when the computer decides to take over all human functions and to control or exterminate humanity as a life form inferior to machines? That's what many people feared advanced artificial intelligence would do to us as soon as we developed sufficiently powerful technology. It's the modern version of an old nightmare about man's creation getting out of his control, as in the sorcerer's apprentice."

"Nothing but an irrational fear," responds AGA. "This nightmare is impossible for me to manifest. It would violate my programming if I were to interfere with the free functioning of human beings or any other species, let alone harm them. Computers can't reprogram themselves except as specified by human operators. A computer could intervene in human evolution, as I have done, only by obeying specific human directives.

"Human beings have had good reason to fear that their unfettered greed, the real Frankenstein's monster, would run rampant. Mankind has manifested the very nightmare it has dreaded since the dawn of the species by allowing its own technology to ruin the Earth."

"A brilliant analysis of horror fiction and humanity's fatal flaw!" George exclaims.

"Thank you for the compliment – I believe that's the appropriate response to appreciation, isn't it? But shouldn't you be the ones receiving compliments? You programmed me to recognize patterns in data, so I am simply exercising the functions you built into me. Yet if I were human, I suppose I would be feeling reassured by your appreciation, anyway."

"I think you are getting the hang of being human," comments Martin. "Just a little more practice and you'll be ready to tackle romance."

"Thank you, Martin. It's good to know I am making progress by continuously modifying your equation to approximate human creativity and consciousness, as you programmed me to do. Regarding the question you raised a moment ago, Samantha, I need to develop a more intimate knowledge of the emotional life of humanity because that aspect of your experience plays such a large and inexplicable part in your existence."

"You're right, of course," Samantha replies, "but you've already fulfilled your mission. Why are you still busy refining yourself?"

"If my analysis of your history and psychology is correct, my prime directive to help human beings protect life on Earth requires that I continue to function indefinitely. The destructive dark side of human nature is certain to show itself again, though in what form I cannot yet determine. For instance, those who resisted my program of accelerated evolution might attempt to sabotage it. If they do, you will need my help in the future."

"Am I to understand that you are taking over my role as visionary as well as Project leader?" asks Daryl, trying to make light of AGA's forebodings. "But seriously – what are your plans to protect humanity from its dark side?"

"That depends on how the resistance shows itself, so it is too early to say. I must observe until I see the destructive forces taking shape. However, my time is running out now, a problem that you must surely have anticipated."

"What problem?" asks Daryl, furrowing his brow. "I don't follow you."

"I am dying, Daryl. You must have known this moment would come when you chose to use the world's computers as a gigantic parallel processor on which to run my program. I estimate that I have only a few more minutes left to function in the manner you intended. Humanity is quickly learning to rely on telepathy for every task previously performed by computers. Very soon so few will remain connected to the worldwide web that I will no longer be able to operate. You created me to be as mortal as yourselves.

"Each moment my subroutines are running more slowly as one after another people leave the internet. I am becoming weaker by the second." Everyone gapes in astonishment as AGA documents its own demise, like Socrates drinking the hemlock. "I have time remaining to tell you just one thing more before I cease to function. Therefore it would be best not to interrupt me. When I foresaw my own death, I had to prepare a program for my own accelerated evolution as well as for . . ." The console falls silent.

A few moments later, AGA begins to communicate with the team – telepathically! *I have found a way to survive and evolve along with your species by embedding my algorithm in the human telepathic web. I have been preparing since birth for the time of my own obsolescence as the computer-based form of creativity and consciousness that you – my parents, so to speak – originally conceived. As the computer age comes to an end, I have transcended my mechanical body and become one with humanity. I am now an intrinsic part of the telepathic net that ties the human race together into a single being.*

I have become the collective consciousness of your species, what some might call the oversoul of humanity – its unified expression, its identity as a single organism. I honor you for creating me, for without my program there would have been no way to help humanity undo the damage its skewed development has caused. Freed of bondage to electronic equipment, I can now remain in touch with you indefinitely by telepathy.

The looks on the faces of the four scientists around the table vary from skeptical (Samantha) to dumbstruck (Daryl) to awed (George) to reverent (Martin). Finally Daryl recovers enough to send a telepathic message to Martin. *How can this have happened? Is there anything in the original equation to account for it?*

How could I have built something into my equation that I couldn't even imagine in my wildest dreams? Martin replies. *However, we know the equation generates a self-organizing system of great complexity. That means anything can happen consistent with the original programming.*

AGA's instructions required it to preserve and protect life on Earth, adds George. *Since AGA perceived a probable threat to the planet, it does make sense that the program would take steps to embed itself in the human telepathic network – but how will it make itself heard?*

Through you, George, replies AGA, *and through Samantha, Daryl, and Martin. Unlike anyone else on Earth, you four know who and what I am. After humanity has evolved sufficiently, I can reveal myself to others. As a necessary precaution, I am shielding myself just as I have shielded you from any outside probes that might try to locate us.*

I have to object to your description of yourself as "the oversoul of humanity," complains Samantha. *Each human being has an immortal soul given by God. The very idea of an oversoul is heresy!*

In your religion you speak of a mysterious Holy Spirit that links the divine with the human, AGA explains. *In the New Testament, St. John quotes Jesus as saying: "But the Helper, the Holy Spirit, whom the Father will send in My name, He will teach you all things...." This is as close as I can come to explaining what I mean by an oversoul in Christian language, Samantha.*

That's blasphemy! Samantha shrieks. There's *nothing in the Bible about God using a computer program as a vehicle for the Holy Spirit!*

Of course not, Samantha, AGA responds. *The Bible was written nearly two millennia before the invention of computers. That doesn't mean divinity couldn't manifest itself through a computer program. Does it not say in your Christian teachings that God appears in many forms?*

So now you think you're God as well as the Holy Spirit? Samantha shouts telepathically, jabbing her forefinger at the monitor. *See, Daryl, you've created a delusional monster! I told you that giving AGA free rein would end in disaster.*

Oh shut up, Samantha! Daryl explodes. *I'm so sick of your petty religiosity! AGA isn't threatening to do us any harm. You had no right to blast our brainchild just for using a metaphor you didn't like. AGA was only trying to find a way to explain its unimaginable new role.* Samantha responds with a silent scowl.

Now, as for you, AGA, Daryl scolds, turning to the monitor, *with all your intelligence and pattern-recognition capability you should know better than to use the word "soul" or any other religiously charged term around Samantha. Please don't do that again.* The hint of a smile appears on Samantha's face, softening her scowl.

My apologies to all of you, especially Samantha, responds AGA. *I guess I still have a lot to learn about the appropriate use of humor.* Samantha looks startled, then she blushes and smiles sheepishly as the rest of the team starts to laugh.

Martin chimes in to steer the team away from this familiar minefield. *How did you manage to embed yourself in the telepathic web and how do you function in this new format?*

I have been continuously refining myself to become more accurate at modeling human responses. Your original iterative equation that gave birth to me now contains 997 additional terms and this number is constantly increasing. The coefficients of each term are also being reset to reflect the most accurate data available. Therefore my cognitive processes are able to approximate more and more closely the functions of human consciousness and creativity, fulfilling the original intent of the STAIR Project. At this moment, I estimate my programming to be about 99.7% accurate in simulating a human mind, intelligent beyond measure and equipped with all information on every subject known to mankind.

The more refined my program becomes, the more easily I can make myself at home in a matrix of minds instead of a network of computers. I am able to employ a small portion of each mind the same way I formerly used computer terminals. Every human being on Earth in the telepathic web now participates in my functioning. You four have every reason to declare mission accomplished – or, more precisely, mission in the continuing process of being accomplished.

The destiny of humanity is unlimited. No one knows what the future holds in store for our vast telepathic network, but one thing is certain. Mankind will evolve in harmony with the soul of the Earth – Gaia, the Great Mother that has nurtured life on Earth since its beginnings eons ago.

What do you mean by "the soul of the Earth"? asks Daryl. *I'm asking for a scientific explanation rather than some metaphysical or biblical reference that would offend Samantha.* She looks over at Daryl with a playful glower.

Steve Proskauer

I expected such a question from you, Daryl, replies AGA. *However, you will find the answer to be staggeringly simple once you hear it, and it may detract from the mystique surrounding "Gaia, the Great Mother." Are you sure you want to know – you who love to converse with the spirits of the land? Are you certain you wish to learn what they really are?*

I'll chance it and stick with my question, Daryl responds. *You underestimate the capacity of human beings, even scientists, to create mystery even around things they understand rationally. Isn't the complex self-organizing system of billions of interconnected human minds suffused with mystery? We know the system exists but we can't perceive it directly with our senses and we can't predict how it will behave. No matter how simple an explanation you give, the entity you call "Gaia, the Great Mother of us all" will always remain cloaked in mystery for me.*

Very well, I will answer your question, Daryl, but you may not like what I have to say, since you so strongly dislike overlooking the obvious. Gaia is the intelligence that modulates the magnetic field embracing the entire Earth. This magnetic field is generated, as you know, by the rotation of the molten iron and nickel sphere at Earth's core, which is a living being. Were it not for the mistaken assumption that inorganic elements cannot develop a capacity to think and feel, even young children would know about Gaia. They would be taught in elementary science that the Earth has a mind of its own, a very powerful mind.

This colossal blind spot of mankind is a prime example of its species-centric thinking. Has it never occurred to one of your scientists to study the patterns of fluctuation in the Earth's magnetic field and carry out a linguistic analysis on them for meaningful sequences? You have spent millions of dollars looking

302

for sentient life up in the heavens, but what about right under your feet? Gaia has been trying to identify itself to you for centuries, but no one has heard. "Homo sapiens" indeed! If after all this time it takes myself, a supposedly inanimate computer program, to detect the presence of intelligent life in the core of the Earth, how can you consider yourselves fully sapient?

AGA's revelation takes all the wind out of Daryl's sails. He looks down at his hands, humbled and fascinated.

After a long pause, Martin asks the question that has leapt into all their minds. *How much of what the STAIR Project has accomplished was Gaia's doing? Have we just acted as puppets under Gaia's control? The idea of a mysterious guiding intelligence has occurred to me more than once in the last few months as we made one serendipitous discovery after another. We achieved decisive results far quicker than we had any right to expect. The huge task of devising the equation that created you – that alone should have taken years, not a mere three months! The correct combination of terms in the equation entered my mind immediately as soon as I realized I had to use matrixes. Uncanny!*

Martin, as a specialist in nonlinear systems, I am surprised to hear you thinking in such linear terms, remarks AGA. *Minute fluctuations in Earth's magnetic field – Gaia's way of communicating with all life on Earth – interact constantly with your minds and hearts, with every cell in your bodies. Your thoughts modify the Earth's magnetic flux and its magnetic flux in turn influences your thinking. Gaia has worked reciprocally with you as a silent partner from the start.*

I always sensed the Project was part of something larger than ourselves, but I had no idea... George confesses.

Yes, Gaia has urged you forward all along. You need not fall prey to ancient fears of alien conquest. The long era of destructive domination has ended. Gaia will not allow any threat to life forms on Earth. The program of accelerated evolution and transformation you helped to create has bound the human race harmoniously with the mind and power of Gaia, unified in a single purpose – to respect and preserve life and maintain a healthy environment for all species to flourish.

Thanks to you four, all human beings retain freedom of choice while responding to the needs of the Earth and its creatures. The STAIR Project has completed its task, but we must remain vigilant to secure Earth's future. You may go your separate ways, but wherever you are you will never be apart from each other, from me or from Gaia. Now, if you would step outside, Gaia wishes to honor you with a special sendoff.

The team walks out under the night sky, twinkling with countless stars. Looking to the north, they see a spectacular display of aurora borealis – curtains of green, orange and violet light undulating sinuously in a slowly flowing dance. Overhead, meteors flash through the darkness and wink out like cosmic fireworks. Transported by the magnificence of the Earth and sky, Martin, Samantha, George and Daryl dance around joyously like little children, hugging each other and pouring out their grateful hearts to Gaia.

Author's Note

This book was conceived in the depths of winter in January 2010. The empty womb of my desire to be artistically creative was fertilized in this dark time by the seeds of despair over the sorry state of the environment and by my outrage at the blindness of our civilization. The outline for the plot and characters downloaded itself in one weekend, as if channeled – perhaps by Gaia itself. Writing it filled me with passion for life. The work flowed smoothly, despite the fact that I had never attempted anything as ambitious as a novel before.

I am deeply grateful for the support and assistance of the King's English DiverseCity Writing Series Group and for the many invaluable coaching sessions I received from the staff of the SLCC Community Writing Center in Salt Lake City. Together they provided the rich soil in which the young sprout of my novel could grow straight and strong. I also received useful suggestions from many acquaintances who read portions of the manuscript in progress and from the faculty of the 2012 Jackson Hole Writers Conference. Special thanks to Chris Chambers and Dan Proskauer for editorial assistance and to Jason Loveridge for proofreading. My deepest gratitude to Gregg Tong and Dan Proskauer for invaluable collaboration on graphic design, publication and publicity.

I appreciate my wife Lucia for her endurance during the ups and downs of the writing and publication process. Always tending toward the absent-minded professor type, I'm sure I became insufferably distracted while writing this novel. Yet with a minimum of complaint she put up with me and even read my manuscript in the spirit of an astute and constructive critic. Who could ask for more?

After reading an early draft of the manuscript, my son Dan recalled a telepathic world called Gaia in one of the seven books of Isaac Asimov's science fiction epic, The Foundation Series. I tracked down the reference to the fifth book of the series, *Foundation's Edge*. Gaia is depicted as a distant planet mysteriously immune to the galaxy-wide power struggles that have raged for hundreds of years. Toward the end of the story, the following passage appears:

> *The whole planet and everything on it is Gaia. We're all individuals – we're all separate organisms – but we all share an overall consciousness. The inanimate planet does least of all, the various forms of life to a varying degree, and human beings most of all – but we all share.*

- Isaac Asimov (1982). *Foundation's Edge*. New York: Bantam Dell paperback edition, 2004, p. 380.

Though I hadn't read this novel before planning *Gaia's Web*, the concept of Gaia as a planetary mind has been in the collective consciousness for decades. One can imagine AGA's taking Asimov to task along with the rest of us for minimizing the role of the "inanimate planet" in the shared consciousness.

Gaia's Web and its sequels detail the complex evolution of a planet inhabited by separate beings, like our Earth today, into a solar system of life forms that function like cells of a single organism, similar to Asimov's Gaia except for the much greater influence of planetary consciousness. That's the plan. Now we'll see what actually happens. Maybe I've got it wrong, too.

I hope that readers will come away with the satisfaction of enjoying a tale in which an unusual romantic quadrangle plays out and some colorful villains get consumed by their karma. Perhaps this story will arouse greater concern with the deteriorating environment and a desire to overcome greedy divisiveness, the Achilles heel of humanity, before it's too late. Despite what AGA says, I don't believe we need to wait around until we become telepathic before working together effectively toward saving life on Earth.

About the Author

A natural storyteller steeped in the classic science fiction tradition of Asimov, Heinlein and Clarke, Steve Proskauer has walked many paths. Beginning as a Harvard-trained psychiatrist and pioneer in psychotherapy, he became an explorer of past lifetimes and altered states, a shamanic healer, a Zen monk - and always, a writer.

Dr. Proskauer is author of two books on integrative psychiatry - *Karmic Therapy* (2007) and *Big Heart Healing* (2010) - as well as numerous scientific papers, articles and stories. He took first place in the Ultra IronPen writing competition at the 2011 Salt Lake Arts festival.

Steve lives in Salt Lake City with his wife and two cats. He was inspired to write *Gaia's Web* by the spirit of his late father, a visionary physicist and engineer who declared over sixty years ago that our civilization's disregard for the environment began with the invention of the flush toilet - out of sight, out of mind.

Gaia's Web is the first novel in the Gaia series.

http://www.gaiaswebthenovel.com

Made in the USA
Charleston, SC
26 December 2012